PENGUIN BOOKS

WRITERS FROM THE OTHER EUROPE
General Editor: Philip Roth

SANATORIUM UNDER THE SIGN
OF THE HOURGLASS

BRUNO SCHULZ was one of the most remarkably gifted
writers to have been produced in Eastern Europe in this
century. By day he taught art to high-school students in
Drogobych, a small town in southern Poland where he
spent most of his life. In his leisure hours Schulz wrote and
drew. His first book, *Cinnamon Shops* (retitled *The Street
of Crocodiles* in its American edition and published by
Penguin Books), was published in 1934. *Sanatorium under
the Sign of the Hourglass*, fiction with drawings, followed
three years later. Schulz produced his drawings by etching
them on spoiled photographic plates he obtained from
drugstores; after putting the plate and sensitive paper into
a frame, he would expose them to sunlight, and the drawing would be reproduced on the paper. A novella, "The
Comet" (included in *The Street of Crocodiles*), assorted
critical writings, letters, a translation of Franz Kafka's *The
Trial*, and a lost work thought to be called *The Messiah*
constitute his entire oeuvre. In 1942, at the age of fifty,
Schulz, a Jew, ventured into the "Aryan" section of his
town and was shot dead in the street by an SS agent.

CELINA WIENIEWSKA was awarded the 1963 Roy Publish-
ers Polish-into-English prize for her superb translation of
The Street of Crocodiles. She has also edited the collection
Polish Writing Today.

JOHN UPDIKE was born in Pennsylvania in 1932 and edu-
cated at Harvard and the Ruskin School of Drawing and
Fine Art at Oxford. His early poems and stories appeared
in *The New Yorker*, for which he still writes. In 1958 he
published his first book, *The Carpentered Hen and Other
Tame Creatures*, a collection of poetry. Since then, he has
written poems, essays, and fiction, including the novels
Rabbit, Run; *The Centaur*; *Couples*; and *The Coup*.

SANATORIUM UNDER THE SIGN OF THE HOURGLASS

Bruno Schulz

Translated from the Polish by
Celina Wieniewska

With 30 illustrations by the author

Introduction by
John Updike

PENGUIN BOOKS

Penguin Books Ltd, Harmondsworth,
Middlesex, England
Penguin Books, 625 Madison Avenue,
New York, New York 10022, U.S.A.
Penguin Books Australia Ltd, Ringwood,
Victoria, Australia
Penguin Books Canada Limited, 2801 John Street,
Markham, Ontario, Canada L3R 1B4
Penguin Books (N.Z.) Ltd, 182–190 Wairau Road,
Auckland 10, New Zealand

First published in Poland under the title
Sanatorium pod Klepsydra 1937
First published in the United States of America by
Walker and Company 1978
First published in Canada by Beayerbooks, Limited, 1978
Published in Penguin Books 1979

LIBRARY OF CONGRESS CATALOGING IN PUBLICATION DATA
Schulz, Bruno, 1892–1942.
Sanatorium under the sign of the hourglass.
(Writers from the other Europe)
Translation of Sanatorium pod klepsydra.
I. Title. II. Series.
PZ4.S3913San 1979 [PG7158.S294] 891.8′5′37 79-17564
ISBN 0 14 00.5272 0

Printed in the United States of America by
Offset Paperback Mfrs., Inc., Dallas, Pennsylvania
Set in Times Roman

WRITERS FROM THE OTHER EUROPE

The purpose of this paperback series is to bring together outstanding and influential works of fiction by Eastern European writers. In many instances they will be writers who, though recognized as powerful forces in their own cultures, are virtually unknown in America. It is hoped that by reprinting selected Eastern European writers in this format and with introductions that place each work in its literary and historical context, the literature that has evolved in "the other Europe" during the postwar decades will be made more accessible to an interested American readership.

PHILIP ROTH

OTHER TITLES IN THIS SERIES

CONTENTS

CONTENTS

Translator's Preface

Sanatorium under the Sign of the Hourglass is the second collection of prose fiction by Bruno Schulz. Published in Warsaw in 1937, it followed three years after *Cinnamon Shops,* his very successful literary debut which is known in the United States as *The Street of Crocodiles.* Like the previous book, *Sanatorium* is, in Schulz's own words: "An attempt at eliciting the history of a certain family, a certain house in a provincial city — not from documents, events, a study of character or of people's destinies — but by a search for the mythical sense, the essential core of that history . . . That dusky, allusive atmosphere, that aura that thickens around any family history, can only occasionally disclose to a poet its second, mythical face: an alternative, a depth in which the secret mystery of blood and race is hidden . . . These mythical elements are inherent in the region of early childish fantasies, intuitions, fears and anticipations characteristic of the dawn of life."

Sanatorium is the poetic recreation of Schulz's autobiography: the memories of a child blessed with an extraordinary sensitivity projected with the eye of an artist; his pilgrimage into a lost and happier past. It is a time when Father was still alive but he is no more the central and dominant preoccupation of his son, as he was in the earlier book. Mother is here as a benevolent, bland presence. Other members of the family make brief appearances; the blue-eyed, temperamental, young servant girl, Adela, is still the household acolyte, the disturbing, sex-charged element. In the masterful central story that gives the book its title, Joseph, dutiful son and observant narrator, visits Father in limbo and reports on its confusion and hidden horrors. Yet *Sanatorium* belongs to Joseph: It chronicles his progress through stages of discovery. The revelation of nature in all its seasons, colors and phases raises him to a feverish frenzy and occasions his dramatic self-recognition of the child-as-artist. The infinite and bewildering variety of the wider world is revealed through the symbols and national emblems in a schoolboy's stamp album (in "Spring"). The evocation of first love in a long, dreamlike sequence in the same story is intertwined with a fantasy about an enchanted house and Joseph's abortive rescue of a would-be princess.

The final stories continue the process of self-discovery, disclosing the basic loneliness, sadness and near despair of Schulz's real existence.

After the publication of his first book, Schulz's life as a teacher of drawing and handicrafts at the Drogobych boys'college began gradually to expand and brighten. He gained friends in the literary world of Warsaw through the novelist Zofia Nalkowska, who was instrumental in the publication of *Cinnamon Shops,* and through Stanislaw Ignacy Witkiewicz, a great admirer of Schulz's prose and one who was also both artist and novelist, as well as a theatrical innovator of genius. Schulz could now supplement his income from teaching by contributing to literary weeklies in Warsaw and Lwow. He began devoting a great deal of time to correspondence (which has been meticulously traced and collected over the years since the end of the last war by Jerzy Ficowski). There were no more letters like those to Deborah Vogel (almost all lost) that spurred Schulz to literary pursuits before any of his work was published. The new letters concerned mostly his work and aspirations: endeavors to get wider recognition, to gain a public, and to have his books translated abroad. The recurrent theme in many of these letters is Schulz's obsession with time: the encroachment on it of the reality of his daily drudgery as a teacher contrasting with his dreams of a limitless quota of uninterrupted time that would provide a *tabula rasa* of pure, virgin hours.

It was not to be. Through the accident of his brother's premature death in 1936, Schulz's financial responsibilities grew: He found himself sole supporter of his widowed sister, her son and an aged cousin. His engagement to a Catholic woman, a relationship already plagued by religious complications, was broken off. His letters reveal ever more frequent bouts of depression, each one lasting for ever longer periods. Although *Cinnamon Shops* brought him a prize from the Polish Academy of Letters (a fact that enhanced his standing in Drogobych: His school gave him the title of "professor," but no rise in salary!), *Sanatorium* failed to win the annual prize awarded by the Warsaw weekly *Wiadomosci Literackie.* With the help of friends in Poland and France and after much persuasion, Schulz did manage to travel to Paris during the summer of 1938. For three weeks he visited art galleries and discussed art and literature. This was already a time of foreboding: Nazi expansionist policies presented a threat to peace in central Europe. The Polish-German pact of 1939 intensified the spread of Nazi ideas in some sections of Polish society. When war broke out in September, 1939, Drogobych was, for a time, occupied by the Russians. Schulz could still teach and was able to write, but his type of writing was too personal, too introspective to be palatable in the harsh climate of war. He therefore reverted to painting and was earning his modest keep as an artist in his native city when, during the German advance into Soviet territory, it was occupied by the Nazis in the summer of 1941.

In the Jewish quarter of Drogobych, on a certain "Black Thursday" in November, 1942, Schulz was bringing home a loaf of bread when he was shot in the street by a Gestapo officer who had a grudge against another Nazi, Schulz's temporary "protector" who liked his paintings. His body was buried by a Jewish friend in a cemetery which no longer exists.

Schulz's fate, as he had written in "Loneliness," was "to be a parasite of metaphors . . . carried away by the first simile that comes along." This particular metaphor does him less than justice: His oeuvre has triumphantly survived. The sixties saw the publication of his work in Germany, France, Italy and Norway. Now, forty years after its publication in Polish, *Sanatorium under the Sign of the Hourglass* is at last published in English in the United States. Schulz's dream of being read by a wider public has at last come true.

CELINA WIENIEWSKA

Introduction

Bruno Schulz was one of the great *writers*, one of the great transmogrifiers of the world into words. In this, his second and final book, the writing, with its ardent accumulations of metaphor and unexpected launching of heavy objects into flight, seems even more rarefied than in his first. The magical town and family melt, shimmering, into the pageant of the calendar and the unfolding of a young consciousness. Sensitivity dawns as entirely artistic: "The fiery beauty of the world" is revealed through the translucent emblems of a schoolmate's stamp album, and the magnificent atmospheric effects of the changing seasons are conjured more than once in terms of deliberately staged theatrics, "a touring show, poetically deceptive, an enormous purple-skinned onion disclosing ever new panoramas under each of its skins." These panoramas disclose themselves to the author through the lens of memory, a cerebral elaboration peculiar to man and requiring the invention of language for its code. The strenuous artifice of the language reaches out to include Nature in its conspiracy:

Who knows the length of time when night lowers the curtain on what is happening in its depth? That short interval is enough, however, to shift the scenery, to liquidate the great enterprise of the night and all its dark fantastic pomp. You wake up frightened, with the feeling of having overslept, and you see on the horizon the bright streak of dawn and the black, solidifying mass of the earth.

The pages are crowded with verbal brilliance, like Schulz's brimming, menacing, amazing skies. But something cruel lurks behind this beauty, bound up with it—the cruelty of myth. Like dreams, myths are a shorthand whose compressions occur without the friction of resistance that reality always presents to pain. In his treasured, detested loneliness Schulz brooded upon his personal past with the weight of generations; how grandly he succeeded can be felt in the dread with which we read even his most lyrical and humorous passages, the dread that something momentous approaches. Something alien may break through these dark, tense membranes of sensation. The scenery-mover, the laboring writer, might rescind his illusion. The rules that hold us safe are somehow awry.

I. B. Singer, a pleasanter genius from the same between-the-wars Poland, said of Schulz, "He wrote sometimes like Kafka, sometimes like Proust, and at times succeeded in reaching depths that neither of them reached." The striking similarities—Marcel Proust's inflation of the past and ecstatic reaches of simile, Franz Kafka's father-obsession and metamorphic fantasies—point toward an elusive difference: the older men's relative orthodoxy within the Judaeo-Christian presumptions of value, and the relative nakedness with which Schulz confronts the mystery of existence. Like Jorge Luis Borges, he is a cosmogonist without a theology. The harrowing effort of his prose (which never, unlike that of Proust or Kafka, propels us onward but instead seems constantly to ask that we stop and reread) is to construct the world anew, as from fragments that exist after some unnameable disaster.

What this disaster might be, our best guess would be his father's madness. "Madness" may be too strong a term—"retreat from reality," certainly. "In reality he was a Drogobych merchant, who had inherited a textile business and ran it until illness forced him to abandon it to the care of his wife. He then retired to ten years of enforced idleness and his own world of dreams": thus Celina Wieniewska, who has so finely translated Schulz's two volumes into English, outlines the facts of the case in her Preface to *The Street of Crocodiles*. In that volume the story "Visitation" says of the father's retirement: "Knot by knot, he loosened himself from us; point by point, he gave up the ties joining him to the human community. What still remained of him—the small shroud of his body and the handful of nonsensical oddities—would finally disappear one day, as unremarked as the gray heap of rubbish swept into a corner, waiting to be taken by Adela to the rubbish dump." The many metamorphoses of Schulz's fictional father-figure, culminating in the horrifying crab form he assumes in the last story of this volume, the sometimes magnificent delusional systems the old man spins, and the terrible war of diminishment versus enlargement in the imagery that surrounds this figure have their basis in an actual metamorphosis that must have been, to the victim's son, more frightening than amusing, more humiliating than poetic.

In Kafka, by contrast, the father threatens by virtue of his potency and emerges as less frail than he at first seems. In both cases the father occupies the warm center of the son's imagination. The mother is felt dimly and coolly and gets small thanks for her efficiency and sanity. At least, however, Schulz's mother is not entirely absent from his recreated world; in the writings of Sören Kierkegaard—another lonely bachelor son of a fascinating, if far from reassuring, father—the mother is altogether absent. From the mother, perhaps, men derive their sense of their bodies; from the father, their sense of the world. From his relationship with his father Kafka construed an enigmatic, stern, yet unimpeachable universe; Schulz presents an antic, soluble, picturesque cosmos, lavish in its inventions but feeble in its authority. In "Tailors' Dummies" (from *The Street of Crocodiles*) he has his father pronounce: "If, forgetting the respect due to the Creator, I were to attempt a criticism of creation, I would say 'Less matter, more form!'"

Sensitive to formlessness, Schulz gives even more attention than Samuel Beckett to boredom, to life's preponderant limbo, to the shoddy swatches of experience, to dead seasons, to those negative tracts of time in which we sleep or doze. His feeling for idle time is so strong that the adamant temporal medium itself appears limp and fickle to him:

We all know that time, this undisciplined element, holds itself within bounds but precariously, thanks to unceasing cultivation, meticulous care, and a continuous regulation and correction of its excesses. Free of this vigilance, it immediately begins to do tricks, run wild, play irresponsible practical jokes, and indulge in crazy clowning. The incongruity of our private times becomes evident.

"The incongruity of our private times"—the phrase encapsulates a problematical feature of modern literature, its immurement in the personal. Abandoning kings and heroes and even those sagas of hearsay that inspired Joseph Conrad and Thomas Hardy, the writer seems condemned to live, like the narrator of "Loneliness" (in *Sanatorium under the Sign of the Hourglass*), in his old nursery. Limited, in a scientific age that has redefined verification, to incidents he has witnessed, to the existence he has lived minute by drab minute, the writer is driven to magnify, and the texture of magnification is bizarre. More purely than Proust or Kafka Schulz surrendered to the multiple distortions of obsessed reflection, giving us now a father as splendid as the glittering meteor, "sparkling with a thousand lights," who leaps into the spread canvas of the fire brigade, and in other places a father reduced to rubbish.

Schulz's last surviving work, the small novella "The Comet" (published at the end of *The Street of Crocodiles*), shows Father himself at the microscope, examining a fluorescent homunculus that a wandering star has engendered in the quiet of the stove's pitch-dark chimney shaft, while Uncle Edward, whom Father's sorcery has transformed into an electric bell, sounds the alarm for the end of the world, which does not come. In these vivid, riddling images an ultimate of strangeness is reached, and a degree of religious saturation, entirely heterodox, unknown in literature since William Blake. Indeed, Schulz's blazing skies, showing "the spirals and whorls of light, the pale-green solids of darkness, the plasma of space, the tissue of dreams," carry us back to the pagan astronomers, their wonder and their desolate inklings of a superhuman order.

Each life makes its myths, as the boredom of days engenders weeds: The intensity of prose needed to reify this message could not have been sustained through a long career. Schulz did not publish until he was over forty and had stopped writing several years before his murder—even in death, in a time of mass slaughter, he was singled out—at the age of fifty. His method lives. "Schulz is my god," I was told not long ago, in Yugoslavia, by the writer Danilo Kiš. One wonders if Schulz's example helped embolden the young Greek novelist Margarita Karapanou to write of childhood with such lyric ferocity; her *Kassandra and the Wolf* has the jagged, fantastic substance of "Spring," with a vicious prepubescent sexual element chillingly added. In the United States an affinity if not an influence can be seen in a writer such as Gilbert Rogin. Rogin, like Schulz, revolves the same small cast of characters, the same dissatisfied but inseparable family, in story after story, refusing to move on, to relinquish the claims to supreme importance that this material has for the author—an importance professed in the lovingly elaborate metaphors and highly intellectual aphorisms that adorn the narrative of those ordinary, rather wretched lives. Where importance is not political, a matter of social consensus (like that of, say, Oedipus, Hamlet, and Kutuzov), it seeks, through metaphor, priorly established planes of importance; *Ulysses* makes of the principle a great mock-heroic machine.

More instinctively, writers in a world of hidden citizens work with an excited precision, pulling silver threads from the coarse texture of daily life. The hypnotized gaze upon local particulars turns objects into signs; objects with some sort of significance painted upon them are treasured, in the absence of symbols derived from an accepted exterior religion. In a recent Rogin story, "The Hard Parts," a heavy cardboard poster of Albrecht Dürer's "Feast of the Rose Garlands" has been placed as a roof on a wire enclosure in a Manhattan garden; from the top floor of his town house the hero repeatedly contemplates this unexpectedly situated sign:

Now, when Albert gazes out his bedroom window, what caught his eye was this weather-beaten *Rosenkranzbild*, resplendent with the roses the nearby bush never produced. . . . Sometimes, as Albert stood and sang, the dark garden seemed to him to be flooded, with just the topmost branches of the privet projecting from the water, and the blistered poster now a raft upon which a desperate swimmer might try to haul himself, only to find it wouldn't support the weight of a child.

For Schulz, the Book full of decals invades the days: "Page after page floated in the air and gently saturated the landscape with brightness." A stamp album even more powerfully offers itself as a substitute for, as a demiurgic activator of, the world:

I opened it, and the glamour of colorful worlds, of becalmed spaces, spread before me. God walked through it, page after page, pulling behind Him a train woven from all the zones and climates. Canada, Honduras, Nicaragua, Abracadabra, Hipporabundia . . . I at last understood you, Oh God. These were the disguises for your riches.

The same eye that so greedily seizes upon the pictorial artifacts translucently afloat on the surface of creation sees symbolic intentions in natural formations like the stars, "the indifferent tribunal of stars, now set in a sky on which the shapes of the instruments floated like water signs or fragments of keys, unfinished lyres or swans, an imitatory, thoughtless starry commentary on the margin of music." Schulz's own illustrations to his stories, though skilled, do not participate in his fluid confusion of the graphic and the actual but, like illustrations by another man, sit athwart the text, obstructing our imagining. Idiosyncratically etched on spoiled photographic plates, the drawings make a dominant impression of shyness—the oversize heads habitually averted, foreshortened from above and unsmilingly wreathed in silence. These efficiently drawn dolls, which yet dwarf the toylike cityscapes they inhabit, disclose none of the radiant depths of their creator's prose; they do suggest the preceding centuries of illustrated fable that lie behind his fabulous relaying of his personal legends.

Personal experience taken cabalistically: This formula fits much modern fiction and, complain though we will, is hard to transcend. Being ourselves is the one religious experience we all have, an experience shareable only partially, through the exertions of talk and art. Schulz's verbal art strikes us—stuns us, even—with its overload of beauty. But, he declares, his art seeks to serve truth, to fill in the gaps that official history leaves. "Where is truth to shelter, where is it to find asylum if not in a place where nobody is looking for it . . . ?" Schulz himself was a hidden man, in an obscure Galician town, born to testify to the paradoxical richness, amid poverty of circumstance, of our inner lives.

JOHN UPDIKE

SANATORIUM UNDER THE SIGN OF THE HOURGLASS

THE BOOK

I

I am simply calling it The Book without any epithets or qualifications, and in this sobriety there is a shade of helplessness, a silent capitulation before the vastness of the transcendental, for no word, no allusion, can adequately suggest the shiver of fear, the presentiment of a thing without name that exceeds all our capacity for wonder. How could an accumulation of adjectives or a richness of epithets help when one is faced with that splendiferous thing? Besides, any *true* reader — and this story is only addressed to him — will understand me anyway when I look him straight in the eye and try to communicate my meaning. A short sharp look or a light clasp of his hand will stir him into awareness, and he will blink in rapture at the brilliance of The Book. For, under the imaginary table that separates me from my readers, don't we secretly clasp each other's hands?

The Book . . . Somewhere in the dawn of childhood, at the first daybreak of life, the horizon had brightened with its gentle glow. The Book lay in all its glory on my father's desk, and he, quietly engrossed in it, patiently rubbed with a wet fingertip the top of decals, until the blank pages grew opaque and ghostly with a delightful foreboding and, suddenly flaking off in bits of tissue, disclosed a peacock-eyed fragment; blurred with emotion, one's eyes turned toward a virgin dawn of divine colors, toward a miraculous moistness of purest azure.

Oh, that shedding of the film, oh, that invasion of brightness, that blissful spring, oh, Father . . .

Sometimes my father would wander off and leave me alone with The Book; the wind would rustle through its pages and the pictures would rise. And as the windswept pages were turned, merging the colors and shapes, a shiver ran through the columns of text, freeing from among the letters flocks of swallows and larks. Page after page floated in the air and gently saturated the landscape with brightness. At other times, The Book lay still and the wind opened it softly like a huge

1

cabbage rose; the petals, one by one, eyelid under eyelid, all blind, velvety, and dreamy, slowly disclosed a blue pupil, a colored peacock's heart, or a chattering nest of hummingbirds.

This was a very long time ago. My mother had not appeared yet. I spent my days alone with my father in our room, which at that time was as large as the world.

The crystals hanging from the lamp filled the room with diffused colors, a rainbow splashed into all the corners, and, when the lamp swayed on its chains, the whole room revolved in fragments of the rainbow, as if the spheres of all nine planets had shifted, one turning around the other. I liked to stand between my father's legs, clasping them from each side like columns. Sometimes he wrote letters. I sat on his desk and watched, entranced, the squiggles of his signature, crabbed and awhirl like the trills of a coloratura singer. Smiles were budding in the wallpaper, eyes hatched, somersaults turned. To amuse me, my father blew soap bubbles through a long straw; they burst in the iridescent space or hit the walls, their colors still hanging in the air.

Then my mother materialized, and that early, bright idyll came to an end. Seduced by my mother's caresses, I forgot my father, and my life began to run along a new and different track with no holidays and no miracles. I might even have forgotten The Book forever, had it not been for a certain night and a certain dream.

II

On a dark wintry morning I woke up early [under the banks of darkness a grim dawn shone in the depths below] and while a multitude of misty figures and signs still crowded under my eyelids, I began to dream confusedly, tormented by various regrets about the old, forgotten Book.

No one could understand me and, vexed by their obtuseness, I began to nag more urgently, molesting my parents with angry impatience.

Barefoot, wearing only my nightshirt and trembling with excitement, I rifled the books on Father's bookshelves, and, angry and disappointed, I tried to describe to a stunned audience that indescribable thing, which no words, no pictures drawn with a trembling and elongated finger, could evoke. I exhausted myself in endless explanations, complicated and contradictory, and cried in helpless despair.

My parents towered over me, perplexed, ashamed of their helplessness. They could not help feeling uneasy. My vehemence, the impatient and feverish urgency of my tone, made me appear to be in the right, to have a well-founded grievance. They came up to me with various books and pressed them into my hands. I threw them away indignantly.

One of them, a thick and heavy tome, was again and again pushed toward me by my father. I opened it. It was the Bible. I saw in its pages a great wandering of animals, filling the roads, branching off into processions heading for distant lands. I saw a sky filled with flocks of birds in flight, and an enormous, upturned pyramid on whose flat top rested the Ark.

I raised my reproachful eyes to Father:

"You must know, Father," I cried, "you must. Don't pretend, don't quibble! This book has given you away. Why do you give me that fake copy, that reproduction, a clumsy falsification? What have you done with The Book?"

My father averted his eyes.

III

Weeks went by. My excitement abated, then passed, but the image of The Book continued to burn in my memory with a bright flame; a large, rustling Codex, a tempestuous Bible, the wind blowing through its pages, plundering it like an enormous, petal-shedding rose.

My father, seeing that I had become calmer, approached me cautiously one day and said in a tone of gentle suggestion:

"As a matter of fact, there are many books. The Book is a myth in which we believe when we are young, but which we cease to take seriously as we get older."

At that time I already held quite a different opinion. I knew then that The Book is a postulate, that it is a goal. I carried upon my shoulders the burden of a great mission. I did not answer; I was scornful and filled with bitter, dogged pride.

In fact, I was already in possession of some tattered remnants of The Book, a few pitiful shreds that by a freak of fate had fallen into my hands. I hid my treasure carefully from everybody, distressed by the utter downfall of that book and knowing that I could not expect anyone to appreciate those mutilated pages. It happened like this:

One day during that winter I surprised Adela tidying up a room. A long-handled brush in her hand, she was leaning against a reading desk, on which lay some papers. I looked over her shoulder, not so much from curiosity as to be close to her and enjoy the smell of her body whose youthful charms had just revealed themselves to my recently awakened senses.

"Look," she said, submitting without protest to my pressing against her. "Is it possible for anyone to have hair reaching down to the ground? I should like to have hair like that."

I looked at the picture. On a large folio page there was a photograph of a rather squat and short woman with a face expressing energy and experience. From her head flowed an enormous stole of hair, which fell heavily down her back trailing its thick ends on the ground. It was an unbelievable freak of nature, a full and ample cloak spun out of the tendrils of hair. It was hard to imagine that its burden was not painful to carry, that it did not paralyze the head from which it grew. But the owner of this magnificence seemed to bear it proudly, and the caption printed under the picture told the history of that miracle, beginning with the words: "I, Anna Csillag, born at Karlovice in Moravia, had a poor growth of hair. . . ."

It was a long story, similar in construction to the story of Job. By divine will, Anna Csillag had been struck with a poor growth of hair. All her village pitied her for this disability, which they tolerated because of the exemplary life she led, although they suspected it could not have been entirely undeserved. But, lo and behold, her ardent prayers were heard, the curse was removed from her head, and Anna Csillag was graced with the blessing of enlightenment. She received signs and portents and concocted a mixture, a miraculous nostrum that restored fertility to her scalp. She began to grow hair, and what is more, her husband, brothers, even cousins were covered overnight with a tough, healthy black coating of hair growth. On the reverse of the page, Anna Csillag was shown six weeks after the prescription was revealed to her,

4

surrounded by her brothers, brothers-in-law, and nephews, bewhiskered men with beards down to their waists, exposed to the admiration of beholders in an eruption of unfalsified, bearlike masculinity. Anna Csillag became the benefactress of her village, on which the blessing of wavy heads of hair and of enormous fringes had descended, and whose male inhabitants, henceforth, could sweep the ground with their beards like broad besoms. Anna Csillag became the apostle of hairiness. Having brought happiness to her native village, she now wanted to make the whole world happy and asked, begged, and urged everyone to accept for their salvation the gift of the gods, the wonderful mixture of which she alone knew the secret.

I read that story over Adela's arm and was struck by a sudden overwhelming thought. This was The Book, its last pages, the unofficial supplement, the tradesmen's entrance full of refuse and trash! Fragments of rainbow suddenly danced on the wallpaper. I snatched the sheaf of paper out of Adela's hands, and in a faltering voice I breathed:

"Where did you find this book?"

"You silly boy," she answered shrugging her shoulders. "It has been lying here all the time; we tear a few pages from it every day and take them to the butcher's for packing meat or your father's lunch . . ."

IV

I rushed to my room. Deeply perturbed, with burning cheeks I began to turn the pages of the old Book with trembling fingers. Alas, not many remained. Not a single page of the real text, nothing but advertisements and personal announcements. Immediately following the prophecies of the long-haired Sibyl was a page devoted to a miraculous nostrum for all illnesses and infirmities. Elsa — the Liquid with a Swan — was a balm that worked wonders. The page was full of authenticated, touching testimonials from people who had experienced its effects.

The enthusiastic convalescents from Transylvania, Slavonia, and Bucovina hurried to bear witness and to relate their stories in warm and moving words. They came bandaged and bent, shaking their now superfluous crutches, tearing plasters from their eyes and bandages from their sores.

Beyond these processions of cripples one imagined distant,

mournful villages under skies white as paper, hardened by the prose of daily drudgery. They were villages forgotten in the depth of time, peopled by creatures chained forever to their tiny destinies. A cobbler was a total cobbler: he smelled of hide; he had a small and haggard face, pale myopic eyes, and a colorless, sniffing moustache; he felt a cobbler through and through. And when their abscesses did not worry them and

their bones did not creak, when dropsy did not force them onto their pallets, these people plunged into a lifeless, gray happiness, smoking cheap, yellow imperial-and-royal tobacco or dully daydreaming in front of kiosks where lottery tickets were sold.

Cats crossed their paths, both from the left and from the right; they dreamed of black dogs, and their palms frequently itched. Once in a while, they wrote a letter copied from a letter-writing manual, carefully stuck a stamp on the envelope, and entrusted it reluctantly to a letter box, which they then struck with their fists, as if to wake it up. And afterward they dreamed of white pigeons that carried letters in their beaks before disappearing in the clouds.

The pages that followed rose over the sphere of daily affairs into the region of pure poetry.

There were harmoniums, zithers, and harps, once played by consorts of angels; now, thanks to the progress of industry, they were accessible at popular prices to ordinary people — to all God-fearing people for their suitable entertainment and for the gladdening of their hearts.

There were barrel organs, real miracles of technology, full of flutes, stops, and pipes, trilling sweetly like nests of sobbing nightingales: priceless treasures for crippled veterans, a source of lucrative income for the disabled, and generally indispensable in every musical family. One imagined these barrel organs, beautifully painted, carried on the backs of little gray old men, whose indistinct faces, corroded by life, seemed covered by cobwebs — faces with watery, immobile eyes slowly leaking away, emaciated faces as discolored and innocent as the cracked and weathered bark of trees, and now like bark smelling only of rain and sky.

These old men had long forgotten their names and identities, and, lost in themselves, their feet encased in enormous heavy boots, they shuffled on bent knees with small, even steps along a straight monotonous line, disregarding the winding and tortuous paths of others who passed them by.

On white, sunless mornings, mornings stale with cold and steeped in the daily business of life, they would disentangle themselves imperceptibly from the crowd and stand the barrel organ on a trestle at street corners, under the yellow smudge of a sky cut by lines of telegraph wires. As people hurried aimlessly with their collars upturned, they would begin their tune — not from the start but from where it had stopped the day before — and play "Daisy, Daisy, give me your answer, do . . . ." while from the chimneys above, white plumes of steam would billow. And — strange thing — that tune, hardly begun, fell at once into its place at that hour and in that landscape as if it had belonged by right to that dreamlike inward-looking day. The thoughts and gray cares of the people hurrying past kept time with the tune.

And when, after a time, the tune ended in a long expansive whizz ripped from the insides of the barrel organ, which now started on something quite else, the thoughts and cares stopped for a moment, like in a dance, to change step, and then at once turned in the opposite direction in time to a new tune now emerging from the pipes of the barrel organ: "Margaretta, treasure of my soul. . . ."

And in the dull indifference of that morning nobody noticed that the sense of the world had completely changed, that it now ran in time not with "Daisy, Daisy . . ." but with "Mar-ga-ret-ta . . ."

I turned another page. . . . What might this be? A spring downpour? No, it was the chirping of birds, which landed like gray shot on open umbrellas, for here I was offered real German canaries from the Harz mountains, cageloads of goldfinches and starlings, basketfuls of winged talkers and singers. Spindle-shaped and light, as if stuffed with cotton wool; jumping jerkily, agile as if running on smooth ball bearings; chattering like cuckoos in clocks — they were destined to sweeten the life of the lonely, to give bachelors a substitute for family life, to squeeze from the hardest of hearts the semblance of maternal warmth brought forth by their touching helplessness. Even when the page was almost turned, their collective, alluring chirping still seemed to persist.

But later on, the miserable remains of The Book became ever more depressing. The pages were now given over to a display of boring quackery. In a long coat, with a smile half hidden by his black beard, who was it who presented his services to the public? Signor Bosco of Milan, a master of black magic, was making a long and obscure appeal, demonstrating something on the tips of his fingers without clarifying anything. And, although in his own estimation he reached amazing conclusions, which he seemed to weigh for a moment before they dissolved into thin air, although he pointed to the dialectical subtleties of his oratory by raising his eyebrows and preparing one for something unexpected, he remained misunderstood, and, what is worse, one did not care to understand him and left him with his gestures, his soft voice, and the whole gamut of his dark smiles, to turn quickly the last, almost disintegrated pages.

These pages quite obviously had slipped into a maniacal babble, into nonsense: A gentleman offered an infallible method of achieving decisiveness and determination and spoke at length of high principles and character. But to turn another page was enough for me to become completely disoriented as far as principles and firmness were concerned.

A certain Mme. Magda Wang, tethered by the train of her gown, declared above a modest décolletage that she frowned on manly determination and principles and that she specialized in breaking the strongest characters. (Here, with a slight kick of her small foot, she rearranged the train of her gown.) There were methods, she continued through clenched teeth, infallible methods she could not divulge here, referring the readers to her memoirs, entitled *The Purple Days* (published by the Institute of Anthroposophy in Budapest); in them she listed the results of her experiences in the Colonies with the "dressage" of men (this last word underlined by an ironical flash of her eyes). And strangely enough, that slovenly and loose-tongued lady seemed to be sure of the approval of those about whom she spoke so cynically, and in the peculiar confusion of her words one felt that their meaning had mysteriously shifted and that we had moved to a totally different sphere, where the compass worked back to front.

This was the last page of The Book, and it left me peculiarly dizzy, filled with a mixture of longing and excitement.

V

Leaning over that Book, my face glowing like a rainbow, I burned in quiet ecstasy. Engrossed in reading, I forgot my mealtimes. My intuition was right: this was the authentic Book, the holy original, however degraded and humiliated at present. And when late in the evening, smiling blissfully, I put the script away in the bottom of a drawer and hid it under a pile of other books, I felt as if I were putting to sleep the Dawn that emits a self-igniting purple flame.

How dull all my other books now seemed!

For ordinary books are like meteors. Each of them has only one moment, a moment when it soars screaming like the phoenix, all its pages aflame. For that single moment we love them ever after, although they soon turn to ashes. With bitter resignation we sometimes wander late at night through the extinct pages that tell their stone dead messages like wooden rosary beads.

The exegetes of The Book maintain that all books aim at being Authentic. That they live only a borrowed life, which at the moment of inspiration returns to its ancient source. This means that as the number of books decreases, the Authentic must increase. However, we don't wish to tire the reader with an exposition of doctrine. We should only like to draw his attention to one thing: The Authentic lives and grows. What

does this mean? Well, perhaps next time, when we open our old script, we may not find Anna Csillag and her devotees in their old place. Perhaps we shall see her, the long-haired pilgrim, sweeping with her cloak the roads of Moravia, wandering in a distant land, through white villages steeped in prose and drabness, and distributing samples of Elsa's balm to God's simpletons who suffer from sores and itches. Ah, and what about the worthy village beavers, immobilized by their enormous beards? What will that loyal commune do, condemned to the care and administration of their excessive growths? Who knows, perhaps they will all purchase the genuine Black Forest barrel organs and follow their lady apostle into the world, looking for her everywhere while playing "Daisy, Daisy"?

Oh Odyssey of beavers, roaming from town to town with barrel organs in pursuit of your spiritual mother! Is there a bard equal to this epic subject, who has been left in their village and is now wielding the spiritual power in Anna Csillag's birthplace? Couldn't they foresee that, deprived of their elite, of their splendid patriarchs, the village will fall into doubt and apostasy and will open its gates — to whom? Whom but the cynical and perverse Magda Wang (published by the Anthroposophical Institute of Budapest), who will open there a school of human dressage and breaking of character?

But let us return to our pilgrims.

We all know that old guard of wandering Cumbrians, those black-haired men with apparently powerful bodies, made of tissue without brawn or vigor. Their whole strength, their whole power, has gone into their hair. Anthropologists have been pondering for a long time over that peculiar tribe of men always clad in dark suits, with thick, silver chains dangling on their stomachs, with fingers adorned with brass signet rings.

I like them, these Caspars or Balthazars; I like their deep seriousness, their funereal decorativeness; I like those magnificent male specimens with beautiful glossy eyes like burnt coffee beans; I like the noble lack of vitality in their overblown and spongy bodies, the morbidezza of decadence, the wheezing breath that comes from their powerful lungs, and even the smell of valerian emanating from their beards.

Like angels of the Presence, they sometimes appear suddenly in the door of our kitchen, enormous and short of breath, and, quickly tired, they wipe off perspiration from their damp brows while rolling the bluish whites of their eyes; for a moment they forget the object of their mission, and, astonished, looking for an excuse, a pretext for their arrival, they stretch out a hand and beg for alms.

Let's return to the Authentic. We have never forsaken it. And here we must stress a strange characteristic of the script, which by now no doubt has become clear to the reader: it unfolds while being read, its boundaries open to all currents and fluctuations.

Now, for instance, no one is offering goldfinches from the Harz Mountains, for from the barrel organs of those dark men the feathery little singers fly out at irregular intervals, and the market square is covered with them as with colored twigs. Ah, what a multiplication of shimmering chattering birds! . . . On all the cornices and flagpoles, colorful bottlenecks are formed by birds fluttering and fighting for position. If you push out of the window the crook of a walking stick, it will be covered with a chirping, heavy bunch of birds before you can draw it back into your room.

We are now quickly approaching the magnificent and catastrophic part of our story, which in our biography is known as the Age of Genius.

Here we must for a moment go completely esoteric, like Signor Bosco of Milan, and lower our voice to a penetrating whisper. By meaningful smiles we must give point to our exposition and grind the delicate substance of imponderables between the tips of our fingers. It won't be our fault if sometimes we shall look like those merchants of invisible fabrics, who display their fake goods with elaborate gestures.

Well then, did the Age of Genius ever occur? It is difficult to answer this question. Yes and no. There are things that cannot ever occur with any precision. They are too big and too magnificent to be contained in mere facts. They are merely trying to occur, they are checking whether the ground of reality can carry them. And they quickly withdraw, fearing to lose their integrity in the frailty of realization. And if they break into their capital, lose a thing or two in these attempts at incarnation, then soon, jealously, they retrieve their possessions, call them in, reintegrate: as a result, white spots appear in our biography — scented stigmata, the faded silvery imprints of the bare feet of angels, scattered footmarks on our nights and days — while the fullness of life waxes, incessantly supplements itself, and towers over us in wonder after wonder.

And yet, in a certain sense, the fullness is contained wholly and integrally in each of its crippled and fragmentary incarnations. This is the phenomenon of imagination and vicarious being. An event may be small and insignificant in its origin, and yet, when drawn close to one's eye, it may open in its center an infinite and radiant perspective because a higher order of being is trying to express itself in it and irradiates it violently.

Thus we shall collect these allusions, these earthly approximations, these stations and stages on the paths of our life, like the fragments of a broken mirror. We shall recreate piece by piece what is one and indivisible — the great era, the Age of Genius of our life.

Perhaps in an attempt at diminution, overawed by the immensity of the transcendental, we have circumscribed, questioned, and doubted too much. Yet, despite all reservations: it did occur.

It was a fact, and nothing can shake our certainty of it: we can still feel its taste on our tongue, its cold fire on our palate, the width of its breath fresh like a draught of pure ultramarine.

Have we to some extent prepared the reader for the things that will follow? Can we risk a return journey into our Age of Genius?

The reader may have caught some of our stage fright: we can feel his anxiety. In spite of appearances our heart is heavy, and we are full of fear.

In God's name, then — let's embark and go!

THE AGE OF GENIUS

I

Ordinary facts are arranged within time, strung along its length as on a thread. There they have their antecedents and their consequences, which crowd tightly together and press hard one upon the other without any pause. This has its importance for any narrative, of which continuity and successiveness are the soul.

Yet what is to be done with events that have no place of their own in time; events that have occurred too late, after the whole of time has been distributed, divided, and allotted; events that have been left in the cold, unregistered, hanging in the air, homeless, and errant?

Could it be that time is too narrow for all events? Could it happen that all the seats within time might have been sold? Worried, we run along the train of events, preparing ourselves for the journey.

For heaven's sake, is there perhaps some kind of bidding for time? Conductor, where are you?

Don't let's get excited. Don't let's panic; we can settle it all calmly within our own terms of reference.

Have you ever heard of parallel streams of time within a two-track time? Yes, there are such branch lines of time, somewhat illegal and suspect, but when, like us, one is burdened with contraband of supernumerary events that cannot be registered, one cannot be too fussy. Let us try to find at some point of history such a branch line, a blind track onto which to shunt these illegal events. There is nothing to fear. It will all happen imperceptibly: the reader won't feel any shock. Who knows? Perhaps even now, while we mention it, the doubtful maneuver is already behind us and we are, in fact, proceeding into a cul-de-sac.

II

My mother rushed in, frightened, and enfolded my screams with her arms, wanting to stifle them like flames and choke them in the warmth of

14

her love. She closed my mouth with hers and screamed together with me.

But I pushed her away, and, pointing to the column of fire, a golden bar that shot through the air like a splinter and would not disappear — full of brightness and spiralling dust specks — I cried: "Tear it out, tear it out!"

The large colored picture painted on the front of the stove grew blood red; it puffed itself up like a turkey, and in the convulsions of its veins, sinews, and all its swollen anatomy, it seemed to be bursting open, trying to liberate itself with a piercing crowing scream.

I stood rigid like a signpost, with outstretched, elongated fingers, pointing in anger, in fierce concentration, hand trembling in ecstasy.

My hand guided me, alien and pale, and pulled me after it, a stiff, waxen hand, like the large votive hands in churches, like angels' palms raised for an oath.

It was toward the end of winter. The world had dissolved in puddles, but sudden waves of heat seemed full of fire and pepper. The honeysweet pulp of day was cut into silvery furrows, into prisms filled with colors and spicy piquancies. Noonday collected within a short space the whole fire of these days and all the moments that glowed.

At that hour, unable to contain the heat, the day shed its scales of silvery tinplate, of crunchy tinfoil, and, layer after layer, disclosed its core of solid brightness. And as if this were not enough, chimneys smoked and billowed with lustrous steam. The bright flanks of the sky exploded into white plumes, banks of clouds dispersed under the shell-fire of an invisible artillery.

The window facing the sky swelled with those endless ascents, the curtains stood in flames, smoking in the fire, spilling golden shadows and shimmering spirals of air. Askew on the carpet lay a quadrilateral of brightness that could not detach itself from the floor. That bar of fire disturbed me deeply. I stood transfixed, legs astride, and barked short, hard curses at it in an alien voice.

In the doorway and in the hall stood frightened, perplexed people: relatives, neighbors, overdressed aunts. They approached on tiptoe and turned away, their curiosity unsatisfied. And I screamed:

"Don't you remember?" I shouted to my mother, to my brother. "I have been telling you that everything is held back, tamed, walled in by boredom, unliberated! And now look at that flood, at that flowering, at that bliss . . . ."

And I shed tears of happiness and helplessness.

"Wake up," I shouted, "come and help me! How can I face this flood alone, how can I deal with this inundation? How can I, all alone, answer the million dazzling questions that God is swamping me with?"

And as they remained silent, I cried in anger: "Hurry up, collect bucketfuls of these riches, store them up!"

But nobody could assist me; bewildered, they looked over their shoulders, hiding behind the backs of neighbors.

Then I realized what I had to do; I began to pull from the cupboards old Bibles and my father's half-filled and disintegrating ledgers, throwing them on the floor under that column of fire that glowed and brightened the air. I wanted more and more sheaves of paper. My mother and brother rushed in with ever new handfuls of old newspapers and magazines and threw them in stacks on the floor. And I sat among the piles of paper, blinded by the glare, my eyes full of explosions, rockets, and colors, and I drew wildly, feverishly, across the paper, over the printed or figure-covered pages. My colored pencils rushed in inspiration across columns of illegible text in masterly squiggles, in breakneck zigzags that knotted themselves suddenly into anagrams of vision, into enigmas of bright revelation, and then dissolved into empty, shiny flashes of lightning, following imaginary tracks.

Oh, those luminous drawings, made as if by a foreign hand. Oh, those transparent colors and shadows. How often, now, do I dream about them, then rediscover them after so many years at the bottom of old drawers, glimmering and fresh like dawn — still damp from the first dew of the day: figures, landscapes, faces!

Oh, those blues that stop your breath with the pang of fear. Oh, those greens greener than wonder. Oh, those preludes of anticipated colors waiting to be given a name!

Why did I squander them at the time with such wanton carelessness in the richness of surfeit? I allowed the neighbors to rummage about and plunder these stacks of drawings. They carried away whole sheaves of them. In what houses did they finally land, which rubbish heaps did they fill? Adela hung them up in the kitchen like wallpaper until the room became light and bright as if snow had fallen during the night.

The drawings were full of cruelty, pitfalls, and aggression. While I sat on the floor taut as a bow, immobile and lurking, the papers around me glowed brightly in the sun. It was enough if a drawing, pinned down by the tip of my pencil, made the slightest move toward escape, for my hand, trembling with new impulses and ideas, to attack it like a cat. Fierce and rapacious, I would, with lightning bites, savage the creation that tried to escape from under my crayon. And that crayon only left the paper when the now dead and immobile corpse displayed its colorful and fantastic anatomy on the page, like a plant in a herbal.

It was a murderous pursuit, a fight to the death. Who could tell the attacker from the attacked in that tangle that spluttered with rage, with squeaks and fears? At times my hand would start to attack twice or three times in vain, only to reach its victim on the fourth or fifth attempt. Often it winced in pain and fear in the fangs and pincers of the monsters writhing under my scalpel.

From hour to hour the visions became more crowded, bottlenecks arose, until one day all roads and byways swarmed with processions and the whole land was divided by meandering or marching columns — endless pilgrimages of beasts and animals.

As in Noah's day, colorful processions would flow, rivers of hair and manes, of wavy backs and tails, of heads nodding monotonously in time with their steps.

My room was the frontier and the tollgate. Here they stopped, tightly packed, bleating imploringly. They wriggled, shuffling their feet anxiously: humped and horned creatures, encased in the varied costumes and armors of zoology and frightened of each other, scared by their own disguises, looking with fearful and astonished eyes through the camouflage of their hairy hides and mooing mournfully, as if gagged under their attires.

Did they expect me to name them and solve their riddle? Or did they ask to be christened so that they could enter into their names and fill them with their being? Strange monsters, question-mark apparitions, blue-print creatures appeared, and I had to scream and wave my hands to chase them away.

17

They withdrew backward, lowering their heads, looking askance, lost within themselves; then they returned, dissolving into chaos, a rubbish dump of forms. How many straight or humped backs passed at that time under my hand, how many heads did my hand touch with a velvety caress!

I understood then why animals have horns: perhaps to introduce an element of strangeness into their lives, a whimsical or irrational joke. An *idée fixe*, transgressing fhe limits of their being, reaching high above their heads and emerging suddenly into light, frozen into matter palpable and hard. It then acquired a wild, incredible, and unpredictable shape, an arabesque, invisible to their eyes yet frightening, an unknown cypher under the threat of which they are forced to live. I understood why these animals are given to irrational and wild panic, to the frenzy of a stampede: pushed into madness, they are unable to extricate themselves from the tangle of these horns, between which — when they lower their heads — they peer wildly or sadly, as if trying to find a passage between the branches. These horned animals have no hope of deliverance and carry on their heads the stigma of their sin with sadness and resignation.

The cats were even further removed from light. Their perfection was frightening. Enclosed in the precision and efficiency of their bodies, they did not know either fault or deviation. They would descend for a moment into the depths of their being, then become immobile within their soft fur, solemnly and threateningly serious, while their eyes became round like moons, sucking the visible into their fiery craters. But a moment later, thrown back to the surface, they would yawn away their vacuity, disenchanted and without illusions. In their lives full of self-sufficient grace, there was no place for any alternative. Bored by this prison of perfection, seized with spleen, they spat with their wrinkled lips, while their broad, striped faces expressed an abstract cruelty.

Lower down martens, polecats, and foxes sneaked stealthily by, thieves among animals, creatures with a bad conscience. They had reached their place in life by cunning, intrigue, and trickery, against the intent of their Creator, and, pursued by hatred, always threatened, always on their guard, always in fear for that place, they passionately loved their furtive, stealthy existence and prepared to be torn to pieces in its defense.

At last, all the processions had filed past, and silence fell on my room once more. I again began to draw, engrossed in my papers that breathed brightness. The window was open, and on the windowsill doves and pigeons shivered in the spring breeze. Turning their heads to one side, they showed their round and glassy eyes in profile, as if afraid and full of flight. The days toward their end became soft, opaline, and translucent, then again pearly and full of a misty sweetness.

Easter came, and my parents went away for a week to visit my married sister. I was left alone in the flat, a prey to my inspirations. Adela brought me breakfast and dinner on a tray. I did not notice her presence when she stopped in the doorway in her Sunday best, smelling of spring in her tulles and silks.

Through the open window gentle breezes entered the room, filling it with the reflections of distant landscapes. For a moment the colors of distance stayed in the air, but not for long; they soon dispersed, dissolving into blue shadows, tender and gentle. The flood of paintings receded a little, the waters of imagination quieted and abated.

I sat on the floor. Spread out around me were my crayons and buttons of paint: godly colors, azures breathing freshness, greens straying to the limits of the possible. And when I took a red crayon in my hand, happy fanfares of crimson marched out into the world, all balconies brightened with red waving flags, and whole houses arranged themselves along streets into a triumphant lane. Processions of city firemen in cherry red uniforms paraded in brightly lighted happy streets, and gentlemen lifted their strawberry-colored bowlers in greeting. Cherry red sweetness and cherry red chirping of finches filled the air scented with lavender.

And when I reached for blue paint, the reflection of a cobalt spring fell on all the windows along the street; the panes trembled, one after the other, full of azure and heavenly fire; curtains waved as if alerted; and a joyful draft rose in that lane between muslin curtains and oleanders on the empty balconies, as if somebody distant had appeared from the other side of a long and bright avenue and was now approaching, somebody luminous, preceded by good tidings, by premonitions, announced by the flight of swallows, by beacons of fire spreading mile after mile.

III

At Easter time, usually at the end of March or the beginning of April,

Shloma, the son of Tobias, was released from prison, where he had been locked up for the winter after the brawls and follies he had been involved in during the summer and autumn. One afternoon that spring I saw him from the window leaving the barber who in our town combined the functions of hairdresser and surgeon; I watched him carefully open the shining glass-paned door of the shop and descend the three wooden steps. He looked fresh and somehow younger, his hair carefully cut. He was wearing a jacket that was too short and too tight for him and a pair of checked trousers; slim and youthful in spite of his forty years.

Trinity Square was at that time empty and tidy. After the spring thaw the slush had been rinsed away by torrential rains that had left the pavements washed clean. The thaw was followed by many days of quiet, discreet fine weather, with long spacious days stretching beyond measure into evenings when dusk seemed endless, empty, and fallow in its enormous expectations. When Shloma had shut the glass door of the barber's after himself, the sky filled it at once, just as it filled all the small windows of the one-story house.

Having come down the steps, he found himself completely alone on the edge of the large, empty square, which that afternoon seemed shaped like a gourd, like a new, unopened year. Shloma stood on its threshold, gray and extinguished, steeped in blueness and incapable of making a decision that would break the perfect roundness of an unused day.

Only once a year, on his discharge from prison, did Shloma feel so clean, unburdened, and new. Then the day received him unto itself, washed from sin, renewed, reconciled with the world, and with a sigh it opened before him the spotless orbs of its horizons.

Shloma did not hurry. He stood at the edge of the day and did not dare cross it, or advance with his small, youthful, slightly limping steps into the gently vaulted conch of the afternoon.

A translucent shadow lay over the city. The silence of that third hour after midday extracted from the walls of houses the pure whiteness of chalk and spread it voicelessly, like a pack of cards. Having dealt one round, it began a second, drawing reserves of whiteness from the large baroque facade of the Church of the Holy Trinity, which, like an enormous divine shift fallen from heaven, folded itself into pilasters, projections, and embrasures and puffed itself up into the pathos of volutes and archvolutes before coming to rest on the ground.

20

Shloma lifted his face and sniffed the air. The gentle breeze carried the scent of oleanders, of cinnamon, and of festive interiors. Then he sneezed noisily, and his famous powerful sneeze frightened the pigeons on the roof of the police station so that they panicked and flew away. Shloma smiled to himself: by the explosion of his nostrils God must have given him a sign that spring was here. This was a surer sign than the arrival of storks, and from then on days would be interrupted by these detonations, which, lost in the hubbub of the city, would punctuate its events from various directions like a witty commentary.

"Shloma," I called out from our low first-floor window.

Shloma noticed me, smiled his pleasant smile, and saluted.

"We are alone in the whole square, you and I," I said softly, because the inflated globe of the sky resounded like a barrel.

"You and I," he repeated with a sad smile. "How empty is the world today!"

We could have divided it between us and renamed it, so open, unprotected, and unattached was the world. On such a day the Messiah advances to the edge of the horizon and looks down on the earth. And when He sees it, white, silent, surrounded by azure and contemplation, He may lose sight of the boundary of clouds that arrange themselves into a passage, and, not knowing what He is doing, He may descend upon earth. And in its reverie the earth won't even notice Him, who has descended onto its roads, and people will wake up from their afternoon nap remembering nothing. The whole event will be rubbed out, and everything will be as it has been for centuries, as it was before history began.

"Is Adela in?" Shloma asked with a smile.

"There is no one at home, come up for a moment and I'll show you my drawings."

"If there is no one in, I shall do so with pleasure if you will open the door."

And looking left and right in the gateway, with the gait of a sneak thief he entered the house.

IV

"These are wonderful drawings," Shloma said, stretching out his arm with the gesture of an art connoisseur. His face lit up with the reflection of color and light. Then he folded his hand round his eye and looked through this improvised spyglass, screwing up his features in a grimace of earnest appreciation.

"One might say," he said, "that the world has passed through your hands in order to renew itself, in order to molt in them and shed its scales like a wonderful lizard. Ah, do you think I would be stealing and committing a thousand follies if the world weren't so outworn and decayed, with everything in it without its gilding, without the distant reflection of divine hands? What can one do in such a world? How can one not succumb and allow one's courage to fail when everything is shut tight, when all meaningful things are walled up, and when you constantly knock against bricks, as against the walls of a prison? Ah, Joseph, you should have been born earlier."

We stood in the semidarkness of my vast room, elongated in perspective toward the window opening on the square. Waves of air reached us in gentle pulsations, settling down on the silence. Each wave brought a new load of silence, seasoned with the colors of distance, as if the previous load had already been used up and exhausted. That dark room came to life only by the reflections of the houses far beyond the window, showing their colors in its depth as in a camera obscura. Through the window one could see, as through a telescope, the pigeons on the roof of the police station, puffed up and walking along the cornice of the attic. At times they rose up all at once and flew in a semicircle over the square. The room brightened for a moment with their fluttering wings, broadened with the echo of their flight, and then darkened when they settled down again.

"To you, Shloma," I said, "I can reveal the secret of these drawings. From the very start I had some doubts whether it was really I who made them. Sometimes they seem to me unintentional plagiarism, something that has been suggested to me or remembered . . . As if something outside me had used my inspiration for an unknown purpose. For I must confess to you," I added softly, looking into his eyes, "I have found the great Original . . ."

"The Original?" he asked, and his face lit up.

"Yes indeed, look for yourself," I said kneeling in front of a chest of drawers. I first took out from it Adela's silk dress, then a box of her ribbons, and finally her new shoes with high heels. The smell of powder and scent filled the air. I took out some books: in the bottom of the drawer lay the long unseen, precious, beloved script.

"Shloma," I said trembling with emotion, "look, here it is . . ."

But he was deep in thought, with one of Adela's shoes in his hand, looking at it meditatively.

"God did not say anything of the kind," he said, "and yet my conviction is total. I cannot find any arguments to the contrary. These lines are irresistible, amazingly accurate, and final, and like lightning illuminate the very center of things. How can you plead innocence, how can you resist when you yourself have been bribed, outvoted, and betrayed by your most loyal allies. The six days of Creation were divine and bright. But on the seventh day God broke down. On the seventh day he felt an unknown texture under his fingers, and frightened, he withdrew his hands from the world, although his creative fervor might have lasted for many more days and nights. Oh, Joseph, beware the seventh day. . . ."

And lifting up with awe Adela's slim shoe, he spoke as if seduced by the lustrous eloquence of that empty shell of patent leather:

"Do you understand the horrible cynicism of this symbol on a woman's foot, the provocation of her licentious walk on such elaborate heels? How can I leave you under the sway of that symbol? God forbid that I should do it. . . ."

Saying this, his skillful fingers stuffed Adela's shoes, dress, and beads into his pocket.

"What are you doing, Shloma?"

But he was already moving quickly toward the door, limping slightly, his checked trousers flapping round his legs. In the doorway he turned his gray, already indistinct face toward me and lifted his hand in a reassuring gesture. And then he was gone.

SPRING

I

This is the story of a certain spring that was more real, more dazzling and brighter than any other spring, a spring that took its text seriously: an inspired script, written in the festive red of sealing wax and of calendar print, the red of colored pencils and of enthusiasm, the amaranth of happy telegrams from far away . . .

Each spring begins like this, with stunning horoscopes reaching beyond the expectations of a single season. In each spring there is everything: processions and manifestations, revolutions and barricades. Each brings with it, at a given moment, the hot wind of frenzy, an infinity of sadnesses and delights that seek in vain their equivalents in reality.

Later on, these exaggerations, culminations, and ecstasies are transformed into blossoming, into the trembling of cool leaves, and are absorbed by the tumultuous rustling of gardens. In this way springs betray their promise; each of them, engrossed in the breathless murmur of flowering parks, forgets its pledges and sheds, one by one, the leaves of its testament.

But that particular spring had the courage to endure, to keep its promise and bond. After many unsuccessful efforts, it succeeded in acquiring a permanent shape and burst upon the world as the ultimate all-embracing spring.

Oh that winds of events, that hurricane of happenings: the successful coups d'état, those grandiose, triumphant, highfalutin days! How I wish that the pace of this story would catch their entrancing, inspired beat, the heroic tone of that epic, the marching rhythm of that springlike "Marseillaise"!

How boundless is the horoscope of spring! One can read it in a thousand different ways, interpret it blindly, spell it out at will, happy to be able to decipher anything at all amid the misleading divinations of birds. The text can be read forward or backward, lose its sense and find it again in many versions, in a thousand alternatives. Because the text of spring is marked by hints, ellipses, lines dotted on an empty azure, and because the gaps between the syllables are filled by the frivolous guesses and surmises of birds, my story, like that text, will follow many different tracks and will be punctuated by springlike dashes, sighs, and dots.

II

During those wild spacious nights that preceded the spring, when the sky was vast, still raw and unscented, and aerial byways led into the starry infinite, my father sometimes took me out to supper in a small garden restaurant hidden between the back walls of the farthest houses of the market square.

We walked in the damp light of streetlamps hissing in the wind, cutting across the large expanse of the square, forlorn, crushed by the immensity of the sky, lost and disoriented by its empty vastness. My father lifted his face bathed in the scanty light and looked anxiously at the starry grit scattered among the shallows of heavenly eddies. Their irregular and countless agglomerations were not yet ordered into constellations, and no figures emerged from the sterile pools. The sadness of the starlit space lay heavily over the town, the lamps pierced the night

below with beams of light, tying them haphazardly into knots. Under these lamps, passers-by stopped in groups of two or three in the circle of light, which for a short moment looked like the glow of a lamp over a dining table, although the night was indifferent and unfriendly, dividing the sky into wild airscapes, exposed to the blows of a homeless wind. Conversations faltered; under the deep shadow of their hats people smiled with their eyes and listened dreamily to the distant hum of the stars.

The paths in the restaurant garden were covered with gravel. Two standard lamps hissed gently. Gentlemen in black frock coats sat in twos or threes at tables covered with white cloths, looking dully at the polished plates. Sitting thus, they calculated mentally the moves on the great chessboard of the sky, each seeing with his mind's eye the jumping knights and lost pawns of which new constellations immediately took the place.

Musicians on the rostrum dipped their mustaches in mugs of bitter beer and sat around idly, deep in thought. Their violins and nobly shaped cellos lay neglected under the voiceless downpour of the stars. From time to time one of them would reach for his instrument and try it, tuning it plaintively to harmonize with his discreet coughing. Then he would put it aside as if it were not yet ready, not yet measuring up to the night, which flowed along unheeding. And then, as the knives and forks began to clank softly above the white tablecloths, the violins would rise alone, now suddenly mature although tentative and unsure just a short while before; slim and narrow-waisted, they eloquently proceeded with their task, took up again the lost human cause, and pleaded before the indifferent tribunal of stars, now set in a sky on which the shapes of the instruments floated like water signs or fragments of keys, unfinished lyres or swans, an imitatory, thoughtless starry commentary on the margin of music.

The town photographer, who had for some time been casting meaningful glances at us from a neighboring table, joined us at last and sat down, putting his mug of beer on the table. He smiled equivocally, fought with his own thoughts, snapped his fingers, losing again and again some elusive point. We had felt for some time that our improvised restaurant encampment under the auspices of distant stars was doomed to collapse miserably, unequal to the ever increasing demands of the night. What could we set against these bottomless wastes? The night simply canceled our human undertaking, even though it was supported by the sound of the violins, and moved into the gap, shifting its constellations to their rightful positions.

We looked at the disintegrating camp of tables, the battlefield of half-folded tablecloths and crumpled napkins, across which the night trod in triumph, luminous and immense. We got up as well, and our thoughts, forestalling our bodies, followed the movements of starry carts on their great and shiny paths.

And so we walked off under the stars, anticipating with half-closed eyes the ever more splendid illuminations. Ah, the cynicism of such a triumphant night! Having taken possession of the whole sky, it now played dominoes in space, lazily and without calculation, indifferently losing or winning millions. Then, bored, it traced on the battlefield of overturned tiles transparent squiggles, smiling faces, the same smile in a thousand copies, which a moment later rose toward the stars, already eternal, and dispersed into starry indifference.

On our way home we stopped at a pastry shop to get cakes. No sooner had we entered the white, icing sugar room than the night suddenly tensed up and became watchful lest we should escape. It waited for us patiently, outside the door, showing the unmoving stars through the window panes of the shop while we were inside selecting our cakes with great deliberation.

It was then that I saw Bianca for the first time. She stood sideways in front of the counter with her governess; she was slim and linear in a white dress as if she had just left the zodiac. She did not turn her head but stood with the perfect poise of a young girl, eating a cream bun. I could not see her clearly, for the zigzags of starry lines still lingered under my eyelids. It was the first time that our still confused horoscopes had crossed, met, and dissolved in indifference. We did not anticipate our fate from that early aspect of the stars, and we left the shop casually, making the glass-fronted door rattle.

The photographer, my father and I walked home in a roundabout way, through distant suburbs. The few houses there were small, and eventually houses disappeared altogether. We entered a climate of gentle warm spring; the silvery reflection of a young, violet moon just risen crept on the muddy path. That pre-spring night antedated itself, feverishly anticipating its later phases. The air, a short while before seasoned with the usual tartness of the time of year, became sweetly insipid, filled with the smell of rain, of damp loam, and of the first snowdrops that bloomed spectrally in the white, magic light. And it was strange that under that benevolent moon frogs' spawn did not spread on the silvery mud, that the night did not resound with a thousand gossiping mouths on those graveled river banks saturated with shiny drops of sweet water. And one had to imagine the croaking of frogs in the night, which was filled with the murmur of subterranean springs, so that — after a moment of stillness — the moon might continue on its way and climb higher in the sky, spreading wide its whiteness, ever more luminous, more magical and transcendental.

We walked thus under the waxing moon. My father and the photographer half-carried me between them, for I was stumbling with tiredness and hardly able to walk. Our steps crunched in the moist sand. It had been a long time since I had slept while walking, and under my eyelids I now saw the whole phosphorescence of the sky, full of luminous signs, of signals and starry phenomena. At last we reached an open field. My father laid me down on a coat spread on the ground. With closed eyes I saw the sun, the moon, and eleven stars aligned in the sky and parading before me.

"Bravo, Joseph!" my father exclaimed and clapped his hands in praise. I committed an unconscious plagiarism of another Joseph and the circumstances were not the same, but no one held it against me. My father, Jacob, shook his head and smacked his lips, and the photographer stood his tripod on the sand, pulled out his camera like a concertina, and hid himself entirely in the folds of its black cloth: he was photographing the strange phenomenon, a shining horoscope in the sky, while I, my head swimming in brightness, lay blinded on the ground and limply held up my dream to exposure.

III

The days became long, light, and spacious — maybe too spacious for their content, which was still poor and tenuous. They were days with an allowance for growth, days pale with boredom and impatience and full of waiting. A light, bright breeze cut their emptiness, yet untroubled by the exhalations of the bare and sunny gardens; it blew the streets clean, and they looked long and festively swept, as if waiting for someone's announced but uncertain arrival. The sun headed for the equinoctial position, then braked and almost reached the point at which it would seem to stand immobile, keeping an ideal balance and throwing out streams of fire, wave after wave, onto the empty and receptive earth.

A continuous draft blew through the whole breadth of the horizon, creating avenues and lanes. It calmed itself while blowing and stopped at

last, breathless, enormous and glassy as if wishing to enclose in its all-embracing mirror the ideal picture of the city, a Fata Morgana magnified in the depth of its luminous concavity. Then the world stood motionless for a while, holding its breath, blinded, wanting to enter whole into that illusory picture, into that provisional eternity that opened up before it. But the enticing offer passed, the wind broke its mirror, and Time took us into his possession once again.

The Easter holidays came, long and opaque. Free from school, we young scholars wandered about the town without aim or necessity, not knowing how to make use of our empty, undefined leisure. Undefined ourselves, we expected something from Time, which was unable to provide a definition and wasted itself in a thousand subterfuges.

In front of the café, tables were already put out on the pavement. Ladies sat at them in brightly colored dresses, and in small gulps they swallowed the breezes as if they were ice cream. Their skirts rustled, the wind worried them from below like a small angry dog. The ladies became flushed, their faces burned from the dry wind, and their lips were parched. This was still an interval with its customary boredom, while the world moved slowly and tremulously toward some boundary.

In those days we all ate like wolves. Dried out by the wind, we rushed home to eat in dull silence enormous chunks of bread and butter, or else we would buy on street corners large cracknels smelling of freshness, or we would sit in a row without a single thought in our heads in the vast vaulted porch of a house in the market square. Through the low arcades we could see the white and clean expanse of the square. Empty, strong-smelling wine barrels stood under the walls of the hall. We sat on a long bench, on which colored peasants' kerchiefs were displayed on market days, and we thumped the planks with our heels in listlessness and boredom.

Suddenly Rudolph, his mouth still full of cracknel, produced from his pocket a stamp album and spread it before me.

IV

I realized in a flash why that spring had until then been so empty and dull. Not knowing why, it had been introverted and silent — retreating, melting into space, into an empty azure without meaning or definition — a questioning empty shell for the admission of an unknown content. Hence that blue (as if just awakened) neutrality, that great and indifferent readiness for everything. That spring was holding itself ready: deserted and roomy, it was simply awaiting a revelation. Who could foresee that this would emerge — ready, fully armed, and dazzling — from Rudolph's stamp album?

In it were strange abbreviations and formulae, recipes for civilizations, handy amulets that allowed one to hold his thumb and finger between the essence of climates and provinces. These were bank drafts on empires and republics, on archipelagoes and continents. Emperors and usurpers, conquerors and dictators could not possess anything greater. I suddenly anticipated the sweetness of domination over lands and peoples, the thorn of that frustration that can only be healed by power. With Alexander of Macedonia, I wanted to conquer the whole world and not a square inch of ground less.

V

Ignorant, eager, full of chafing desire, I took the march-past of creation, the parade of countries, shining processions I could see only at intervals, between crimson eclipses, caused by the rush of blood from my heart beating in time with the universal march of all the races. Rudolph paraded before my eyes those battalions and regiments; he took the salute fully absorbed and diligent. He, the owner of the album, degraded himself voluntarily to the role of an aide, reported to me solemnly, somewhat disoriented by his equivocal part. At last, very excited in a rush of fierce generosity, he pinned on me, like a medal, a pink Tasmania, glowing like May, and a Hyderabad swarming with a gypsy babble of entangled lettering.

VI

It is then that the revelation took place: the vision of the fiery beauty of the world suddenly appeared, the secret message of good tidings, the special announcement of the limitless possibilities of being. Bright, fierce, and breathtaking horizons opened wide, the world trembled and shook in its joints, leaning dangerously, threatening to break out from its rules and habits.

What attraction, dear reader, has a postage stamp for you? What do you make of the profile of Emperor Franz Joseph with his bald patch crowned by a laurel crown? Is it a symbol of ordinariness, or is it the ultimate within the bounds of possibility, the guarantee of unpassable frontiers within which the world is enclosed once and for all?

At that time, the world was totally encompassed by Franz Joseph I. On all the horizons there loomed this omnipresent and inevitable profile, shutting the world off, like a prison. And just when we had given up hope and bitterly resigned ourselves inwardly to the uniformity of the world — the powerful guarantor of whose narrow immutability was Franz Joseph I — then suddenly Oh God, unaware of the importance of it, you opened before me that stamp album, you allowed me to cast a look on its glimmering colors, on the pages that shed their treasures, one after another, ever more glaring and more frightening. . . . Who will hold it against me that I stood blinded, weak with emotion, and that tears flowed from my eyes? What a dazzling relativism, what a Copernican deed, what flux of all categories and concepts! Oh God, so there were uncounted varieties of existence, so your world was indeed vast and infinite! This was more than I had ever imagined in my boldest dreams. So my early anticipation that, in spite of all evidence to the contrary, continued to nag at me and insist that the world was immeasurable in its variety had been proven right at last!

VII

The world at that time was circumscribed by Franz Joseph I. On each stamp, on every coin, and on every postmark his likeness confirmed its stability and the dogma of its oneness. This was the world, and there were no other worlds besides, the effigies of the imperial-and-royal old man proclaimed. Everything else was make-believe, wild pretense, and usurpation. Franz Joseph I rested on top of everything and checked the world in its growth.

By inclination we tend to be loyal, dear reader. Being also affable and easygoing, we are not insensitive to the attractions of authority. Franz Joseph I was the embodiment of the highest authority. If that authoritarian old man threw all his prestige on the scales, one could do nothing but give up all one's aspirations and longings, manage as well as one could in the only possible world — that is, a world without illusions and romanticism — and forget.

But when the prison seemed to be irrevocably shut, when the last bolt-hole was bricked up, when everything had conspired to keep silent about You, Oh God, when Franz Joseph had barred and sealed even the last chink so that one should not be able to see You, then You rose wearing a flowing cloak of seas and continents and gave him the lie. You, God, took upon Yourself the odium of heresy and revealed this enormous, magnificent, colorful blasphemy to the world. Oh splendid Heresiarch! You struck me with the burning book, with that explosive stamp album from Rudolph's pocket. I did not know at that time that stamp albums could be pocket-size; in my blindness I at first took it for a paper pistol with which we sometimes pretended to fire at school, from under the seats, to the annoyance of teachers. Yet this little album symbolized God's fervent tirade, a fiery and splendid philippic against Franz Joseph and his estate of prose. It was the book of truth and splendor.

I opened it, and the glamour of colorful worlds, of becalmed spaces, spread before me. God walked through it, page after page, pulling behind Him a train woven from all the zones and climates. Canada, Honduras, Nicaragua, Abracadabra, Hipporabundia . . . I at last understood you, Oh God. These were the disguises for your riches, these were the first random words that came to your mind. You reached into your pocket and showed me, like a handful of marbles, the possibilities that your world contained. You did not attempt to be precise; you said whatever came into your mind. You might equally well have said Panphibrass and Halleleevah, and the air among palms would flutter with motley parrot wings, and the sky, like an enormous sapphire, cabbage rose, blown open to its core, would show in its dazzling center your frightening peacock eye, would shine with the glare of your wisdom, and would spread a super-scent. You wanted to dazzle me, Oh God, to seduce me, perhaps to boast, for even You have moments of vanity when you succumb to self-congratulation. Oh, how I love these moments!

How greatly diminished you have become, Franz Joseph, and your gospel of prose! I looked for you in vain. At last I found you. You were among the crowd, but how small, unimportant, and gray. You were marching with some others in the dust of the highway, immediately following South America, but preceding Australia, and singing together with the others: Hosanna!

VIII

I became a disciple of the new gospel. I struck up a friendship with Rudolph. I admired him, feeling vaguely that he was only a tool, that the album was destined for somebody else. In fact, he seemed to me only its guardian. He catalogued, he stuck in and unstuck the stamps, he put the album away and locked the drawer. In reality he was sad, like a man who guesses that he is waning while I am waxing. He was like the man who came to straighten the Lord's paths.

IX

I had reasons to believe that the album was predestined for me. Many signs seemed to point to its holding a message and a personal commission for me. There was, for instance, the fact that no one felt himself to be the owner of the album, not even Rudolph, who acted more like its servant, an unwilling and lazy servant in the bond of duty. Sometimes envy would flood his heart with bitterness. He rebelled inwardly against the role of keeper of a treasure that did not really belong to him. He looked with envy on the reflection of distant worlds that flooded my face with a gamut of color. Only in that reflection did he notice the glow of these pages. His own feelings were not really engaged.

X

I once saw a prestidigitator. He stood in the center of the stage, slim and visible to everybody, and demonstrated his top hat, showing its empty white bottom. Thus having assured us that his art was above suspicion of fraudulent manipulation, he traced with his wand a complicated magic sign and at once, with exaggerated precision and openness, began to produce from the top hat paper strips, colored ribbons by the foot, by the yard, finally by the mile. The room filled with the rustling mass of color, became bright from the heaps of light tissue, while the artist still pulled at the endless weft, despite the spectators' protests, their cries of ecstasy and spasmodic sobs until it became clear that all this effort was nothing to him, that he was drawing this plenty, not from his own, but from supernatural resources that had been opened to him and that were beyond human measures and calculations.

But some people who could perceive the real sense of this demonstration went home deep in thought and enchanted, having had a glimpse of the truth that God is boundless.

XI

Now perhaps is the time for drawing a parallel between Alexander the Great and my modest self. Alexander was susceptible to the aroma of countries. His nostrils anticipated untold possibilities. He was one of those men on whose head God lays His hand while they are asleep so that they get to know what they don't know, so that they are filled with intuitions and conjectures, while the reflections of distant worlds pass across their closed eyelids. Alexander, however, took divine allusions too literally. As a man of action — that is to say, of a shallow spirit — he interpreted his mission as that of conqueror of the world. He felt as unfulfilled as I was, his breast heaved with the same kind of sighs, and he hungered after ever new horizons and landscapes. There was no one who could point out his mistake. Not even Aristotle could understand him. Thus, although he had conquered the whole world, he died disappointed, doubting the God who kept eluding him and doubting God's miracles. His likeness adorned the coins and seals of many lands. In the end, he became the Franz Joseph of his age.

XII

I should like to give the reader at least an approximate idea of that album in which the events of that spring were adumbrated, then finally arranged. An indescribable, alarming wind blew through the avenue of these stamps, the decorated street of crests and standards, and unfurled these emblems in an ominous silence, under the shadow of clouds that loomed threateningly over the horizon. Then the first heralds appeared in the empty street, in dress uniforms with red brassards, perspiring, perplexed, full of the sense of their mission. They gestured silently, preoccupied and solemn, the street immediately darkened from the advancing procession, and all the side streets were obscured by the steps of the demonstrating throngs. It was an enormous manifestation of countries, a universal May Day, a march-past of the world. The world was demonstrating with thousands of hands raised as for an oath, it averred in a thousand voices that it was *not* behind Franz Joseph but behind somebody infinitely greater. The demonstration was bathed in a pale red, almost pink light, the liberating color of enthusiasm. From Santo Domingo, from San Salvador, from Florida came hot and panting delegations, clothed in raspberry red, who waved cherry pink bowler hats from which chattering goldfinches escaped in twos and threes. Happy breezes sharpened the glare of trumpets, brushed softly against the surface of the instruments, and brought forth tiny sparks of electricity. In spite of the large numbers taking part in the march-past, everything was orderly, the enormous parade unfolded itself in silence and according to plan. There were moments when the flags, waving violently from balconies, writhing in amaranthine spasms, in violent silent flutters, in frustrated bursts of enthusiasm, became still as for a roll call: the whole street then turned red and full of a silent threat, while in the darkened distance the carefully counted salvoes of artillery resounded dully, all forty-nine of them in the dusk-filled air.

And then the horizon suddenly clouded over as before a spring storm, with only the instruments of the bands brassily shining, and in the silence one could hear the murmur of the darkening sky, the rustle of distant spaces, while from nearby gardens the scent of bird cherry floated in concentrated doses and dissolved imperceptibly in the air.

XIII

One day toward the end of April the morning was warm and gray; people walking in the streets and looking ahead did not notice that the trees in the park were splitting in many places and showing sweet, festering wounds.

Enmeshed in the black net of tree branches, the gray, sultry sky lay heavily on human shoulders. People scrambled from under its weight like June bugs in a warm dampness or, without a thought in their heads, sat hunched on the benches of the park, a sheet of faded newspaper on their laps.

Then at about ten o'clock the sun appeared like a luminous smudge from under the swollen body of cloud, and suddenly among the tree branches all the fat buds began to shine and a veil of chirruping uncovered the now pale golden face of the day. Spring had come.

And at once the avenue of the park, empty a moment before, filled with people hurrying in all directions, as if this were the hub of the city, and blossomed with women's frocks. Quick and shapely girls were hurrying — some to work in shops and offices, others to assignations — but for a few moments, while they passed the openwork basket of the avenue, which now exuded the moisture of a greenhouse and was filled with birds' trills, they seemed to belong to that avenue and to that hour, to be the extras in a scene of the theater of spring, as if they had been reborn in the park together with the delicate branches and leaves. The park avenue seemed crowded with their refreshing hurry and the rustle of their underskirts. Ah, these airy, freshly starched shifts, led for a walk under the openwork shadow of the spring corridor, shifts damp under the armpits, now drying in the violet breezes of distance! Ah, these young, rhythmical steps, those legs hot from exercise in their new crunchy silk stockings that covered red spots and pimples, the healthy spring rash of hot-blooded bodies! The whole park became shamelessly pimply, and all the trees came out in buddy spots, which burst with the voices of birds.

And then the avenue became empty, and under the vaults of trees one could hear the soft squeaks of a perambulator on high wheels. In the small varnished canoe, engulfed in highly starched bands of linen, like in a bouquet, slept something more precious than a flower. The girl who slowly pushed the pram would lean over it from time to time, tilt to its back wheels the swinging, squeaking basket that bloomed with white freshness, and blow caressingly into the bouquet of tulle until she had reached its sweet sleepy core, across whose dreams tides of cloud and light floated like a fairy tale.

At noon the paths of the park were crisscrossed with light and shadow, and the song of birds hung continuously in the air, but the women passing on the edge of the promenade were already tired, their hair matted with migraine, and their faces fatigued by the spring. Later still, the avenue emptied completely, and in the silence of the early afternoon smells began slowly to drift across from the park restaurant.

XIV

Every day at the same time, accompanied by her governess, Bianca could be seen walking in the park. What can I say about Bianca, how can I describe her? I only know that she is marvelously true to herself, that she fulfills her program completely. My heart tight with pleasure, I notice again and again how with every step, light as a dancer, she enters into her being and how with each of her movements she unconsciously hits the target.

Her walk is ordinary, without excessive grace, but its simplicity is touching, and my heart fills with gladness that Bianca can be herself so simply, without any strain or artifice.

Once she slowly lifted her eyes to me, and the seriousness of that look pierced me like an arrow. Since then, I have known that I can hide nothing from her, that she knows all my thoughts. At that moment, I put myself at her disposal, completely and without reservation. She accepted this by almost imperceptibly closing her eyes. It happened without a word, in passing, in one single look.

When I want to imagine her, I can only evoke one meaningless detail: the chapped skin on her knees, like a boy's; this is deeply touching and guides my thoughts into tantalizing regions of contradiction, into blissful antinomies. Everything else, above and below her knees, is transcendental and defies my imagination.

XV

Today I delved again into Rudolph's stamp album. What a marvelous study! The text is full of cross-references and allusions. But all the lines converge toward Bianca. What blissful conjectures! My expectations and hopes are ever more dazzling. Ah, how I suffer, how heavy is my heart with the mysteries that I anticipate!

XVI

A band is now playing every evening in the city park, and people on their spring outings fill the avenues. They walk up and down, pass one another, and meet again in symmetrical, continuously repeated patterns. The young men are wearing new spring hats and nonchalantly carrying gloves in their hands. Through the hedges and between the tree trunks the dresses of girls walking in parallel avenues glow. The girls walk in pairs, swinging their hips, strutting like swans under the foam of their ribbons and flounces; sometimes they land on garden seats, as if tired by the idle parade, and the bells of their flowered muslin skirts expand on the seats, like roses beginning to shed their petals. And then they disclose their crossed legs — white irresistibly expressive shapes — and the young men, passing them, grow speechless and pale, hit by the accuracy of the argument, completely convinced and conquered.

At a particular moment before dusk all the colors of the world become more beautiful than ever, festive, ardent yet sad. The park quickly fills with pink varnish, with shining lacquer that makes every other color glow deeper; and at the same time the beauty of the colors becomes too glaring and somewhat suspect. In another instant the thickets of the park strewn with young greenery, still naked and twiggy, fill with the pinkness of dusk, shot with coolness, spilling the indescribable sadness of things supremely beautiful but mortal.

Then the whole park becomes an enormous, silent orchestra, solemn and composed, waiting under the raised baton of the conductor for its music to ripen and rise; and over that potential, earnest symphony a quick theatrical dusk spreads suddenly as if brought down by the sounds swelling in the instruments. Above, the young greenness of the leaves is pierced by the tones of an invisible oriole, and at once everything turns somber, lonely, and late, like an evening forest.

A hardly perceptible breeze sails through the treetops, from which dry petals of cherry blossom fall in a shower. A tart scent drifts high

40

under the dusky sky and floats like a premonition of death, and the first stars shed their tears like lilac blooms picked from pale, purple bushes.

It is then that a strange desperation grips the youths and young girls walking up and down and meeting at regular intervals. Each man transcends himself, becomes handsome and irresistible like a Don Juan, and his eyes express a murderous strength that chills a woman's heart. The girls' eyes sink deeper and reveal dark labyrinthine pools. Their pupils distend, open without resistance, and admit those conquerors who stare into their opaque darkness. Hidden paths of the park reveal themselves and lead to thickets, ever deeper and more rustling, in which they lose themselves, as in a backstage tangle of velvet curtains and secluded corners. And no one knows how they reach, through the coolness of these completely forgotten darkened gardens, the strange spots where darkness ferments and degenerates, and vegetation emits a smell like the sediment in long-forgotten wine barrels.

Wandering blindly in the dark plush of the gardens, the young people meet at last in an empty clearing, under the last purple glow of the setting sun, over a pond that has been growing muddy for years; on a rotting balustrade, somewhere at the back gate of the world, they find themselves again in pre-existence, a life long past, in attitudes of a distant age; they sob and plead, rise to promises never to be fulfilled, and, climbing up the steps of exaltation, reach summits and climaxes beyond which there is only death and the numbness of nameless delight.

XVII

What is a spring dusk?

Have we now reached the crux of the matter, and is this the end of the road? We are beginning to be at a loss for words: they become confused, meandering, and raving. And yet it is beyond these words that the description of that unbelievable, immense spring must begin. The miracle of dusk! Again, the power of our magic has failed and the dark element that cannot be embraced is roaring somewhere beyond it. Words are split into their components and dissolved, they return to their etymology, re-enter their depths and distant obscure roots. This process is to be taken literally. For it is getting dark, our words lose themselves among unclear associations: Acheron, Orcus, the Underworld . . . Do you feel darkness seeping out of these words, molehills crumbling, the smell of cellars, of graves slowly opening? What is a spring dusk? We ask this question once more, the fervent refrain of our quest that must remain unrewarded.

When the tree roots want to speak, when under the turf a great many old tales and ancient sagas have been collected, when too many whispers have been gathered underground, inarticulate pulp and dark nameless things that existed before words — then the bark of trees blackens and disintegrates into thick, rough scales which form deep furrows. You dip your face into that fluffy fur of dusk, and everything becomes impenetrable and airless like under the lid of a coffin. Then you must screw up your eyes and bully them, squeeze your sight through the impenetrable, push across the dull humus — and suddenly you are at your goal, on the other side; you are in the Deep, in the Underworld. And you can see . . .

It is not quite as dark here as we thought. On the contrary, the interior is pulsating with light. It is, of course, the internal light of roots, a wandering phosphorescence, tiny veins of light marbling the darkness, an evanescent shimmer of nightmarish substances. Likewise, when we sleep, severed from the world, straying into deep introversion, on a return journey into ourselves, we can see clearly through our closed eyelids, because thoughts are kindled in us by internal tapers and smolder erratically. This is how total regressions occur, retreats into self, journeys to the roots. This is how we branch out into anamnesis and are shaken by underground subcutaneous shivers. For it is only above ground, in the light of day, that we are a trembling, articulate bundle of tunes; in the depth we disintegrate again into black murmurs, confused purring, a multitude of unfinished stories.

It is only now that we realize what the soil is on which spring thrives and why spring is so unspeakably sad and heavy with knowledge. Oh, we would not have believed it had we not seen it with our own eyes! Here are labyrinths of depth, warehouses and silos of things, graves that are still warm, the litter, and the rot. Age-old tales. Seven layers (like in ancient Troy), corridors, chambers, treasure chests. Numerous golden masks — one next to another — flattened smiles, faces eaten out, mummies, empty cocoons . . . Here are columbaria, the drawers for the

42

dead, in which they lie desiccated, blackened like roots, awaiting their moment. Here are great apothecary storerooms where they are displayed in lachrymatories, crucibles, and jars. They have been standing on the shelves for years in a long, solemn row, although no one has been there to buy them. Perhaps they have come alive in their pigeonholes, completely healed, clean as incense, and scented — chirruping specifics, awakened impatient drugs, balms, and morning unguents — balancing their early taste on the tip of the tongue. These walled-in pigeon perches are full of chicks hatching out and making their first attempts at chirping. How dew-fresh and time-anticipating are these long, empty lanes where the dead wake up in rows, deeply rested — to a completely new dawn!

But we have not finished yet; we can go deeper. There is nothing to fear. Give me your hand, take another step: we are at the roots now, and at once everything becomes dark, spicy, and tangled like in the depth of a forest. There is a smell of turf and tree rot; roots wander about, entwined, full with juices that rise as if sucked up by pumps. We are on the nether side, at the lining of things, in gloom stitched with phosphorescence. There is a lot of movement and traffic, pulp and rot, tribes and generations, a brood of bibles and iliads multiplied a thousand times! Wanderings and tumult, the tangle and hubbub of history! That road leads no farther. We are here at the very bottom, in the dark foundations, among the Mothers. Here are the bottomless infernos, the hopeless Ossianic spaces, all those lamentable Nibelungs. Here are the great breeding grounds of history, factories of plots, hazy smoking rooms of fables and tales. Now at last one can understand the great and sad machinery of spring. Ah, how it thrives on stories, on events, on chronicles, on destinies! Everything we have ever read, all the stories we have heard and those we have never heard before but have been dreaming since childhood — here and nowhere else is their home and their motherland. Where would writers find their ideas, how would they muster the courage for invention, had they not been aware of these reserves, this frozen capital, these funds salted away in the underworld? What a buzz of whispers, what persistent purr of the earth! Continuous persuasions are throbbing in your ears. You walk with half-closed eyes in a warmth of whispers, smiles, and suggestions, importuned endlessly, pin-pricked a thousand times by questions as though by delicate insect proboscides. They would like you to take something from them, anything, a pinch at least of these disembodied, timeless stories, absorb it into your young life, into your bloodstream; save it, and try to live with it. For what is spring if not a resurrection of history? It alone among these disembodied things is alive, real, cool, and unknowing. Oh, how attracted are these specters and phantoms, larvae and lemurs, to its young green blood, to its vegetative ignorance! And spring, helpless and naïve, takes them into its slumber, sleeps with them, wakes half-conscious at dawn, and remembers nothing. This is why it is heavy with the sum of all that is forgotten and sorrowful, for it alone must live vicariously on these rejected lives, and must be beautiful to embody all that has been lost. . . . And to make up for all this, it has only the heady smell of cherry blossom to offer, streaming in one eternal, infinite flood in which everything is contained. . . . What does forgetting mean? New greenery has grown overnight on old stories, a soft green tuft, a bright, dense mass of buds has sprouted from all the pores in a uniform growth like the hair on a boy's head on the day after a haircut. How green with oblivion spring becomes: old trees regain their sweet nescience and wake up with twigs, unburdened by memories although their roots are steeped in old chronicles. That greenness will once more make them new and fresh as in the beginning, and stories will become rejuvenated and start their plots once again, as if they had never been.

There are so many unborn tales. Oh, those sad lamenting choruses among the roots, those stories outbidding one another, those inexhaustible monologues among suddenly exploding improvisations! Have we the patience to listen to them? Before the oldest known legend there were others no one has ever heard; there were nameless forerunners; novels without a title; enormous, pale, and monotonous epics; shapeless bardic tales; formless plots; giants without a face; dark texts written for the drama of evening clouds. And behind these lays, sagas, unwritten books, books — eternal pretenders, and lost books *in partibus infidelium*.

Among all the stories that crowd at the roots of spring, there is one that long ago passed into the ownership of the night and settled down forever at the bottom of the firmament as an eternal accompaniment and background to the starry spaces. During every spring night, whatever might happen in it, that story unfolds itself above the croaking of frogs and the endless working of mills. A man walks under the milky stars strewn by the handmills of night; he walks hugging a child in the folds of his cloak; he walks across the sky, constantly on his way, a perpetual wanderer through the endless spaces. Oh, the sadness of loneliness, the pathos of orphanhood in the vastness of night. Oh, glare of distant stars! In that story time can never change anything. The story appears on the starry horizons and will do so forever, always afresh, for once derailed from the tracks of time, it has become unfathomable, never to be exhausted by repetition. There goes that man who hugs the child in his arms — we are repeating on purpose that refrain, that pitiful motto of the night, in order to express the intermittent continuity of walking, sometimes obstructed by the tangle of stars, sometimes completely invisible during long, silent intervals in which one can feel the breeze of eternity. The distant worlds come within reach, glaring frighteningly, they send violent signals through eternity in an unspoken, mute language — while he walks on and on and soothes the little girl endlessly, monotonously, and without hope, helpless against the whispers and sweet persuasions of the night, against the only word formed on the lips of silence, when no one is listening to it. . . .

The story is about a princess kidnapped and changed for another child.

XVIII

When late at night they return to the spacious villa among gardens, to a low white room where a black shining piano stands with all its strings silent, when through the wide glass wall, as if through the panes of a greenhouse, the spring night looks in, pale and blinking with stars, and the scent of cherry blossom floats from bottles and containers over the cool white bedding — then anxious listening fills the sleepless night and the heart speaks in sleep, sobs, races, and stumbles through the long, dewy, moth-swarming night, luminous and scented with bird cherry.

. . . Ah, it is the bird cherry that gives depth to the limitless night; hearts aching from flights, tired from happy pursuits, would like to rest awhile on some airy narrow ridge, but from that endless pale night a new night is born, even paler and more disembodied, cut into luminous lines and zigzags, into spirals of stars and pale flights, pierced a thousand times by the suckers of invisible gnats bloated with the blood of maidens; the tireless heart must again stumble through sleep, mad, engaged in starry and complex affairs, in breathless hurry, in moonlit panics, ascending and enlarged, entangled in pale fascinations, in comatose lunar dreams and lethargic shivers.

Ah, all these rapes and pursuits of that night, the treacheries and whispers, Negroes and helmsmen, balcony railings and night-blinds, muslin frocks and veils trailing behind hurried escapes! . . . Until at last, after a sudden blackout, a dull black pause, a moment comes when all the puppets are back in their boxes, all the curtains are drawn, and all the bated breaths are quietly exhaled, while on the vast calm sky dawn is building noiselessly its distant pink and white cities, its delicate, lofty pagodas and minarets.

XIX

Only now will the nature of that spring become clear and legible to an attentive reader of the Book. All these morning preparations, all the day's early ablutions, all its hesitations, doubts, and difficulties of choice will disclose their meaning to one who is familiar with stamps. Stamps introduce one to the complex game of morning diplomacy, to the prolonged negotiations and atmospheric deceits that precede the final version of any day. From the reddish mists of the ninth hour, the motley and spotted Mexico with a serpent wriggling in a condor's beak is trying to emerge, hot and parched by a bright rash, while in a gap of azure amid the greenery of tall trees, a parrot is stubbornly repeating "Guatemala, Guatemala" at even intervals, with the same intonation, and that green word infects things that suddenly become fresh and leafy. Slowly, among difficulties and conflicts, a voting takes place, the order of ceremonies is established, the list of parades, the diplomatic protocol of the day.

In May the days were pink like Egyptian stamps. In the market square brightness shone and undulated. On the sky billows of summery clouds — volcanic, sharply outlined — folded under chinks of light [Barbados, Labrador, Trinidad], and everything was running with redness, as if seen through ruby glasses or the color of blood rushing to the head. There sailed across the sky the great corvette of Guiana, exploding with all its sails. Its bulging canvas towered amid taut ropes and the noise of tugboats, amid storms of gulls and the red glare of the sea. Then there rose to the sky and spread wide an enormous, tangled rigging of ropes, ladders, and masts and, with a full spread of canvas, a manifold, many-storied aerial spectacle of sails, yards, and braces, of holds from which small agile Negro boys shot out for a moment and were lost again in the labyrinths of canvas, among the signs and figures of the fantastic tropical sky.

Then the scenery changed in the sky: in massed clouds three simultaneous pink eclipses occurred, shiny lava began to smolder, outlining luminously the fierce contours of clouds [Cuba, Haiti, Jamaica] and the center of the world receded, its glaring colors became deeper. Roaring tropical oceans, with their azure archipelagos, happy currents and tides and equatorial and salty monsoons made their appearance. With the stamp album in my hand, I was studying the spring. Was it not a great commentary on the times, the grammar of its days and nights?

The main thing was not to forget, like Alexander the Great, that no Mexico is final, that it is a point of passage which the world will cross, that beyond each Mexico there opens another, even brighter one, a Mexico of super-colors and hyper-aromas. . . .

XX

Bianca is all gray. Her dark complexion has a tinge of burned-out ashes. The touch of her hand must be unimaginable.

The careful breeding of whole generations flows in her disciplined blood. Her resigned submission to the rules of tact, proof of conquered contrariness, broken rebellion, secret sobbing, and violence done to her pride, is quite touching. Every one of her gestures expresses submission, with good will and sad grace, to the prescribed forms. She does nothing that is unnecessary, each step is avariciously measured, just complying with the conventions, entering into their spirit without enthusiasm and only from a passive sense of duty. From these daily victories Bianca draws her premature experience and wisdom. Bianca knows what there is to know, and she does seem to enjoy her knowledge, which is serious and full of sadness. Her mouth is closed in lines of infinite beauty, her eyebrows traced with severe accuracy. No, her wisdom does not lead to relaxation of rules, to softness or self-indulgence. On the contrary. The truth, at which she gazes with her sad eyes, can only be borne by a tense attention to forms and their strictest observance. And that unfailing tact and loyalty to convention obscures a whole sea of sadness and suffering gallantly overcome.

And yet, although broken by form, she has emerged from it victorious. But with what sacrifice has that triumph been achieved!

When she walks — slim and straight — it is not clear what kind of pride she carries so simply in the unsophisticated rhythm of her walk, whether her own pride overcome, or the triumph of principles to which she has submitted.

But when she lifts her eyes and looks straight at you, nothing can be hidden from her. Her youth has not protected her from being able to guess the most secret things. Her quiet serenity has been achieved after long days of weeping and sobbing. This is why her eyes are deeply circled and have in them the moist, hot glow and that spare purposefulness that never misses anything.

XXI

Bianca, enchanting Bianca, is a mystery to me. I study her with obstinacy, passion, and despair — with the stamp album as my textbook. Why am I doing this? Can a stamp album serve as a textbook of psychology? What a naïve question! A stamp album is a universal book, a compendium of knowledge about everything human. Naturally, only by allusion, implication, and hint. You need some perspicacity, some courage of the heart, some imagination in order to find the fiery thread that runs through the pages of the book.

One thing must be avoided at all costs: narrow-mindedness, pedantry, dull pettiness. Most things are interconnected, most threads lead to the same reel. Have you ever noticed swallows rising in flocks from between the lines of certain books, whole stanzas of quivering pointed swallows? One should read the flight of these birds. . . .

But to return to Bianca. How movingly beautiful are her movements! Each is made with deliberation, determined centuries ago, begun with resignation, as if she knew in advance the course and the inevitable sequence of her destiny. It happens that I want to ask her something with my eyes, to beg for something in my thoughts, while I sit facing her in the park. And before I have formulated my plea, she has already answered. She has answered sadly by one short, penetrating look.

Why does she hold her head lowered? What is she gazing at with attention, with such thoughtfulness? Is her life so hopelessly sad? And yet, in spite of everything, doesn't she carry that resignation with dignity, with pride, as if things had to remain as they were, as if that knowledge, which deprives her of joy, had given her some untouchability instead, some higher freedom found only in voluntary submission? Her obedience has the grace of triumph and of victory.

With her governess she sits on a bench facing me, and both are reading. Her white dress — I have never seen her wear any other color — lies like an open flower on the seat. Her slim dark legs are crossed in front of her with indescribable grace. To touch her body must, I imagine, be painful from the sheer holiness of such a contact.

Then having closed their books, they both rise. With one quick look Bianca acknowledges and returns my ardent greeting and walks away, disengaged, weaving her feet, meandering, melodiously keeping pace with the rhythm of the long, elastic steps of her governess.

XXII

I have investigated the whole area around the estate. I have walked several times around the high fence that surrounds that vast terrain. I have seen the white walls of the villa with its terraces and broad verandas from all angles. Behind the villa spreads a park and, adjoining it, a large plot of land without any trees. Strange structures, partly factories, partly farm buildings, stand there. I put my eye against a chink in the fence, and what I saw must have been an illusion. In the spring air, thinned by the heat, you can sometimes see distant things mirrored through miles of quivering air. All the same my head is splitting from contradictory thoughts. I must consult the stamp album again.

XXIII

Is it possible? Could Bianca's villa be an extraterritorial area under the safeguard of international treaties? To what astonishing assumptions does the study of the stamp album lead me! Am I alone in possession of this amazing truth? And yet one cannot treat lightly the evidence and arguments provided on this point by the stamp album.

Today I investigated the whole villa from nearby. For weeks I have been hanging around the crested wrought iron gate. My opportunity came when two large empty carriages drove out of the garden. The gates were left wide open and there was nobody in sight. I entered nonchalantly, produced my drawing book from my pocket and, leaning against a pillar of the gate, pretended to draw some architectural detail. I stood on a graveled path trod so many times by Bianca's light feet. My heart would stop still from blissful anticipation at the thought that I might see her emerging in a flimsy white dress from one of the French windows. But all the windows and doors had green sunshades drawn over them. Not even the slightest sound betrayed the life hidden in that house. The sky on the horizon was overcast; there was lightning in the distance. No breeze moved the warm rarefied air. In the quietness of that gray day only the chalk white walls of the villa spoke with the voiceless but expressive eloquence of their ornate architecture. Its elegance was repeated in pleonasms, in a hundred variations on the same motif. Along a blindingly white frieze, bas-relief garlands ran in rhythmic cadenzas to the left and right and stopped undecided at the corners. From the height of the central terrace a marble staircase descended, ceremonious and solemn, between smoothly running balusters and architectural vases, and, flowing broadly to the ground, seemed to arrange its train with a deep curtsy.

I have quite an acute sense of style. The style of that building worried and irritated me, although I could not explain why. Behind its restrained classicism, behind a seemingly cool elegance, some other, elusive influences were hiding. The design was too intense, too sharply pointed, too full of unexpected adornments. A drop of an unknown poison inserted into the veins of the architect made his design recondite, explosive, and dangerous.

Inwardly disoriented, trembling from contradictory impulses, I walked on tiptoe along the front of the villa, scaring the lizards asleep on the steps.

By the round pool, now dry, the earth was parched from the sun and still bare; only here and there, from a crack in the ground, sprang a tuft of an impatient fantastical green. I pulled out some of these weeds and put them into my drawing book. I was shaking with excitement. Over the pool the air hung translucent and glossy, undulating from the heat. A barometer on a nearby post showed a catastrophic low. There was calm everywhere. Not a twig moved. The villa was asleep, its curtains drawn, and its chalky whiteness glared in the dullness of the gray air. Suddenly, as if the stagnation had reached its critical point, the air shook with a colored ferment.

Enormous, heavy butterflies coupling in amorous frolics appeared. The clumsy, vibrating fluttering continued for a moment in the dull air. The butterflies flew past, as if racing one another, then rejoined their partners, dealing out in flight like cards whole packs of colorful shimmers. Was it only a quick decomposition of the overripe air, a mirage in an atmosphere that was full of hashish and visions? I waved my cap and a heavy, velvety butterfly fell to the ground, still fluttering its wings. I lifted it up and hid it. It was one more proof. . . .

XXIV

I have discovered the secret of the villa's style. The lines of its architecture repeated one incomprehensible pattern so many times and so insistently that I finally understood their mystifying code: the masquerade was really quite transparent. In those elaborate and mobile lines of exaggerated elegance there was too much spice, an excess of hot piquancy, something fidgety, too eager, too showy — something, in a word, colorful and colonial . . . Indeed, the style was in effect rather repulsive — lustful, overelaborate, tropical, and extremely cynical.

XXV

I need not say how this discovery shook me. The clues became clearer, the various reports and hints suddenly fit. Most excited, I shared my discovery with Rudolph. He did not seem concerned. He even snorted angrily, accusing me of exaggeration and invention. He has been accusing me for some time of lying and willful mystification. I still had some remains of regard for him as the owner of the stamp album, but his envious and bitter outbursts set me more and more against him. I didn't show any resentment, as I was unfortunately dependent on him. What would I do without the stamp album? He knew this and exploited his advantage.

XXVI

Too much has been happening during the spring. Too many aspirations, pretensions, and boundless ambitions are hidden in its dark depths. Its expansion knows no limits. The administration of that enormous, widespread, and overgrown enterprise is sapping my strength. Wishing to share part of the burden with Rudolph, I have nominated him co-regent. Anonymously of course. Together with the stamp album we form, we three, an unofficial triumvirate, on which rests the burden of responsibility for the whole impenetrable and convoluted affair of the spring.

XXVII

I did not have enough courage to go round to the back of the villa. I should certainly have been noticed by someone. Why, in spite of this, did I have the feeling of having been there already — a long time ago? Don't we in fact know in advance all the landscapes we see in our life? Can anything occur that is entirely new, that, in the depths of our being, we have not anticipated for a long time? I know, for instance, that one day at a late hour I shall stand on the threshold of these gardens, hand in hand with Bianca. We shall find forgotten corners where, between old walls, poisonous plants are growing, where Poe's artificial Edens, full of hemlock, poppies, and convolvuli, glow under the grizzly sky of very old frescoes. We shall wake up the white marble statue sleeping with empty eyes in that marginal world beyond the limits of a wilting afternoon. We shall scare away its only lover, a red vampire bat with folded wings asleep on its lap. It will fly away soundlessly, soft and undulating, a helpless, disembodied, bright red scrap without bone or substance; it will circle, flutter, and dissolve without trace in the deadly air. Through a small gate we shall enter a completely empty clearing. Its vegetation will be charred like tobacco, like a prairie during an Indian summer. It will perhaps be in the State of New Orleans or Louisiana — countries are after all only a pretext. We shall sit on the stone wall of a square pond. Bianca will dip her white fingers in the warm water full of yellow leaves and will not lift her eyes. On the other side of the pond, a black, slim, veiled figure will be sitting. I shall ask about it in a whisper, and Bianca will shake her head and say softly: "Don't be afraid, she is not listening; this is my dead mother who lives here." Then she will talk to me about the sweetest, quietest, and saddest things. No comfort will be possible. Dusk will be falling. . . .

XXVIII

Events are following one another at a mad pace. Bianca's father has arrived. I was standing today at the junction of Fountain and Scarab streets when a shining, open landau as broad and shallow as a conch drove by. In that white, silk-lined shell I saw Bianca, half-lying, in a tulle dress. Her gentle profile was shaded by the brim of her hat tied under her chin with ribbons. She was almost drowned in swathes of white satin. Next to her sat a gentleman in a black frock coat and a white piqué waistcoat, on which glistened a heavy gold chain with innumerable trinkets. Under his black bowler hat a grim, gray face with sideburns was visible. I shivered when I saw him. There could be no doubt. This was M. de V. . . .

As the elegant carriage passed me, discreetly rumbling with its well-sprung box, Bianca said something to her father, who turned back and stared at me through his large dark glasses. He had the face of a gray lion without a mane.

Excited, almost demented from contradictory feelings, I cried out: "Count on me!" and "until the last drop of my blood . . ." and fired into the air a pistol produced from my breastpocket.

XXIX

Many things seem to point to the fact that Franz Joseph was in reality a powerful but sad demiurge. His narrow eyes, dull like buttons embedded in triangular deltas of wrinkles, were not human eyes. His face, with its milky white sideburns brushed back like those of Japanese demons, was the face of an old mopish fox. Seen from a distance, from the height of the terrace at Schönbrunn, that face, owing to a certain combination of wrinkles, seemed to smile. From nearby that smile unmasked itself as a grimace of bitterness and prosaic matter-of-factness, unrelieved by the spark of any idea. At the very moment when he appeared on the world stage in a general's green plumes, slightly hunched and saluting, his blue coat reaching to the ground, the world reached a happy point in its development. All the set forms, having exhausted their content in endless metamorphoses, hung loosely upon things, half wilted, ready to flake off. The world was a chrysalis about to change violently, to disclose young, new, unheard-of colors and to stretch happily all its sinews and joints. It was touch and go, and the map of the world, that patchwork blanket, might float in the air, swelling like a sail. Franz Joseph took this as a personal insult. His element was a world held by the rules of prose, by the pragmatism of boredom. The atmosphere of chanceries and police stations was the air he breathed. And, a strange thing, this dried-up dull old man, with nothing attractive in his person, succeeded in pulling a great part of creation to his side. All the loyal and provident fathers of families felt threatened along with him and breathed with relief when this powerful demon laid his weight upon everything and checked the world's aspirations. Franz Joseph squared the world like paper, regulated its course with the help of patents, held it within procedural bounds, and insured it against derailment into things unforeseen, adventurous, or simply unpredictable.

Franz Joseph was not an enemy of godly and decent pleasures. It was he who invented, under the spur of kindliness of a sort, the imperial-and-royal lottery for the people, Egyptian dream books, illustrated calendars, and the imperial-and-royal tobacco shops. He standardized the servants of heaven, dressed them in symbolic blue uniforms, and let them loose upon the world, divided into ranks and divisions — angelic hordes in the shape of postmen, conductors, and tax collectors. The meanest of those heavenly messengers wore on his face a reflection of age-old wisdom borrowed from his Creator and a jovial, gracious smile framed by sideburns, even if his feet, as a result of his considerable earthly wanderings, reeked of sweat.

But has anyone ever heard of a frustrated conspiracy at the foot of the throne, of a great palace revolution nipped in the bud at the beginning of the glorious rule of the All-Powerful? Thrones wilt when they are not fed with blood, their vitality grows with the mass of wrongs committed, with life-denials, with the crushing of all that is perpetually different and that has been ousted by them. We are disclosing here secret and forbidden things; we are touching upon state secrets hidden away and secured with a thousand seals of silence.

Demiurge had a younger brother of an entirely different cast of mind, with different ideas. Who hasn't a brother under one form or another who follows him like a shadow, an antithesis, the partner in an eternal dialogue? According to one version, he was only a cousin; according to another, he had never been born. He was only suggested by the fears and ravings of the Demiurge, overheard while he was asleep. Perhaps he had only invented him anyway, substituted someone else for him, in order to play out the symbolic drama, to repeat once more, for the thousandth time, ceremoniously and ritually that prelegal and fatal act that, in spite of the thousand repetitions, occurs again and again. The conditionally born, unfortunate antagonist, professionally wronged, as it were, because of his role, bore the name of Archduke Maximilian. The very sound of that name, mentioned in a whisper, renews our blood, makes it redder and brighter, makes it pulsate quickly in the clear colors of enthusiasm, of postal sealing wax, and of the red pencil in which happy messages are printed. Maximilian had pink cheeks and shining, azure eyes. All human hearts went out to him, and swallows, squeaking with joy, cut across his path. The Demiurge himself loved him secretly while he plotted his downfall. First, he nominated him commander of the Levant Squadron in the hope that he would drown miserably on an expedition to the South Seas. Soon afterward he concluded a secret alliance with Napoleon III, who drew him by deceit into the Mexican adventure. Everything had been planned in advance. The young man, full of fantasy and imagination, enticed by the hope of creating a new, happier world on the Pacific, resigned all his rights as an agnate of the crown and heir to the Hapsburgs. On the French liner *Le Cid* he sailed straight into a prepared ambush. The documents of that secret conspiracy have never seen the light of day.

Thus the last hope of the discontented was dashed. After Maximilian's tragic death, Franz Joseph forbade the use of red under the pretext of court mourning. The black and yellow colors of mourning became official. The amaranth of enthusiasm has since been fluttering secretly only in the hearts of its adherents. But the Demiurge did not succeed in extirpating it completely from nature. After all, it is potentially present in sunlight. It is enough to close one's eyes in the spring sun in order to absorb it under one's eyelids in each wave of warmth. Photographic paper burns that same red in the spring glare. Bulls led along the sunny streets of the city with a cloth on their horns see it in bright patches and lower their heads, ready to attack imaginary torreros fleeing in panic in sun-drenched arenas.

Sometimes a whole bright day passes in explosions of the sun, in banks of clouds edged with a red glow. People walk about dizzy with light, with closed eyes that inwardly see rockets, Roman candles, and barrels of powder. Later, toward the evening, the hurricane fire of light abates, the horizon becomes rounder, more beautiful, and filled with azure like a glass globe with a miniature panorama of the world, with happily arranged plans, over which clouds tower like a crown of gold medals or church bells ringing for evensong.

People gather in the market square, silent under the enormous cupola of light, and group themselves without thinking into a great, immobile finale, a concentrated scene of waiting; the clouds billow in ever deepening pinks; in all eyes there is calm and the reflection of luminous distances. And suddenly, while they wait, the world reaches its zenith, achieves in a few heartbeats its highest perfection. The gardens arrange themselves on the crystal bowl of the horizon, the May greenery foams and overflows like wine about to spill, hills are formed in the shape of clouds; having passed its supreme peak, the beauty of the world dissolves and takes off to make an entry into eternity.

And while people remain immobile, lowering their heads still full of visions, bewitched by the great luminous ascent of the world, the man whom they had unconsciously all been waiting for runs out from among the crowd, a breathless messenger, pink of face, wearing raspberry-colored tights, and decorated with little bells, medals, and orders. He circles the square slowly six or seven times in order to be in everybody's view, his eyes downcast, as if ashamed, his hands on his hips. His rather heavy stomach is shaken by the rhythmical run. Red from exertion, the face shines with perspiration under the black Bosnian mustache, and the medals, orders, and bells jump up and down in time on his chest like a harness. One can see him from the distance as, turning the corner in a taut parabolic line, he approaches with the Janissary band of his bells, handsome as a god, incredibly pink, with an immobile torso, and drives away with a short whip the pack of barking dogs that has been following him.

Then Franz Joseph, disarmed by the universal harmony, discreetly

57

proclaims an amnesty, concedes the use of red color, allows it for one May evening in a watered-down, candy shade, and, reconciled with the world, appears in the open window of the Schönbrunn Palace; at that moment he is seen all over the world — wherever pink messengers are running on clean-swept market squares, bordered by silent crowds. One can see him in an enormous imperial-and-royal apotheosis against the background of cloud, leaning with gloved hands on the windowsill, clad in a turquoise coat with the ribbon of Commander Grand Cross of the Order of Malta; his eyes, blue buttons without kindness or grace, are narrowed in a kind of smile in the delta of wrinkles. Thus he stands, his snowy sideburns brushed back, made up to represent kindliness: an embittered fox who, for distant onlookers, fakes a smile without humor or genius.

XXX

After hesitating for a long time, I told Rudolph about the events of the last few days. I could no longer keep to myself the secret that weighed me down. His face darkened; he screamed, said I was lying, and finally burst out with an open show of jealousy. Everything was an invention, a complete lie, he shouted, running with his arms raised. Extraterritorialism! Maximilian! Mexico! Ha, ha!! Cotton plantations! Enough of that, this is the end, he is not going to lend me his stamp album anymore. End of partnership. Cancellation of contract. He pulled his hair in agitation. He was completely out of control, ready for anything.

Very frightened, I began to plead with him. I admitted that my story seemed improbable on first hearing, even unbelievable. I myself, I agreed, was quite amazed. No wonder that it was difficult for him, unprepared as he was, to accept it at once. I appealed to his heart and honor. Would his conscience allow him to refuse me his help just when matters were about to reach a decisive stage? Would he now spoil everything by withdrawing his participation? At last I undertook to prove, on the basis of the stamp album, that everything was, word for word, the truth.

Somewhat mollified, Rudolph opened the album. Never before had I spoken with such force and enthusiasm. I outdid myself. Supporting my reasoning with the evidence of stamps, not only did I refute all his accusations and dispel his doubts, but what is more, I reached such revealing conclusions that I myself was amazed by the perspectives that opened up. Rudolph remained silent and defeated, and no more was said about dissolving the partnership.

XXXI

Can one consider it a coincidence that at about the same time a great theater of illusion, a magnificent wax figure exhibition, came to town and pitched its tent in Holy Trinity Square? I had been anticipating it for a long time and told Rudolph the news with great excitement.

The evening was windy; rain hung in the air. On the yellow and dull horizon the day was getting ready to depart, hastily putting weatherproof gray covers over the train of its carts, about to proceed in rows toward the cool beyond. Under a half-drawn, darker curtain the last streaks of sunset appeared for a moment, then sank into a flat, endless plain, a lakeland of watery reflections. A frightened, yellow, foredoomed glare shone from these streaks across half the sky; the curtain was falling quickly. The pale roofs of houses shone with a moist reflection; it was getting dark and the gutter pipes were beginning to sing in monotone.

The wax figure exhibition was already open. Crowds of people sheltering under umbrellas were outlined in the dim light of the sinking day in the forecourt of the tent, where they ceremoniously gave money for their tickets to a décolletaged lady, glittering with jewels and gold teeth: a live, laced-up, and painted torso, her lower extremities lost in the shadow of velvet curtains.

Through a half-open flap we entered a brightly lighted space. It was full of people. Groups of them in wet overcoats with upturned collars ambled in silence from place to place, stopping in attentive semicircles. Without difficulty I recognized among them those who belonged to this world only in appearance, who in reality led a separate, dignified, and embalmed life on pedestals, a life on show, festively empty. They stood in grim silence, clad in somber made-to-measure frock coats and morning suits of good-quality cloth, very pale, and on their cheeks the feverish flush of the illnesses from which they had died. They had not had a single thought in their heads for quite a time, only the habit of showing themselves from every angle, of exhibiting the emptiness of their existence. They should have been in their beds a long time before, tucked under their cold sheets, their dose of medicine administered. It was a presumption to keep them up so late on their narrow pedestals and in chairs on which they sat so stiffly, in tight patent-leather footwear, miles from their previous existence, with glazed eyes entirely deprived of memory.

All of them had hanging from their lips, dead like the tongue of a strangled man, a last cry, uttered when they left the lunatic asylum where, taken for maniacs, they had spent some time in purgatory before entering this ultimate abode. No, they were not authentic Dreyfuses, Edisons, or Lucchenis; they were only pretenders. They may have been real madmen, caught red-handed at the precise moment a brilliant *idée fixe* had entered their heads; the moment of truth was skillfully distilled and became the crux of their new existence, pure as an element and unalterable. Ever since then, that one idea remained in their heads like an exclamation mark, and they clung to it, standing on one foot, suspended in midair, or stopped at half a gesture.

Passing anxiously from group to group, I looked in the crowd for Maximilian. At last I found him, not in the splendid uniform of admiral of the Levant Squadron, in which he sailed from Toulon on the way to Mexico in the flagship *Le Cid*, nor in the green tail coat of a cavalry general he wore in his last days. He was in an ordinary suit of clothes, a frock coat with long, folding skirts and light-colored trousers, his chin resting on a high collar with a cravat. Rudolph and I stopped reverently in the group of people forming a semicircle in front of him. Suddenly, I froze. A few steps from us, in the first row of the onlookers, stood Bianca in a white dress, accompanied by her governess. She stood there and looked. Her small face had become paler in the last few days, and her eyes, darkly circled and full of shadow, wore an expression of profound sadness.

She was standing immobile, with folded hands hidden in the pleats of her dress, looking from under her serious eyebrows with mournful eyes. My heart bled at the sight of her. Unconsciously I followed the direction of her gaze, and this is what I saw: Maximilian's features moved, as if awakened, the corner of his mouth curled up in a smile, his eyes shone and began to roll in their orbits, his breast covered with decorations heaved with a sigh. It was not a miracle, but a simple mechanical trick. Suitably wound up, the Archduke held court in accordance with the principles of his mechanism, graciously and ceremoniously as he had done when alive. He was now scanning the spectators, his eyes looking attentively at everybody in turn.

His eyes rested on Bianca's for a moment. He winced, hesitated, swallowed hard, as if he had wanted to say something; but a moment later, obedient to his mechanism, he continued to run his eyes over other faces with the same inviting and radiant smile. Had he become aware of Bianca's presence, had it reached his heart? Who could tell? He was not even fully himself, merely a distant double of his former being, much reduced and in a state of deep prostration. On the basis of mere fact, one must admit that in a way he was his own closest relative, perhaps he was even as much himself as possible under the circumstances, so many years after his death. In that waxen resurrection it must have been very difficult to become one's real self. Something quite new and frightening

must have sneaked into his being; something foreign must have detached itself from the madness of the ingenious maniac who conceived him in his megalomania — and this now seemed to be filling Bianca with awe and horror. Even a very sick person changes and becomes detached from his own self, let alone someone so clumsily resuscitated. For how did he behave now toward his own flesh and blood? With an assumed gaiety and bravado he continued to play his clowning imperial comedy, magnificent and smiling. Had he much to conceal, or was he perhaps afraid of the attendants who were watching him while he was on exhibition in that hospital of wax figures where he and the others stayed under hospital regulations? Distilled laboriously from somebody's madness; clean, cured, and saved at last — didn't he have to tremble at the possibility of being returned to chaos and turmoil?

When I turned to Bianca again, I saw that she had covered her face with a handkerchief. The governess put an arm around her, gazing inanely at her with her enamel blue eyes. I could not look any longer at Bianca's suffering and felt like sobbing. I pulled Rudolph's sleeve and we walked toward the exit.

Behind our backs, that made-up ancestor, that grandfather in the prime of life, continued to bestow on all and sundry his radiant imperial salutes: in an excess of zeal he even lifted his hand and was almost blowing kisses to us in the immobile silence, amid the hissing of acetylene lamps and the quiet dripping of rain on the canvas of the tent; he rose on tiptoe with the last remnants of his strength, mortally ill like the rest of them and longing for the death shroud.

In the vestibule the made-up torso of the lady cashier said something to us while her diamonds and gold teeth glittered against the black background of magic draperies. We went out into a dewy night, warm from rain. The roofs shone with water, the gutter pipes gurgled monotonously. We ran through the downpour, lighted by street lamps, jingling under the rain.

XXXII

Oh abysmal human perversity, truly infernal intrigue! In whose mind could have arisen that venomous and devilish idea, bolder than the most elaborate flights of fancy? The deeper I penetrate its malevolence, the greater my wonder at the perfidy, the flash of evil genius, in that monstrous idea.

So my intuition has not led me astray. Here, at hand, in the midst of an apparent legality, in time of peace guaranteed by treaties, a crime was being committed that made one's hair stand on end. A somber drama was being enacted in complete silence, a drama so shrouded in secrecy that nobody could guess at it and detect it during the innocent aspects of that spring. Who could suspect that between that gagged, mute wax figure rolling its eyes and the delicate, carefully raised, and beautifully mannered Bianca a family tragedy was being enacted? Who really was Bianca? Are we to reveal the secret at last? What if she was not descended either from the legitimate empress of Mexico or even from the morganatic wife, Izabella d'Orgaz, who, from the stage of a touring opera, conquered Archduke Maximilian by her beauty?

What if her mother was the little Creole girl whom he called Conchita and who under that name has entered history through the back door as it were. Information about her that I have been able to collect with the help of the stamp album can be summarized in a few words.

After the Emperor's fall, Conchita left with her small daughter for Paris, where she lived on a widow's pension, keeping unbroken faith with the memory of her imperial lover. There, history lost track of that touching figure, giving way to hearsay and reconstruction. Nothing is known about the daughter's marriage and her subsequent fate. Instead, in 1900, a certain Mme. de V., a lady of extraordinary and exotic beauty, left France with her small daughter and her husband on false passports and proceeded to Austria. At Salzburg, on the Austro-Bavarian frontier, when changing trains for Vienna, the family was stopped by the Austrian gendarmerie and arrested. It was remarkable that, after his false papers had been examined, M. de V. was freed but did not try to get his wife and daughter released. He returned the same day to France, and all trace of him has since been lost. Thereafter the story becomes very entangled. I was therefore very thrilled when the stamp album helped me to find the fugitives' trace. The discovery was entirely mine. I succeeded in identifying the said M. de V. as a highly suspect individual who appeared in a different country under a completely different name. But hush! . . . Nothing more can be said about it yet. Suffice it to say that Bianca's genealogy has been established beyond any doubt.

XXXIII

So much for canonical history. But the official history remains incomplete. There are in it intentional gaps, long pauses that spring fills swiftly with its fantasies. One needs a lot of patience to find a grain of truth in the tangle of springtime vagaries. This might be achieved by a careful, grammatical analysis of the phrases and sentences of spring. Who? Whose? What? One must eliminate the seductive cross talk of birds — their pointed adverbs and prepositions, their skittish pronouns — and work oneself slowly to a healthy grain of sense. The stamp album serves as a compass in my search. Stupid, indiscriminating spring! It covers everything with growth, mingles sense with nonsense, cracking jokes, light-hearted to a degree. Could it be that it, too, is in league with Franz Joseph, that it is tied to him by a bond of common conspiracy? Every ounce of sense breaking through is at once covered up by a hundred lies, by an avalanche of nonsense. The birds obliterate all evidence, obscure all traces by their faulty punctuation. Truth is cornered by the luxuriance that immediately fills each empty plot, each crevice, with its spreading foliage. Where is truth to shelter, where is it to find asylum if not in a place where nobody is looking for it: in fairground calendars and almanacs, in the canticles of beggars and tramps, which in direct line are derived from stamp albums?

XXXIV

After many sunny weeks came a period of hot and overcast days. The sky darkened as on old frescoes, and in the oppressive silence banks of clouds loomed like tragic battlefields in paintings of the Neapolitan school. Against the background of these leaden, ashen cumuli, the chalky whiteness of houses shone brightly, accentuated by the sharp shadows of cornices and pilasters. People walked with heads bowed, their mood dark and tense as before a storm charged with static electricity.

Bianca had not been seen again in the park. She was obviously closely supervised and not allowed out. They must have smelled danger.

I saw in town a group of gentlemen in black morning coats and top hats walking through the market square with the measured steps of diplomats. Their white shirt fronts glared in the leaden air. They looked in silence at the houses, as if valuing them, and walked with slow, rhythmic steps. They had coal black mustaches on carefully shaven faces with shining expressive eyes, which turned in their orbits smoothly, as if oiled. From time to time they doffed their hats and wiped their brows. They were all slim, tall, and middle-aged, and they had the sultry faces of gangsters.

XXXV

The days became dark, cloudy, and gray. A distant, potential storm lay in wait day and night over the horizon, not discharging itself in a downpour. In the great silence, a breath of ozone would pass at times through the steely air, with the smell of rain and a moist, fresh breeze.

Afterward the gardens filled the air with enormous sighs and grew their leaves hastily, doing overtime by day and by night. All flags hung down heavy and darkened, helplessly pouring out the last streaks of color into the dense aura. Sometimes at the opening of a street someone turned to the sky half a face, like a dark cut-out with one frightened and shining eye, and listened to the rumble of space, to the electric silence of passing clouds while the air was cut by the flight of trembling, pointed, arrow-sharp, black and white swallows.

Ecuador and Colombia are mobilizing. In the ominous silence lines of infantry in white trousers, white straps crossed on their breasts, are crowding the quays. The Chilean unicorn is rearing. One can see it in the evening outlined against the sky, a pathetic animal, immobile with terror, its hooves in the air.

XXXVI

The days are sinking ever deeper into shadow and melancholy. The sky has blocked itself and hangs low, swelled with a dark, threatening storm. The earth, parched and motley, is holding its breath; only the gardens, crazy and drunken, continue to grow, to sprout leaves and fill all their free spaces with a cool greenery. (The fat buds were sticky like an itchy rash, painful and festering; now they are healing with cool foliage, forming leafy scars, gaining green health, multiplied beyond measure and without count. They have already stifled under their greenness the forlorn call of the cuckoo, and its distant voice now rises faintly from deep thickets, dulled by the happy flood of leaves.)

Why are the houses shining so bright in that dusky landscape? As the rustling parks become darker, the whitewash on houses sharpens and glows in the sunless air with the hot reflection of burnt earth, as if it were to be spattered in a moment by the feverish spots of an infectious disease.

Dogs run dizzily, their noses in the air. Crazed and excited, they sniff among the fluffy greenness. Something revealing and enormous prepares to spring forth from the closeness of these overcast days.

I am trying to guess what event could match the negative sum of expectations contained in this enormous load of electricity; what could equal this catastrophic barometrical low.

The thing that is growing is preparing nature for a trough that the gardens cannot fill although they are equipped with the most enchanting smell of lilac.

XXXVII

Negroes, crowds of Negroes, were in the city! People had seen them here and there, in many places at once. They were running in the streets in a noisy, ragged gang, rushing into grocery shops, and stealing food. They joked, nudged one another, laughed, rolled the whites of their eyes, chattered gutturally, and bared their white, shining teeth. Before the militia could be mobilized, they disappeared into thin air.

I have felt it coming; it was unavoidable. It was the natural consequence of meteorological tension. Only now do I realize what I have felt all along: that the spring was announcing the Negroes' arrival. Where had they come from? Why did the hordes of black men in striped cotton pajamas suddenly appear here? Was it the great Barnum who had opened his circus in the neighborhood, having traveled with an endless train of people, animals, and demons? Had his wagons, crowded with an endless chatter of beasts and acrobats, stopped anywhere near us? Not at all. Barnum was far away. I have my suspicions, but I won't breathe a word. For you, Bianca, I'll remain silent, and no torture will extract any confession from me.

XXXVIII

On that day I dressed slowly and with great care. Finally, in front of the mirror, I composed my face into an expression of calm and relentless determination. I carefully loaded my pistol, before slipping it in the back pocket of my trousers. I glanced into the mirror once more and with my hand patted the breastpocket of my jacket where I had hidden some documents. I was ready to face the man.

I felt completely calm and determined. Bianca's future was at stake, and for her I was prepared to do anything! I decided not to confide in Rudolph. The better I knew him, the stronger I felt that he was a prosaic fellow, unable to rise above triviality. I have had enough of his face, alternatively freezing in consternation and growing pale with envy at each of my new revelations.

Deep in thought, I quickly walked the short distance. When the great iron gates clanged shut behind me with suppressed vibrations, I at once entered a different climate, different currents of air, the cool and unfamiliar region of a great year. The black branches of trees pointed to another, abstract time; their bare forked tops were outlined against the white sky of another, foreign zone; the avenues closed in. The voices of birds, muted in the vast spaces of the sky, cut the silence, a silence heavy and loaded that spread into gray meditation, into a great, unsteady paleness without end or goal.

With my head raised, cool and self-possessed, I asked to be announced. I was admitted to a darkened hall that exuded an aura of quiet luxury. Through a high open window the garden air flowed in gentle, balmy waves. These soft influxes, penetrating across the gentle filter of billowing curtains, made objects become alive; furtive chords resounded along rows of Venetian tumblers in a glass-fronted cabinet, and the leaves on the wallpaper rustled, silvery and scared.

It is strange how old interiors reflect their dark turbulent past, how in their stillness bygone history tries to be reenacted, how the same situations repeat themselves with infinite variations, turned upside down and inside out by the fruitless dialectic of wallpapers and hangings. Silence, vitiated and demoralized, ferments into recriminations. Why hide it? The excessive excitements and paroxysms of fever have had to be soothed here, night after night by injections of secret drugs, and the wallpapers have provided imagined visions of gentle landscapes and of distant mirrored waters.

I heard a rustle. Preceded by a valet, a man was coming down the stairs, short but well-built, economic of gesture, blinded by the light reflected on his large horn-rimmed spectacles. For the first time I faced him closely. He was inscrutable, but I noticed, not without satisfaction, that after my first words two furrows of worry and bitterness appeared on his face. While behind his spectacles he was composing his face into a mask of magnificent haughtiness, I could see panic slowly getting hold of him. As he gradually became more interested, it was obvious from his concentrated attention that at last he was beginning to take me seriously. He invited me into his study next door. When we entered it, a woman in a white dress leapt away from the door, as if she had been listening, and disappeared inside the house. Was it Bianca's governess? When I entered the room, I felt as if I were entering a jungle. The opaque greenish twilight was striped by the watery shadows of Venetian blinds drawn over the windows. The walls were hung with botanical prints; small colorful birds fluttered in large cages. Probably wishing to gain time, the man showed me specimens of primitive arms — jereeds, boomerangs, and tomahawks — which were displayed on the walls. My acute sense of smell detected the smell of curare. While he was handling a sort of primitive halberd, I suggested that he should be careful, and supported my warning by producing my pistol. He smiled wryly, a little put out, and put the weapon back in its place. We sat down at a very large ebony desk. I thanked him for the cigar he offered, saying that I did not smoke. My abstemiousness obviously impressed him. With a cigar in the corner of his hanging lips, he looked at me with a friendliness that did not inspire confidence. Then, turning the pages of his checkbook, he suddenly proposed a compromise, naming a four-figure sum, while his pupils rolled into the corners of his eyes. My ironical smile made him abruptly change the subject. With a sigh he opened a large ledger. He began to explain the state of his affairs. Bianca's name was not mentioned even once, although every word we uttered concerned her. I looked at him without moving, and the ironical smile never left my lips. At last, quite exhausted, he leaned back in his chair.

"You are intractable," he said as if to himself, "what exactly do you want?"

I began to speak again. I spoke softly, with restrained passion. A flush came to my cheeks. Trembling, I mentioned several times the name Maximilian, stressing it, and observed how my adversary's face became successively paler. At last I finished, breathing heavily. He sat there shaken. He could not master the expression on his face, which suddenly became old and tired.

"Your decision will show me," I ended, "whether you have really understood the new state of affairs and whether you are ready to follow it by your actions. I demand facts, and nothing but facts . . ."

With a shaking hand he reached for the bell. I stopped him by raising my hand, and with my finger on the trigger of the pistol, I withdrew backward from the room. At the door, the servant handed me my hat. I found myself on a terrace flooded by sunshine, my eyes still full of the eddying twilight. I walked downstairs, not turning my head, triumphant and now certain that no assassin's gun would be aimed at me from behind the drawn Venetian blinds of the mansion.

XXXIX

Important matters, highest affairs of state, force me now to have frequent confidential talks with Bianca. I prepare for them scrupulously, sitting at my desk late into the night, poring over genealogical details of a most delicate nature. Time goes by, the night stops softly outside the open window, matures, grows more solemn — suggesting deeper stages of initiation — and finally disarms itself with a helpless sigh. In long, slow gulps the dark room inhales the air of the park, its fluffy seeds and pollens, its silent plushy moths that fly softly around the walls. The wallpaper bristles with fear; cool ecstasies and flights of fancy begin, the panic and the folly of a night in May, long after midnight. Its transparent and glassy fauna, the light plankton of gnats, falls on me as I lean over my papers and work far into the small hours. Grasshoppers and mosquitoes land on my papers — blown-glass squiggles, thin monograms, arabesques invented by the night — and grow larger and more fantastic, as large as bats or vampires.

On such extramarginal nights that know no limits, space loses its meaning. Surrounded by the bright circle of midges, with a sheaf of papers ready at last, I make a few steps into an unknown direction, into one of the blind alleys of the night that must end at a door, Bianca's white door. I press the handle and enter, as if from one room to another. When

I cross the threshold, my black wide-brimmed hat flutters as if blown by the wind. My fantastically knotted tie rustles in the draft as I press to my heart an attaché case filled with most secret documents. It feels as if I have stepped from the vestibule of night into the night proper. How deeply one can breathe the nightly ozone! Here is the thicket, here is the core of the night scented with jasmine.

It is here that the night begins its real story. A large lamp with a pink shade is lighted at the head of the bed. In its pink glow Bianca rests on enormous pillows, sailing on the bedding like on a night tide, under a wide, open window. Bianca is reading, leaning on her white forearm. To my deep bow she replies with a quick look from over her book. Seen from nearby, her beauty is muted, not overwhelming. With sacrilegious pleasure I notice that her nose is not very nobly shaped and her complexion far from perfect. I notice it with a certain relief, although I know that she controls her glamour with a kind of pity in order that I do not become breathless and tongue-tied. Her beauty regenerates through the medium of distance and then becomes painful, peerless, and unbearable.

Emboldened by her nod, I sit down by her bed and begin my report, with the help of the documents prepared. Through the open window behind Bianca's head the crazy rustle of the trees is heard. Processions of trees pass by, penetrate through the walls, spread themselves, and become all-embracing. Bianca listens to me somewhat distractedly. It is quite irritating that she does not stop reading. She allows me to argue each matter thoroughly, to enumerate the pros and cons; then lifting her eyes from the book and fluttering her lids a little absently, she makes a quick, perfunctory, but astonishingly apt decision. Attentive and concentrating on her words, I listen carefully to the tone of her voice, so as to understand her hidden intentions. Then I humbly submit the papers for her signature; Bianca signs, with downcast eyes, her eyelashes casting long shadows, and watches me with slight irony as I countersign them.

Perhaps the late hour, past midnight, does not favor concentration on affairs of state. The night, having reached its last frontiers, leans toward dissolution. While we are talking, the illusion of a room fades; we are now practically in the middle of a forest. Tufts of fern grow in every corner; behind the bed a screen of bushes moves animated and entangled. From that leafy wall, big-eyed squirrels, woodpeckers, and sundry night creatures materialize and look immobile at the lamplight with shining, bulging eyes. At a certain moment, we have entered an illegal time, a night beyond control, liable to all kinds of excesses and crazes. What is happening now does not really count and consists of trifles, reckless misdemeanors, and nightly frolics. This must be the reason for the strange changes that occur in Bianca's behavior. She, always so self-possessed and serious, the personification of beautiful discipline, becomes now whimsical, contrary, and unpredictable. The papers are spread out on the great plain of her counterpane. Bianca picks them up nonchalantly, casts an eye on them, and lets them fall again from between her loosened fingers. Pouting, a pale arm laid under her head, she postpones her decisions and makes me wait. Or else she turns away from me, clamps her hands over her ears, and is deaf to my entreaties and persuasions. Then without a word, with one kick of her foot under the bedclothes, she makes all the papers slip to the floor, and with wide open eyes she watches over her arm from the height of her pillows how, crouching, I pick them up carefully from the ground, blowing the pine needles from them. These whims, quite charming in themselves, do not make my difficult and responsible task as regent any easier.

During our conversation the rustle of the forest and the scent of jasmine evoke in the room visions of landscapes. Innumerable trees and bushes, whole woodland sceneries, move past us. And then it becomes clear that we find ourselves in a kind of train, a nightly forest train, rolling slowly along a ravine in the wooded outskirts of the city. Hence the delightful breeze that flows through the compartment. A conductor with a lantern appears from nowhere, emerges from among the trees, and punches our tickets with his machine. The darkness deepens, the draft becomes more piercing. Bianca's eyes shine, her cheeks are flushed, an enchanting smile opens her lips. Does she want to confide in me? Reveal a secret? Bianca talks of treason, and her face burns with ecstasy, her eyes narrow in a paroxysm of delight when, wriggling like a lizard under her counterpane, she accuses me of having betrayed my most sacred mission. She stubbornly fixes my face, now pale, with her sweet eyes, which are beginning to squint.

"Do it," she whispers intently, "do it. You will become one of them, one of the dark Negroes . . ."

72

And when in despair I put my finger to my lips in a gesture of entreaty, her little face suddenly becomes mean and venomous.

"You are ridiculous with your inflexible loyalty and your sense of mission. God knows why you imagine you are indispensable. And what if I should choose Rudolph? I prefer him to you, you boring pedant. Ah, he would be obedient and follow me into crime, into self-destruction!"

Then, with a triumphant expression she asks:

"Do you remember Lonka, the washerwoman Antonia's daughter, with whom you played when you were small?"

I look at her amazed.

"It was I," she says giggling, "only I was a boy at that time. Did you like me then?"

O there is something very rotten and dissolute at the very center of spring. Bianca, Bianca, must you disappoint me, even you?

XL

I am afraid to reveal my trump card too soon. I am playing for too high a stake to risk it. It's a long time since I have ceased to report to Rudolph about developments. Besides, his behavior has recently undergone a change. Envy, which had been the dominant feature of his character, has given way to some sort of magnanimity. Whenever we meet by chance, an eager, rather embarrassed friendliness now shows in his gestures and clumsy remarks, whereas formerly, under the grumpy expression of a silent and expectant reserve, there was at least a devouring curiosity, a hunger for new details concerning the affair. Now he has become strangely calm and seems uninterested in what I might have to say. This suits me because every night I attend extremely important meetings at the Wax Figures Exhibition, meetings that must remain secret for the time being. The attendants, stupefied by drink, which I generously supply, sleep the sleep of the just in their closets, while I, in the light of a few smoking candles, confer with the distinguished company of exhibits. There are among them some Royals, and negotiations with them are never an easy matter. From their past they have preserved an instinctive gallantry now inapplicable, a readiness to burn in the fire of some principle, to put their lives at stake. The ideals that once guided their lives have been discredited one after another in the prose of daily life, their fires have burned out: here they stand, played out yet full of unspent energy, and, their eyes shining crazily, they await the cue for their last role. When they are so uncritical and defenseless, how easy it is to give them the wrong cue, to suggest any idea that comes along! This simplifies my task, of course. On the other hand, it is extremely difficult to reach them, to light in them the spark of interest, so empty have they become.

To wake them up at all has cost me a lot of effort. They were all in their beds, mortally pale and laboring for breath. I had to lean over each of them and whisper the vital words, words that should shock them like electric current. They would open one lazy eye. They were afraid of the attendants, pretended to be deaf or dead. Only when reassured that we

were alone would they lift themselves up on their beds, bandaged, made of bits and pieces, feeling their wooden limbs, their false lungs and imitation livers. At first they were very mistrustful and wanted to recite the roles they had learned. They could not understand why anyone should ask them for anything different. And so they sat dully, groaning from time to time, these once splendid men, the flower of mankind: Dreyfus and Garibaldi, Bismarck and Victor Emmanuel I, Gambetta, Mazzini, and many others. The most difficult to persuade was Archduke Maximilian himself. When, whispering in his ear, I kept repeating Bianca's name, he only blinked his eyes and no glimmer of understanding showed on his face. It's only when I uttered distinctly the name of Franz Joseph that a wild grimace appeared on his face, a pure conditional reflex, in which his feelings were not involved. That particular complex had long ago been eliminated from his consciousness: how else could he live with it, with that burning hatred, he, who had been put together from pieces after the bloody execution at Querétaro? I had to teach him about his life from the beginning. His memory was very poor. I had to recur to the subconscious glimmers of feeling. I was implanting in him elements of love and hate, but already on the following night he did not remember anything. His more intelligent colleagues tried to help him, to prompt the reactions he should show; his reeducation advanced slowly, step by step. He had been very neglected, innerly ravaged by the attendants, yet in spite of this I finally succeeded in making him reach for his sword at the sound of Franz Joseph's name. He very nearly stabbed Victor Emmanuel I, who did not give way to him quickly enough.

In fact, most of that splendid assembly absorbed my idea with much more eagerness and much quicker than the plodding, luckless Archduke. Their enthusiasm was boundless, and I had to use all my strength to restrain them. It is difficult to say whether they understood in all its implications the ideal for which they were to fight, but the merit of the case was not their concern. Destined to burn in the fire of some dogma, they were enchanted at having acquired, thanks to me, a catchword for which they could die fighting in exultation. I calmed them with hypnosis, taught them patiently how to keep a secret. I was proud of their progress. What leader had ever had under his command such illustrious subordinates, generals who were such fiery spirits, a guard composed of geniuses, cripples though they all might be!

At last the date came; on a stormy and windy night all that was being prepared had to happen. Lightning pierced the sky, opening up the gory, frightening interior of the earth and shutting it again. Yet the world continued to turn with the rustling of trees, processions of forests, shifting of horizons. Under cover of darkness we left the exhibition. I walked at the head of the inspired cohort, advancing among the violent limping and rattling, the clatter of crutches and metal. Lightning licked the bared blades of sabers. Stumbling, we reached the gate of the villa. We found it open. Worried, anticipating treachery, I gave the order to light flares. The air became red from burning resinous chips, flocks of frightened birds shot up high into the glare, and in this Bengal light we saw clearly the villa, its terraces and balconies illuminated by the flames. From the roof a white flag was waving. Struck by a bad premonition, I marched into the courtyard at the head of my warriors. The majordomo appeared on the terrace. Bowing, he descended the monumental staircase and approached hesitantly, with uncertain gestures. I pointed my blade at him. My loyal troops stood immobile, lifting high their smoking flares: in the silence one could hear the hissing of the flames.

"Where is M. de V.?" I asked.

He spread his hands helplessly.

"He has gone away, sir," he answered.

"We shall see if this is so. And where is the Infanta?"

"Her Highness has also left, they have all gone away . . ."

I had no reason to doubt his words. Someone must have betrayed me. There was no time to be lost.

"Company mount horse!" I cried. "We must cut off their flight!"

We broke into the stables. In the warm darkness we found the horses. Within a moment we were all mounted on the rearing and neighing steeds. Galloping, we formed a long cavalcade and reached the road.

"Through the woods toward the river," I commanded and turned into a forest path. The forest engulfed us. We rode amid waterfalls of noise, amid disturbed trees, the flares lighting the progress of our extended file. Confused thoughts rushed through my head. Had Bianca been kidnapped, or had her father's lowly ancestry overruled the voice of her mother's blood and the sense of mission I had been trying in vain to implant in her? The path became narrower and changed into a ravine, at the end of which there opened a large forest clearing. There at last we caught up with them. They saw us coming and stopped their carriage. M. de V. got out and crossed his arms on his breast. He was walking toward us, his glasses shining crimson in the light of the flares. Twelve bared blades were pointed at his breast. We approached in a large semicircle, in silence, the horses at a trot. I shielded my eyes in order to see better. The light of the flares now fell on the carriage, and inside it I saw Bianca, mortally pale, and, sitting next to her, Rudolph. He was holding her hand and pressing it against his breast. I slowly dismounted and advanced shakily toward the carriage. Rudolph rose as if wanting to get out and speak to me.

Stopping by the carriage, I turned to the cavalcade following me slowly, their sabers at the ready, and said:

"Gentlemen, I have troubled you unnecessarily. These people are free and can proceed if they wish, unmolested. No hair of their heads is to be touched. You have done your duty, gentlemen. Please sheath your sabers. I don't know how completely you have understood the ideal that I engaged you to serve, and how profoundly it has fired your imagination. That ideal, as you can see, has now completely failed. I believe that, as far as you are concerned, you might survive its failure without much damage, for you have already survived once before the failure of your own ideals. You are indestructible now; as for me . . . but never mind that. I should not like you to think," and here I turned to those in the carriage, "that what has happened has found me entirely unprepared. This is not so. I have been anticipating it all for a long time. If I had persisted in my error for so long, not wishing to admit the truth to myself, it was only because it would not have been seemly for me to know things that exceed my competence, or openly to anticipate events. I wanted to remain in the role destiny had allotted to me, I wanted to fulfil my task and remain loyal to the position I had usurped. For, I must now confess with regret, despite the promptings of my ambition, I have only been a usurper. In my blindness, I undertook to comment on the text, to be the interpreter of God's will; I misunderstood the scanty traces and indications I believed I found in the pages of the stamp album. Unfortunately, I wove them into a fabric of my own making. I have imposed my own direction upon this spring, I devised my own program to explain its immense flourishing and wanted to harness it, to direct it according to my own ideas. The spring has carried me away for a time; it was patient and indifferent and hardly aware of me. I took its lack of response for tolerance, for solidarity, even for complicity. I thought that I could decipher, better than spring itself, its features, its deepest intentions, that I could read in its soul or anticipate what, overcome by its own immensity, it could not express. I ignored all the signs of its wild and unchecked independence, I overlooked its violent and incalculable perturbations.

"In my megalomania I went so far as to dare to pry into the dynastic affairs of the highest powers, and I have mobilized you, gentlemen, against the Demiurge. I have abused your receptiveness to ideas, your noble credulity, in order to implant in you a false and iconoclastic doctrine, to harness your fiery idealism for a wanton, inconsiderate action. I don't want to determine whether I have been suited to the highest duties to which my ambition has driven me. I was probably called only to initiate them, to be abandoned later. I have exceeded my competence, but even that has been foreseen. In reality, I have known my fate from the outset. As the fate of that luckless Maximilian, my fate was that of Abel. There was a moment when my sacrifice seemed sweet and pleasing to God, when your chances seemed nil, Rudolph. But Cain always wins. The dice were loaded against me."

At that moment a distant detonation shook the air, and a column of fire rose above the forests. All those present turned their heads.

"Stay calm," I said, "it is the Wax Figures Exhibition on fire. I left there, before our departure, a barrel of powder with a lighted fuse. You have lost your home, noble gentlemen, and now you are homeless. I hope that this does not affect you too much?"

But these once powerful individuals, these leaders of mankind, stood silent, helplessly rolling their eyes, crazily keeping a battle formation in the distant glare of the fire. They looked at one another, blinking, without a thought.

"You, Sire," I addressed myself to the archduke, "were wrong. Perhaps you too were guilty of megalomania. I had no right to try to reform the world on your behalf. Perhaps this has never been your intention either. Red is, after all, only a color like all the others, and only all colors put together contribute to the wholeness of light. Forgive me for having misused your name for purposes that were alien to you. Long live Franz Joseph the First!"

The Archduke shook at the sound of that name, reached for his saber, then hesitated and thought better of it; but a more vivid flush colored his painted cheeks, the corners of his mouth lifted, his eyes began to turn in their orbits, and in a measured step, with great distinction, he began to hold court, moving from one person to the other with a radiant smile. They moved away from him, scandalized. The revival of imperial manners at this unsuitable moment created the worst possible impression.

"Stop this, Sire," I said, "I don't doubt that you know by heart the ceremonial of your court, but this is not the time for it. I want to read to you, noble gentlemen, and to you, Infanta, the act of my abdication. I am abdicating completely. I am dissolving the triumvirate. I am giving up the regency in favor of Rudolph. You, noble gentlemen," here I turned to my staff, "are free to go now. Your intentions were excellent, and I thank you most sincerely in the name of our dethroned idea" — tears sprung to my eyes — "which, in spite of everything . . ."

Just then a shot was fired somewhere nearby. We all turned our heads in that direction. M. de V. stood with a smoking pistol in his hand, strangely stiff and leaning to one side. He grimaced, then staggered and fell on his face.

"Father, Father!" screamed Bianca and threw herself upon the prostrate man. Confusion followed. Garibaldi, an old hand who knew everything about wounds, leaned over him. The bullet had pierced his heart. The King of Piedmont and Mazzini lifted him carefully by the arms and laid him on a stretcher. Bianca was sobbing, supported by Rudolph. The Negroes who just then appeared under the trees crowded round their master. "Massa, Massa, our kind massa," they chanted in chorus.

"This night is truly fatal!" I cried. "This tragedy won't be the last. But I must confess that this is something I had not foreseen. I have wronged him. In reality, a noble heart beat in his breast. I hereby revoke my judgment of him, which has obviously been shortsighted and prejudiced. He must have been a good father, a good master to his slaves. My reasoning has failed even in this instance, but I admit it without regret. It is your duty, Rudolph, to comfort Bianca, to redouble your love, to replace her father. You will probably want to take his body on board; we shall therefore form a procession and march to the harbor. I can hear the siren of the steamship."

Bianca got back into the carriage; we mounted our horses. The Negroes took the stretcher on their shoulders and we all turned toward the harbor. The cavalcade of riders brought up the rear of that sorry procession. The storm had abated during my speech, the light of flares opened deep long cracks among the trees, and fleeting black shadows formed a semicircle behind our backs. At last we left the forest. We could see in the distance the steamship with its large paddles.

Not much remains to be added, the story is nearing its end. Accompanied by the sobbing of Bianca and the Negroes, the body of the dead man was taken aboard. For the last time we re-formed our ranks.

"One more thing, Rudolph," I said, taking hold of a button of his jacket. "You are leaving now as heir to an enormous fortune. I don't wish to make any suggestions, and it should be my task to provide for the old age of these homeless heroes, but, unfortunately, I am a pauper."

Rudolph at once reached for his checkbook. We conferred shortly and privately and quickly came to an agreement.

"Gentlemen," I exclaimed, addressing myself to my guard, "my generous friend here has decided to compensate you for my action, which has deprived you of your livelihood and a roof over your heads. After what has happened, no wax-figure cabinet will ever admit you, especially since the competition is very great. You will have to give up some of your ambitions. Instead, you will become free men, which, I know, will appeal to you. As you have not been trained, unfortunately, for any practical work, having been destined for purely representative duties, my friend here has made a donation sufficient for the purchase of twelve barrel organs from the Black Forest. You will disperse all over the world, playing for people's pleasure. The choice of music is left to you. Why mince words, anyway, since you are not completely real Dreyfuses, Edisons, and Napoleons? You have assumed these names vicariously, for lack of anything better. Now you will swell the numbers of many of your predecessors, those anonymous Garibaldis, Bismarcks, and MacMahons who wander in their thousands, unacknowledged, all over the world. In the depths of your hearts you will remain forever what you are. And now, dear friends and noble gentlemen, let's wish together all happiness to the bridal pair: Long live Rudolph and Bianca!"

"Long live Rudolph and Bianca!" they cried in chorus.

The Negroes were singing a Negro spiritual. When they had finished, I regrouped them again with a wave of my hand, and then, producing my pistol, I cried:

"And now farewell, gentlemen, and take warning from what you are about to see now and never attempt to guess at divine intentions. No one has ever penetrated the designs of the spring. *Ignorabimus*, gentlemen, *ignorabimus!*"

I lifted the pistol to my temple and was about to pull the trigger, when someone knocked it from my hand. An officer of the Feldjägers stood by me and, holding some papers in his hand, asked:

"Are you Joseph N.?"

"Yes," I answered.

"Haven't you some time ago," asked the officer, "dreamed the standard dream of the biblical Joseph?"

"Perhaps. . . ."

"So you admit it," said the officer consulting his papers. "Do you know that the dream has been noticed in the highest places and has been severely criticized?"

"I cannot answer for my dreams," I said.

"Yes, you can. I am arresting you in the name of His Majesty the Emperor-and-King!"

I smiled.

"How slow are the mills of justice. The bureaucracy of His Majesty the Emperor-and-King grinds rather slowly. I have outpaced that early dream by actions that are much more dangerous and that I wanted to expiate by taking my own life, yet it is this obsolete dream that has saved my life. . . . I am at your disposal."

I saw an approaching column of troops. I stretched out my arms so that I could be handcuffed and turned my head once more. I saw Bianca for the last time. Standing on board the steamship, she was waving her handkerchief. The guard of veterans was saluting me in silence.

A NIGHT IN JULY

During the long holiday of my last year in school I became acquainted for the first time with summer nights. Our house, exposed all day long to the breezes and glares of the hot summer days that entered through the open windows, now contained a new lodger, my sister's small son, a tiny, pouting, whimpering creature. He made our home revert to primitive conditions, he reduced us to the nomadic and harem-like existence of a matriarchal encampment where bedding, diapers, and sheets were forever being washed and dried, where a marked neglect of feminine appearance was accompanied by a predilection for frequent strippings of a would-be innocent character, an acid aura of infancy and of breasts swelling with milk.

After a very difficult confinement, my sister left to convalesce at a spa, my brother-in-law began to appear only at mealtimes, and my parents stayed in their shop until late at night. The household was ruled by the baby's wet-nurse, whose expansive femininity was further enhanced by her role as mother-provider. That majestic dignity, coupled with her large and weighty presence, impressed a seal of gynecocracy on the whole house. It was a gynecocracy based on the natural advantages of a replete and fully grown carnality shared cleverly between herself and two servant girls, whose activities allowed them to display a whole gamut of feminine self-absorption. The blossoming and ripening of the garden full of rustling leaves, silvery flashes of light, and shadowy meditations was balanced inside the house by an aroma of femininity and maternity that floated over the white linen and the budding flesh. At the hotly glaring hour of noon all the curtains in the wide-open windows rose in fright and all the diapers drying on lines fluttered in a row: through this white avenue of linens and muslins feathery seeds, pollens, and lost petals flowed in; the garden tides of light and shadow, the intermittent rustle and calm slowly entered the rooms as if this hour of Pan had lifted all walls and partitions and allowed an all-embracing unity to rule the whole world.

I spent the evenings of that summer in the town's only cinema, staying there until the end of the last performance.

From the darkness of the cinema hall, with its fleeting lights and shadows, one entered a quiet, bright lobby like the haven of an inn on a stormy night.

After the fantastic adventures of the film, one's beating heart could calm down in the bright waiting room, shut off from the impact of the great pathetic night; in that safe shelter, where time stood still, the light bulbs emitted waves of sterile light in a rhythm set by the dull rumbling of the projector, and kept by the shake of the cashier's box.

That lobby, plunged into the boredom of late hours like a railway waiting room after the departure of the last train, seemed at times to be the background for the final minutes of existence, something that would remain after all else had passed, after the tumult of life was exhausted. On a large colored poster, Asta Nielsen staggered forever with the black stigma of death on her forehead, her mouth open in a last scream, her eyes supremely beautiful and wide with superhuman effort.

The cashier had long since left for home. By now she was probably bustling by an unmade bed that was waiting in her small room like a boat to carry her off to the black lagoons of sleep, into the complicated world of dreams. The person sitting in the box office was only a wraith, an illusory phantom looking with tired, heavily made-up eyes at the emptiness of light, fluttering her lashes thoughtlessly to disperse the golden dust of drowsiness scattered by the electric bulbs. Occasionally she smiled palely to the sergeant of the fire brigade, who, himself empty of reality, stood leaning against the wall, forever immobile in his shining helmet, in the shallow splendor of his epaulettes, silver braids, and medals. The glass panes of the door leading into the late July night shook in time with the rhythm of the projector, but the reflection of the electric lamp in the glass refuted the night, contributing to the illusion of a shelter safe from the immense spreading darkness. Then at last the enchantment of the lobby was broken: the glass door opened and the red curtain swelled from the breath of night which overruled everything.

Imagine the sense of adventure felt by a slim and sickly high school boy when he opens the glass door of a safe haven and walks out all alone into the immensity of a July night. Will he forever wade through the black morasses and quagmires of the endless night, or will he come one morning to a safe harbor? How many years will his lonely wanderings last?

No one has ever charted the topography of a July night. It remains unrecorded in the geography of one's inner cosmos.

A night in July! What can be likened to it? How can one describe it? Shall I compare it to the core of an enormous black rose, covering us with the dreams of hundreds of velvety petals? The night winds blow open its fluffy center, and in its scented depth we can see the stars looking down on us.

Shall I compare it to the black firmament under our half-closed eyelids, full of scattered speckles, white poppy seeds, stars, rockets, and meteors? Or perhaps to a night train, long as the world, driving through an endless black tunnel; walking through a July night is like passing precariously from one coach to another, between sleeping passengers, along narrow drafty corridors, past stuffy compartments.

A night in July! The secret fluid of dusk, the living, watchful, and mobile matter of darkness, ceaselessly shaping something out of chaos and immediately rejecting every shape. Black timber out of which caves, vaults, nooks, and niches along the path of a sleepy wanderer are constructed. Like an insistent talker, the night accompanies a lonely pilgrim, shutting him within the circle of its apparitions, indefatigable in invention and in fantasies, evoking for him starry distances, white milky ways, the labyrinths of successive Coliseums and Forums. The night air, that black Proteus playfully forming velvety densities streaked with the scent of jasmine, cascades of ozone, sudden airless wastes rising like black globes into the infinite, monstrous grapes of darkness flowing with dark juice! I elbow my way along these tight passages, I lower my head to pass under arches and low vaults, and suddenly the ceiling breaks open with a starry sigh, a wide cupola slides away for a moment, and I am led again between narrow walls and passages. In these airless bays, in these nooks of darkness, scraps of conversation left by nightly wanderers hang in the air, fragments of inscriptions stick to posters, lost bars of laughter are heard, and skeins of whispers undispersed by the breeze of night unfold. Sometimes the night closes in around me like a small room without a door. I am overcome by drowsiness and cannot make out whether my legs are still carrying me forward or whether I am already at rest in that small chamber of the night. But then I feel again a velvety hot kiss left floating in space by some scented lips, some shutters open, I take a long step across a windowsill and continue to wander under the parabolas of falling stars.

From the labyrinth of night two wanderers emerge. They are weaving something together and pull from the darkness a long, hopeless plait of conversation. The umbrella of one of them knocks monotonously against the pavement (such umbrellas are carried as protection from the rain of stars and meteors), and large heads in globelike bowlers start rolling about. At other times I am stopped for a moment by the conspiratorial look of a black squinting eye, and a large bony hand with protruding joints limps through the night clutching the crutch of a stick, tightly grasping a handle made from a stag's horn (in such sticks long thin swords are sometimes hidden).

At last, at the city boundary the night gives up its games, removes its veil, discloses its serious and eternal face. It stops constructing around us illusory labyrinths of hallucination and nightmare and opens wide its starry eternity. The firmament grows into infinity, constellations glow in their splendor in time-hallowed positions, drawing magic figures in the sky as if they wanted to announce something, to proclaim something ultimate by their frightening silence. The shimmering of these distant worlds is a silvery starry chatter like the croaking of frogs. The July sky scatters an unbelievable dust of meteors, quietly soaked up by the cosmos.

At some hour of the night — the constellations still dreaming their eternal dreams — I found myself again in my own street. A star shone over the end of it, emitting an alien scent. When I opened the gate of the house, a draft could be felt like that in a dark tunnel. In the dining room the light was still on, four candles burned in a brass candlestick. My brother-in-law was not yet in. Since my sister's departure, he had frequently been late for supper, sometimes not returning until late at night. Waking up from sleep, I often saw him undressing with a dull and meditative expression. Then he would blow out the candle, take all his clothes off, and, naked, lie for a long while sleepless on the cool bed. Sleep would only gradually overpower his large body. He would restlessly murmur something, breathe heavily, sigh, struggle with an imaginary burden on his breast. At times he would sob softly and dryly. Frightened, I asked in the darkness: "Are you all right, Charles?" but in the meantime he was off on the steep path of his dreams, scrambling laboriously up some hill of snoring.

Through the open window the night was now breathing slowly. Into its large formless mass a cool, odorous fluid was being poured, the dark joints became looser, allowing thin rivulets of scent to seep through. The dead matter of darkness sought liberation in inspired flights of jasmine scent, but the unformed depths of the night remained still dead and unliberated.

The chink of light under the door to the next room shone like a golden string, sonorous and sensitive, like the sleep of the infant whining in his cradle. The chatter of caressing talk could be heard from there, an idyll between the wet-nurse and the baby, the idyll of first love, in the midst of a circle of nightly demons that assembled in the darkness behind the window, lured by the warm spark of life glimmering inside.

On the other side was an empty room, and beyond it the bedroom of my parents. Straining my ear, I could hear how my father, on the threshold of sleep, glided in ecstasy over its aerial roads, wholly dedicated to this flight. His melodious and penetrating snoring told the story of his wandering along unknown impasses of sleep.

Thus did the souls slowly enter the aphelion, the sunless side of life, which no living creature has ever seen. They lay like people in the throes of death, rattling terribly and sobbing, while the black eclipse held their spirits in bond. And when at last they passed the black nadir, the deepest Orcus of the soul, when in mortal sweat they had fought their way through its strange promontories, the bellows of their lungs began to swell with a different tune, their inspired snores persisting until dawn.

A dense darkness still oppressed the earth when a different smell, a different color announced the slow approach of dawn. This was the moment when the most sober, sleepless head is visited for a time by the oblivion of sleep. The sick, the very sad, and those whose souls are torn apart have at that time a moment of relief. Who knows the length of time when night lowers the curtain on what is happening in its depth? That short interval is enough, however, to shift the scenery, to liquidate the great enterprise of the night and all its dark fantastic pomp. You wake up frightened, with the feeling of having overslept, and you see on the horizon the bright streak of dawn and the black, solidifying mass of the earth.

MY FATHER JOINS
THE FIRE BRIGADE

At the beginning of October my mother and I usually returned home from our holiday in the country. The place where we stayed was in a neighboring county, in a wooded valley of the River Slotvinka, which resounded with the murmur of innumerable underground springs. With our ears still filled with the rustle of beech trees and the chirping of birds, we rode in a large old landau, crowned with an enormous hood. We sat underneath it among numerous bundles in a kind of velvet-lined cavernous alcove, looking through the window at the changing landscape, colorful like pictures slowly dealt out from a pack.

At dusk we reached a plateau — the vast, startled crossroads of the country. The sky over it was deep, breathless, and windswept. Here was the farthest tollgate of the country, the last turning, beyond which the landscape of early autumn opened lower down. The frontier too was here, marked by an old, rotting frontier post with a faded inscription on a board that swayed in the wind.

The great wheels of the landau creaked as they sank in the sand, and the chattering spokes fell silent; only the large hood droned dully and flapped darkly in the crosswinds, like an ark that had landed in a desert.

Mother paid the toll, the bar of the turnpike squeaked when lifted, and the landau rolled heavily into the autumn.

We entered the wilted boredom of an enormous plain, an area of faded pale breezes that enveloped dully and lazily the yellow distance. A feeling of forlornness rose from the windswept space.

Like the yellowed pages of an old fable, the landscape became paler and more brittle as if it would disintegrate in an enormous emptiness. In that windy nowhere, in that yellow nirvana, we might have ridden to the limits of time and reality, or remained in it forever, amid the warm, sterile draftiness — an immobile coach on large wheels, stuck in the clouds of a parchment sky; an old illustration; a forgotten woodcut in an old-fashioned, moldy novel — when the coachman suddenly jerked the reins and from the lethargy of the crossroads pulled the landau into a forest.

We entered the thickets of dry fluff, a tobacco-colored wilting. Everything around us was sheltered and tawny like the inside of a box of trabucos. In that cedar semidarkness we passed tree trunks that were dry and odorous like cigars. We drove on and the forest became darker, smelling more aromatically of tobacco, until at last it enclosed us like a dry cello box, resounding faintly to its last tune. The coachman had no matches, so he could not light the lanterns. The horses, breathing heavily, found their way by instinct. The rattling of the spokes became less loud, the wheels began to turn softly in the sweet-smelling needles. My mother fell asleep. Time passed uncounted, making unfamiliar knots and abbreviations in its passage. The darkness was impenetrable; the dry rustle of the forest still resounded over the hood as the ground under the horses' hooves became solid and the carriage turned round and stopped, almost brushing a wall. Holding the door of the landau, my mother blindly felt for the gate to our house. The coachman was already unloading our bundles.

We entered a large vaulted hallway. It was dark, warm, and quiet like an old empty bakery at dawn, when the oven is cool, or like a Turkish bath late at night, when the forsaken tubs and basins grow cold in the darkness, in a silence measured by the dripping of taps. A cricket was patiently pulling from the darkness the tacking stitches of light, so fine that they could not lighten it at all. We groped around blindly until we found the stairs.

When we reached the creaking landing, my mother said:

"Wake up, Joseph, you are dropping off; only a few more steps to go."

But, almost unconscious with drowsiness, I clung closer to her and fell completely asleep.

Afterward, I never could learn from my mother how real were the things that I saw that night through my closed eyelids, overwhelmed as I was by tiredness and falling again and again into dull oblivion, and how much of it was the product of my imagination.

A great debate was taking place between my father, my mother, and Adela, the chief protagonist of that scene — a debate, I now realize, of capital importance. The gaps in my memory must be at fault if I cannot reconstruct its sense, also the blind spots of sleep I am now trying to fill with guesswork, supposition, and hypothesis. Inert and unconscious, I swam away again and again while the breezes of the starry night coming from the open windows swept over my closed eyes. The night's breathing was regular and pure; as if uncovered by removing a transparent curtain, the stars appeared at times to look at my sleep. From under my eyelids I saw a room lighted by a candle, its glow casting a pattern of golden lines and curlicues.

It is possible, of course, that the scene took place at some other time. Many things seem to indicate that I had been its witness much later, when, with my mother and the shop assistants, I returned home late one day, after the shop had been closed.

On entering our apartment, my mother exclaimed in amazement and wonder and the shop assistants stopped still, transfixed. In the middle of the room stood a splendid knight clad in brass, a veritable Saint George, looming large in a cuirass of polished golden tinplate, a sonorous armor complete with golden armlets. With astonishment and pleasure I recognized my father's bristling mustache and beard, which could be seen from under the heavy praetorian helmet. The armor was undulating on his breast, its strips of metal heaving like the scales on the abdomen of some huge insect. Looking tall in that armor, Father, in the glare of golden metal resembled the archstrategist of a heavenly host.

"Alas, Adela," my father was saying, "you have never been able to understand matters of a higher order. Over and over again you have frustrated my activities with outbursts of senseless anger. But encased in armor, I am now impervious to the tickling with which you had driven me to despair when I was bedridden and helpless. An impotent rage has now taken hold of your tongue, and the vulgarity and grossness of your language is only matched by its stupidity. Believe me, I am full of sorrow and pity for you. Unable to experience noble flights of fancy, you bear an unconscious grudge against everything that rises above the commonplace."

Adela directed at my father a look of utter contempt and, turning to my mother, said in an angry voice, while shedding tears of irritation:

"He pinches all our raspberry syrup! He has already taken away

90

from the larder all the bottles of syrup we made last summer! He wants to give it all to these good-for-nothing firemen. And, what is more, he is being rude to me!" Adela sobbed.

"Captain of the fire brigade, captain of some crowd of lay-abouts!" she continued, looking at Father with loathing. "The house is full of them. In the morning, when I want to fetch the rolls, I cannot open the front door. Two of them are lying asleep in the hallway barring it. On the staircase a few more are spread on the steps, asleep in their brass helmets. They force their way into my kitchen; they push in their rabbit faces, lift up two fingers like schoolboys in class, and beg plaintively: 'Sugar, sugar, please . . .' They snatch the bucket from my hands and run to the pump to get water for me; they dance around me, smile at me, very nearly wag their tails. And all the time they leer at me and odiously lick their lips. If I glance at any one of them, he immediately becomes red in the face like an obscene turkey. And to that horrible lot I am supposed to give our raspberry syrup?"

"Your vulgarity," said my father, "defiles everything it comes into contact with. You have given us a picture of these sons of fire as seen by your profane eyes. As to me, all my sympathy is with that unfortunate tribe of salamanders, those poor, disinherited creatures of fire. The mistake committed by that once-so-splendid tribe was that they devoted themselves to the service of mankind, that they sold themselves to man for a spoonful of miserable broth. They have been repaid by scorn because the stupidity of plebeians is boundless. Now these once-so-sensitive creatures have to live in degradation. Can one wonder that they don't like their dull and coarse fare, cooked by the wife of the beadle of the city school in a communal pot that they have to share with men under arrest? Their palates, the delicate and refined palates of fiery spirits, crave noble and dark balms, aromatic and colorful potions. Therefore, on the festive night when we shall all sit in the great city hall at tables covered with white cloth and when the light of a thousand illuminations will sparkle over the city, each of us will dip his roll of bread in a beaker of raspberry juice and slowly sip that noble liquor. This is the way to fortify the firemen, to regenerate all the energy they squander under the guise of fireworks, rockets, and Bengal fires. My heart is full of fellow feeling for their misery and undeserved abasement. I have accepted from their hands the saber of a captain in the hope that I might lead them from their present degradation to a future pledged to new ideas."

"You are completely transformed, Jacob," said my mother, "you are magnificent! All the same, I hope that you will stay at home tonight. Don't forget that we have not had a chance to talk seriously since my return from the country. And as for the firemen," she added, turning to Adela, "I really think that you are a little prejudiced. Though ne'er-do-wells, they are decent boys. I always look with pleasure at those slim young men in their shapely uniforms; I must say, though, that their belts are drawn in a shade too tightly at the waist. They have a natural elegance, and their eagerness and readiness to serve the ladies at any time is really touching. Whenever I drop my umbrella in the street or stop to tie a bootlace, there is always one of them at hand, ready to help and to please. I daren't disappoint them so I always wait patiently for one of them to appear and to perform the little service that seems to make them so happy. When, having performed his duty, he walks away, he is at once surrounded by a group of his colleagues who discuss the event with him eagerly, while the hero illustrates with gestures what actually happened. If I were you, Adela, I would willingly make use of their gallantry."

"I think that they are nothing but a bunch of loafers," said Theodore, the senior shop assistant. "We don't even let them fight fires anymore because they are as irresponsible as children. It is enough to see how enviously they watch groups of boys throwing buttons against a wall to understand that they have brains like hares. Whenever you look out a window at boys playing in the street, you are sure to see among them one of these large chaps breathlessly running about, almost crazy with pleasure at the boys' game. At the sight of a fire, they jump for joy, clap their hands, and dance like savages. No, one cannot rely on them to put out the fires. Chimney sweeps and city militiamen are the people to use. This would leave fairs and popular festivals to the firemen. For instance, at the so-called storming of the Capitol on a dark morning last autumn, they dressed up as Carthaginians and lay siege, with a devilish noise, at the Basilian Hill, while the people who watched them sang: 'Hannibal, Hannibal ante portas!' Toward the end of autumn, they become lazy and somnolent, fall asleep standing up, and, with the first snows, disappear completely from sight. I have been told by an old stove fitter that when he repairs chimneys, he often finds firemen clinging to the air duct, immobile like pupae and still in their scarlet uniforms and shiny helmets. They sleep upright, drunk with raspberry syrup, filled up with its sticky sweetness and fire. You must pull them out by their ears and take them back to their barracks, sleep-drunk and semiconscious, along morning streets whitened by hoarfrost, while street urchins throw stones at them, and they, in return, smile the embarrassed smiles of guilt and bad conscience and sway about like drunkards."

"Be that as it may," said Adela, "they can't have any of my syrup. I did not spend hours at the hot kitchen range making syrup and spoiling my complexion so that these idlers should drink it now."

Instead of answering, my father produced a tin whistle and blew a piercing note. At once, four slim young men rushed into the room and arranged themselves in a row under the wall. The room brightened from the glare of their helmets, and they, dark and sunburnt under their hats, having adopted a military posture, waited for father's orders. At a sign from my father, two of them got hold of a large carboy, full of raspberry syrup, and before Adela could stop them, ran downstairs with their precious loot. The two remaining men gave a smart military salute and followed suit.

For a moment it seemed that Adela would throw a fit: her beautiful eyes blazed with rage. But Father did not wait for her outburst. With one leap, he reached the windowsill and spread his arms wide. We rushed after him. The market square, brightly lighted, was crowded. Under our house, eight firemen held fully extended a large sheet of canvas. Father turned round, the plate of his armor flashing in the light; he saluted us silently, then, with arms outspread, bright like a meteor, he leaped into the night sparkling with a thousand lights. The sight was so beautiful that we all began to cheer in delight. Even Adela forgot her grievance and clapped and cheered. Meanwhile, my father jumped onto the ground from the canvas sheet and, having shaken his clanking breastplate into position, went to the head of his detachment, which, two by two, slowly marched in formation past the dark lines of the watching crowd, lights playing on the brass of their helmets.

A SECOND FALL

Among the many scientific researches undertaken by my father in rare periods of peace and inner serenity between the blows of disasters and catastrophes in which his adventurous and stormy life abounded, studies of comparative meteorology were nearest to his heart, particularly those of the climate of our province, which had many peculiarities. It was my father who laid the foundations of a skillful analysis of climatic trends. His *Outline of General Systematics of the Fall* explained once and for all the essence of that season, which in our provincial climate assumed a prolonged, parasitical, and overgrown form known also by the name of *Chinese summer*, extending far into the depths of our colorful winters. What more can I say? My father was the first to explain the secondary, derivative character of that late season, which is nothing other than the result of our climate having been poisoned by the miasmas exuded by degenerate specimens of baroque art crowded in our museums. That museum art, rotting in boredom and oblivion and shut in without an outlet, ferments like old preserves, oversugars our climate, and is the cause of this beautiful malarial fever, this extraordinary delirium, to which our prolonged fall is so agonizingly prone. For beauty is a disease, as my father maintained; it is the result of a mysterious infection, a dark forerunner of decomposition, which rises from the depth of perfection and is saluted by perfection with signs of the deepest bliss.

A few factual remarks about our provincial museum might be apposite here. Its origins go back to the eighteenth century, and it stems from the admirable collecting zeal of the Order of Saint Basil, whose monks bestowed their treasure on the city, thus burdening its budget with an excessive and unproductive expense. For a number of years the Treasury of the Republic, having purchased the collection for next to nothing from the impoverished order, ruined itself grandly by artistic patronage, a pursuit worthy of some royal house. But already the next generation of city fathers, more practical and mindful of economic necessities, after fruitless negotiations with the curators of an archducal collection to whom they had tried to sell the museum, closed it down, dismissed its trustees, and granted the last keeper a pension for life. During these negotiations, it has been authoritatively stated by experts, the value of the collection had been greatly exaggerated by local patriots. The kindly Fathers of Saint Basil had, in their praiseworthy enthusiasm, bought more than a few fakes. The museum did not contain even a single painting by a master's hand but owned the whole *oeuvre* of third- and fourth-rate painters, whole provincial schools, known only to specialist art historians.

A strange thing: the kindly monks had militaristic inclinations, and the majority of the paintings represented battle scenes. A burnt, golden dusk darkened these canvases decayed with age. Fleets of galleons and caravels and old forgotten armadas moldered in enclosed bays, their swelled sails carrying the majestic emblems of remote republics. Under smoky and blackened varnishes, hardly visible outlines of equestrian engagements could be discerned. Across the emptiness of sun-scorched plains under a dark and tragic sky, cavalcades passed in an ominous silence balanced on the left and right by the distant flashes and smoke of artillery.

In paintings of the Neapolitan school a sultry, cloudy afternoon grows old in perpetuity, as if seen through a bottle darkly. A pale sun seems to wilt under one's eyes in those landscapes, forlorn as if on the eve of a cosmic catastrophe. And this is why the ingratiating smiles and gestures of dusky fisherwomen, selling bundles of fish to wandering comedians, seem so futile. All that world has been condemned and forgotten a long time ago. Hence the infinite sweetness of the last gestures that alone remain, frozen forever. And deeper still in that country, inhabited by a carefree race of merrymakers, harlequins, and birdmen with cages, in that country without any reality or earnestness, small Turkish girls with fat little hands pat honey cakes lying in rows on wooden boards; two boys in Neapolitan hats carry a basket of noisy pigeons on a pole that sways slightly under the burden of its cooing, feathered load. And still farther in the background, on the very edge of the evening, on the last plot of soil where a wilting bunch of acanthus sways on the border of nothingness, a last game of cards is still being played before the arrival of the already looming darkness.

That whole lumber room of ancient beauty has been subjected to a painful distillation under the pressure of years of boredom.

"Can you understand," my father used to ask, "the despair of that condemned beauty, of its days and nights? Over and over again it had to rouse itself to fictitious auctions, stage successful sales and noisy, crowded exhibitions, become inflamed with wild gambling passions, await a slump, scatter riches, squander them like a maniac, only to realize on sobering up that all this was in vain, that it could not get anywhere beyond a self-centered perfection, that it could not relieve the pain of excess. No wonder that the impatience and helplessness of beauty had at last to find its reflection in our sky, that it therefore glows over our horizon, degenerates into atmospheric displays, into these enormous arrangements of fantastic clouds I call our second or spurious fall. That second fall of our province is nothing but a sick mirage projected through an expanse of radiation into our sky by the dying, shut-in beauty in our museums. Fall is a great touring show, poetically deceptive, an enormous purple-skinned onion disclosing ever new panoramas under each of its skins. No center can ever be reached. Behind each wing that is moved and stored away new and radiant scenes open up, true and alive for a moment, until you realize that they are made of cardboard. All perspectives are painted, all the panoramas made of board, and only the smell is authentic, the smell of wilting scenery, of theatrical dressing rooms, redolent of grease paint and scent. And at dusk there is disorder and chaos in the wings, a pileup of discarded costumes, among which you can wade endlessly as if through yellowed fallen leaves. There is great confusion: everybody is pulling at the curtain ropes, and the sky, a great autumnal sky, hangs in tatters and is filled with the screeching of pulleys. And there is an atmosphere of feverish haste, of belated carnival, a ballroom about to empty in the small hours, a panic of masked people who cannot find their real clothes.

"Fall, the Alexandrian time of the year, collecting in its enormous library the sterile wisdom of three hundred and sixty-five days of the sun's race. Oh those elderly mornings, yellow like parchment, sweet with wisdom like late evenings! Those forenoons smiling slyly like wise palimpsests, the many-layered texts of yellowed books! Ah, days of fall, that old crafty librarian, groping his way up ladders in a faded dressing gown and trying spoonfuls of sweet preserves from all the centuries and cultures! Each landscape is for him like the opening chapter of an old novel. What fun he has letting loose the heroes of old stories under that misty, honey-colored sky into an opaque and sad, late sweetness of light! What new adventures will Don Quixote find at Soplicowo?* How will Robinson Crusoe fare upon his return to his native Drohobycz?"

On close, immobile evenings, golden after fiery sunsets, my father read us extracts from his manuscript. The flow of ideas allowed him sometimes to forget about Adela's ominous presence.

Then came the warm winds from Romania, establishing an enormous yellow monotony, a feel of the south. The fall would not end. Like soap bubbles, days rose ever more beautiful and ethereal, and each of them seemed so perfect that every moment of its duration was like a miracle extended beyond measure and almost painful.

In the stillness of those deep and beautiful days, the consistency of leaves changed imperceptibly, until one day all the trees stood in the straw fire of completely dematerialized leaves, in a light redness like a coating of colored confetti, magnificent peacocks and phoenixes; the slightest move or flutter would cause them to shed the splendor of their plumage — the light, molted, superfluous leafy feathers.

*Name of the estate in Lithuania where the action of *Pan Tadeusz* by Adam Mickiewicz takes place.

DEAD SEASON

I

At five o'clock in the morning, an hour glaring with early sunshine, our house was already enveloped in an ardent but quiet brightness. At that solemn hour, unobserved by anyone — while the rooms in the semidarkness of drawn blinds were still filled with the harmonious breathing of sleeping people — its facade bathed in the sun, in the silence of the early haze, as if its surface were decorated by blissfully sleeping eyelids. Thus, in the stillness of these early hours, it absorbed the first fires of the morning with a sleepy face melting in brilliance, its features slightly twitching from intense dreams. The shadow of the acacia in front of the house slid in waves down the hot surface, trying in vain to penetrate into the depth of golden sleep. The linen blinds absorbed the morning heat, portion after portion, and sunbathed fainting in the glare.

At that early hour, my father, unable to sleep any longer, went downstairs loaded with books and ledgers, in order to open the shop, which was on the street level of the building. For a moment he stood still in the gateway, sustaining with half-closed eyes the powerful onslaught of the sun. The sun-drenched wall of the house pulled him tenderly into its blissfully leveled, smooth surface. For a moment Father became flat, grown into the facade, and felt his outstretched hands, quivering and warm, merging into its golden stucco. (How many other fathers have grown forever into the facades of houses at five o'clock in the morning, while on the last step of the staircase? How many fathers have thus become the concierges of their own gateways, flatly sculpted into the embrasure with a hand on the door handle and a face dissolved into parallel and blissful furrows, over which the fingers of their sons would wander, later, reminiscing about their parent, now incorporated forever into the universal smile of the house front?) But soon he wrenched himself away, regained a third dimension, and, made human once more, freed the metal-framed door of the shop from its bolts, bars, and padlocks.

While he was opening that heavy, ironclad door, the grumbling dusk took a step back from the entrance, moved a few inches deeper, changed position, and lay down again inside. The morning freshness, rising like smoke from the cool tiles of the pavement, stood shyly on the threshold in a tiny, trembling stream of air. Inside the shop the darkness of many preceding days and nights lurked in the unopened bales of cloth, arranged itself in layers, then spent itself at the very heart of the shop — in the storeroom — where it dissolved, undifferentiated and self-saturated, into a dully looming archmatter of cloth.

My father walked along that high wall of cheviots and cords, passing his hand caressingly along the upright bales. Under his touch the rows of blind torsos ever ready to fall over or break order, calmed down and entrenched themselves in their cloth hierarchy and precedence.

For my father our shop was the place of eternal anguish and torment. This creature of his hands had for some time, in the years of its growth, been pushing against him ever more violently from day to day, and it had finally outgrown him. The shop became for him a task beyond his strength, at once immense and sublime. The immensity of its claims frightened him. Even his life could not satisfy their awful extent. He looked with despair at the frivolity of his shop assistants, their silly, carefree optimism, their jokes and thoughtless manipulations, occurring at the margins, as it were, of that great business enterprise. With bitter irony he watched that gallery of faces undisturbed by any worry, those foreheads innocent of any idea; he looked into the depths of those trusting eyes never troubled by even the slightest shadow of doubt. For all her loyalty and devotion, how could my mother help him? The realization of matters of a higher order was outside the scope of her simple and uncomplicated mind. She was not created for heroic tasks. For he did notice that behind his back she occasionally exchanged quick and understanding looks with the shop assistants, glad of any moment without supervision, when she could take part in their fatuous clowning.

My father separated himself more and more from that world of lightheartedness and escaped into the hard discipline of total dedication. Horrified by the laxity spreading everywhere, he shut himself off in the lonely service of his high ideal. His hand never strayed from the reins, he never allowed himself a relaxation of rules or the comfort of facile solutions.

That was good enough for Balanda & Co. and these other dilettanti of the trade, who knew not the hunger for perfection nor the asceticism of high priesthood. My father suffered when he saw the downfall of the retail textile trade. Who of the present generation of textile merchants remembered the good traditions of their ancient art? Which of them knew, for instance, that pieces of cloth, laid in a stack on display shelves in accordance with the principles of textile art, could emit under the touch of a finger running downward, a sound like a descending scale? Which among his contemporaries was conversant with the finer points of style in the exchange of notes, memos, and letters? How many still remembered the charm of merchant diplomacy, the diplomacy of the good old school, the exciting stages of negotiation: beginning with irreconcilable stiffness and intransigent reserve at the visit of the representative of a foreign firm, through gradual thaw under the influence of the indefatigable persuasions and blandishments of that envoy, until the invitation to a working supper with wine — served at the desk, on top of papers, in an exalted mood, with some pinching of Adela's bottom while she served the meal, amid peppery jokes and a free flow of talk, as behooves gentlemen who know what is expected in the circumstances — was crowned with a mutually profitable business deal?

In the quietness of the morning hours, while the heat was slowly rising, my father expected to find a happy and inspired phrase that would give the required weight to his letter to Messrs. Christian Seipel & Sons, Spinners and Mechanical Weavers. It was to be a cutting riposte to the unfounded demands of these gentlemen, the reply *ad rem*, concise at the decisive point, so that the letter could rise to a strong and witty final plea to produce the desired shock effect and could then be rounded off with one energetic, elegant, and final irrevocable sentence. He could almost feel the form of that phrase that had been eluding him for many days, he could almost touch it with his fingertips, but he could not lay his hands on it. He waited for a flash of carefree humor to take by storm the obstacle that stubbornly barred his way. He reached for yet another clean sheet of paper, in order to give fresh impetus to the conquest of the obstacle that had been defying all his efforts.

Meanwhile the shop became gradually peopled with his assistants. They entered flushed from the early morning heat and avoided Father's desk, at which they cast frightened and guilt-ridden looks.

Exhausted after the night and conscious of it, they felt the weight of his silent disapproval, which nothing they did could dispel. Nothing could placate the master, brooding over his worries; no show of eagerness could pacify him as he sat lurking like a scorpion behind his desk, his glasses flashing ominously as he foraged like a mouse among his papers. His excitement increased, his latent temper intensified in step with the heat. The square patch of sunlight on the floor glared. Shiny, metallic flies flashed like lightning in the entrance to the shop, settling for a moment on the sides of the door, glass bubbles blown from the hot pipe of the sun, from the glassworks of that radiant day: they sat with wings outspread, full of flight and swiftness, then changed places in furious zigzags. Through the bright quadrilateral of the doorway one could see the lime trees of the city park fainting in the sunlight, the distant bell tower of the church outlined clearly in the translucent and shimmering air, as if in the lenses of binoculars. The tinplated roofs were burning; the enormous, golden globe of heat was swelling all over the world.

Father's irritation grew. He looked round helplessly, doubled up with pain, exhausted by diarrhea. He felt in his mouth a taste more bitter than wormwood.

The heat intensified, sharpening the fury of the flies, making the metal on their abdomens shine. The quadrilateral of light now reached Father's desk, and the papers burned like the Apocalypse. Father's eyes, blinded by the sunlight, could not stand their white uniformity. Through his thick glasses he saw everything he looked at in crimson, greenish, or purple frames and was filled with despair at this explosion of color, the anarchy raging over the world in an orgy of brightness. His hands shook. His palate was bitter and dry, heralding an attack of sickness. His eyes, embedded in the furrows of wrinkles, watched with attention the development of events in the depth of the shop.

II

When, at noon, my father, exhausted by the heat, trembling with futile excitement and almost on the verge of madness, retreated upstairs and the ceilings of the floor above cracked here and there under his skulking step, the shop experienced a momentary pause and relaxation: the hour of the afternoon siesta.

The shop assistants turned somersaults on the bales of cloth, pitched tents of fabric on the shelves, made swings from draperies. They unwound the cloth, set free the smooth, tightly rolled ancient darkness. The shopworn, felted dusk, now liberated, filled the spaces under the ceiling with the smell of another time, with the odor of past days patiently arranged in innumerable layers during the cool falls of long ago. Blind moths scattered in the darkened air, fluffs of feathers and wool circled with them all over the shop, and the smell of finishing, deep and autumnal, filled this dark encampment of cloth and velvet. Picnicking in that camp the shop assistants devised practical jokes. They let their colleagues wrap them tightly up to their ears in dark, cool cloth and lay in a row blissfully immobile under the stack of bales — living bolts of cloth like mummies, rolling their eyes with an assumed fear at their own immobility. Or else they let themselves be swung up to the ceiling on enormous, outspread blankets of cloth. The dull thudding of these blankets and the current of air that arose made them mad with joy. It seemed as if the whole shop was taking off in flight, the fabrics rising in inspiration, the shop assistants, with their coattails flowing, swinging upward like prophets on short ascensions. My mother looked indulgently at these games, the relaxation due in the hours of siesta justified in her eyes even the worst transgressions.

In the summer the back of the shop was dark because of the weeds growing in the courtyard. The storeroom window overlooking it became all green and iridescent like submarine depths from the movement of leaves and their undulating reflections. Flies buzzed there monotonously in their semiobscurity of long afternoons; they were monstrous specimens bred on Father's sweet wine, hairy hermits lamenting their accursed fate day in, day out in long, monotonous sagas. These flies, inclined to wild and unexpected mutations, abounded in unnatural specimens, bred from incestuous unions, degenerated into a super-race of top heavy giants, of veterans emitting a deep melancholy buzz. Toward the end of the summer some specimens were posthumously hatched out with wasted wings — mute and voiceless, the last of their race, resembling large, bluish beetles — and ended their sad lives running up and down the green windowpanes on busy, futile errands.

The rarely opened door became covered with cobwebs. My mother slept behind the desk, in a cloth hammock swinging between the shelves. The shop assistants, bothered by flies, winced and grimaced, stirring in an uneasy sleep. Meanwhile, the weeds took over the courtyard. Under the ruthless heat of the sun, the rubbish heap sprouted enormous nettles and mallows.

The heat of the sun falling on the subterranean water on this plot of soil produced a fermentation of venomous substances, some poisonous derivatives of chlorophyll. This morbid process brought forth malformed wrinkled leaves of astonishing lightness that spread until the space under the window was filled with a tissue-thin tangle of green pleonasms, of weedy rubbish degenerating into a papery, tawdry patchwork clinging to the walls of the storeroom. The shop assistants woke with flushed faces from a quick nap. Strangely excited, they got up with feverish energy, ready for even more heroic buffooneries; corroded by boredom, they climbed on tall shelves and drummed with their feet, looking fixedly at the empty expanse of the market square, longing for any kind of diversion.

Once a peasant from the country, barefoot and smock-clad, stopped in the doorway of the shop and looked in shyly. For the bored shop assistants this was a heaven-sent opportunity. They quickly swept down the ladders, like spiders at the sight of a fly; the peasant, surrounded, pulled, and pushed, was asked a hundred questions, which he tried to parry with a bashful smile. He scratched his head, smiled, and looked with suspicion at the assiduous young men. So he wanted tobacco? But what kind? The best, Macedonian, golden as amber? Not that kind? Would ordinary pipe tobacco do? Shag perhaps? Would he care to step in? To come inside? There was nothing to fear. The shop assistants prodded him gently deeper into the shop, toward a side counter. Leon went behind the counter and pretended to pull out a nonexistent drawer. Oh, how he worked at it, how he bit his lip with effort! It was stuck and would not move. One had to thump the top of the counter with one's fists, with all one's might. The peasant, encouraged by the young men, did it with concentration, with proper attention. At last, when there was no result, he climbed, hunched and gray-haired, on top of the counter and stamped it with his bare feet. He had us all in fits of laughter.

It was then that the regrettable incident occurred that filled us all with sadness and shame. Although we did not act in bad faith, we were all equally to blame. It was all due to our frivolity, our lack of seriousness and understanding for Father's worries. Given the unpredictable, insecure, and volatile nature of my father, our thoughtlessness produced consequences that were truly fatal.

While we were all standing in a semicircle, enjoying our little joke, my father quietly entered the shop.

We did not see him come in. We noticed him only when the sudden understanding of our little game distorted his face in a grimace of wild horror. My mother came running, very frightened:

"What is the matter, Jacob?" she asked breathlessly.

She began to slap him on the back as one would a person who is choking. It was too late. My father was bristling all over, his face was decomposing quickly, falling apart, changing under our eyes, struck by the burden of an inexplicable calamity. Before we could understand what was happening, he shook himself violently, buzzed, and rose in flight before our eyes, transformed into a monstrous, hairy, steel blue horsefly, furiously circling and knocking blindly against the walls of the shop. Transfixed, we listened to the hopeless lament, the expressively modulated dull plaint, running up and down the registers of boundless pain — an unrelieved suffering under the dark ceiling of the shop.

We stood unmoving, deeply shamed, unable to look at one another. In the depth of our hearts we felt a certain relief that at a critical moment my father had found a way out of an impossible situation. We admired the courage with which he threw himself recklessly into a blind alley of desperation from which, as it seemed, there was no return.

Yet, looking at it dispassionately, one had to take my father's transformation *cum grano salis*. It was much more the symbol of an inner protest, a violent and desperate demonstration from which, however, reality was not absolutely absent. One has to keep in mind that most of the events described here suffer from summer aberrations, the canicular semireality, the marginal time running irresponsibly along the borderline of the dead season.

We listened in silence. My father's revenge was particularly cunning: it was a kind of reprisal. From then on we were condemned to hearing forever that baleful low buzzing — a persistent, doleful complaint, which rose to a pitch and then suddenly stopped. For a moment, we savored the silence with relief, a beneficent respite during which a glimmer of hope arose in us. But after a while the buzzing began again, ever more insistent and plaintive, and we realized that there was no end to that suffering, to that curse, to the homeless beating against all the walls. That monologue of complaint and silence, each time rising even louder and angrier, as if it wanted to cancel the previous moment of short appeasement, jarred on our nerves. Suffering that is limitless, suffering that is stubbornly enclosed within the circle of its own mania, suffering to the point of distraction, of self-mutilation, becomes in the end unbearable for the helpless witnesses of misfortune. That incessant, angry appeal for our sympathy contained too obvious a reproach, too glaring an accusation against our own well-being, not to make us rebellious. We all inwardly writhed, full of protest and fury instead of contrition. Was there really no other way out for him but to throw himself blindly into that pitiful and hopeless condition, and, having fallen into it, no matter whether by his own fault or by ours, couldn't he find more strength of spirit or more dignity to bear it without complaint? My mother could only check her anger with difficulty. The shop assistants, sitting on their ladders in dull amazement, had dreams of retaliation and thought of reckless pursuit along the shelves with a leather flyswatter, and their eyes became bloodshot. The canvas blind over the shop entrance was flapping furiously, the afternoon heat hung over miles of sun-drenched plain and devastated the distant world underneath it, and in the semiobscurity of the shop, under the dark ceiling, my father hopelessly circled and circled, enmeshing himself tighter and tighter in the desperate zigzags of his flight.

III

Yet, in spite of all the evidence to the contrary, such episodes were of no great importance, for, that same evening, my father was poring as usual over his papers, and the incident seemed to be long forgotten, the deep grudge overcome and erased. We, of course, refrained from any allusion to it. We looked with pleasure as, with seeming equanimity, in peaceful concentration, he industriously covered page after page with his calli-graphically precise writing. Instead, it became ever more difficult to forget the compromising presence of the poor peasant. It is well known how stubbornly such unfinished business becomes rooted in certain minds. We ignored him on purpose during these empty weeks, leaving him to stamp on the counter in the dark corner, daily becoming smaller and grayer. Almost unnoticeable now, he was still stamping away on the same spot, smiling benevolently, hunched over the counter, indefatiga-ble, chattering softly to himself. The stamping and knocking became his true vocation, in which he was completely engrossed. We did not interfere with him. He had gone too far; we could not reach him now.

Summer days have no dusk. Before we knew where we were, night would come to the shop, a large oil lamp was lighted, and shop affairs continued. During these short summer nights it was not worth returning home. My father usually sat at his desk in apparent concentration and marked the margins of letters with black scattered stars, ink spots, hair lines that circled in his field of vision, atoms of darkness detached from the great summer night behind the windows. The night meanwhile scattered like a puffball a microcosm of shadows under the globe of the lamp. Father was blinded as his spectacles reflected the lamp. He was waiting, waiting with impatience and listening while he stared at the whiteness of the paper through which flowed the dark galaxies of black stars and dust specks. Behind his back, without his participation, as it were, the great battle for the shop was being fought. Oddly enough, it was fought on a painting hanging behind his head, between the filing cabinet and the mirror, in the bright circle of the lamplight. It was a magic painting, a talisman, a riddle of a picture, endlessly interpreted and passed on from one generation to the next. What did it represent? That was the subject of unending disputations conducted for years, a never-ending quarrel between two opposing points of view. The paint-ing represented two merchants facing one another, two opposites, two worlds.

"I gave credit," cried the slim, down-at-heel little fellow, his voice breaking in despair.

"I sold for cash," answered the fat man in the armchair, crossing his legs and twiddling his thumbs above his stomach.

How my father hated the fat one! He had known both since his childhood. Even as a schoolboy, he was full of contempt for any fat egoist who devoured innumerable buttered rolls in the middle of the morning. But he did not quite support the slim one either. Now he looked amazed as all initiative slipped from his hands, taken over by the two men at loggerheads. With bated breath, blinking his eyes from which the spectacles had slipped, my father now tensely awaited the result of the dispute.

The shop itself was a perpetual mystery. It was the center of all Father's thoughts, of his nightly cogitations, of his frightening silences. Inscrutable and all-embracing, it stood in the background of daily events. In daytime, the generations of fabrics, full of patriarchal dignity, lay in order of precedence, segregated according to their ancestry and origins. But at night the rebellious blackness of the materials broke out and stormed about with silent tirades and hellish improvisations. In the fall the shop bustled, overflowing with the dark stock of winter merchandise, as if whole acres of forest had been uprooted and were marching through a windswept landscape. In the summer, in the dead season, the shop retreated to its dark reservations, inapproachable in its thickets of cloth. The shop assistants banged at night with their wooden yardsticks at the dull wall of bales, listening as the shop roared with pain, immured in the cave of cloth.

In the surrounding darkness my father harked back to the past, to the abyss of time. He was the last of his line, he was Atlas on whose shoulders rested the burden of an enormous legacy. By day and by night, my father thought about the meaning of it all and tried to understand its hidden intention. He often looked askance, full of expectation, at his assistants. Not himself receiving any secret signs, any enlightenment, any directives, he expected that these young and naïve men, just emerging from their cocoons, might suddenly realize the meaning of his trade that stubbornly evaded him. He pestered them with persistent questioning, but they, stupid and inarticulate, avoided his looks, turned their eyes away, and mumbled some confused nonsense. In the mornings, using a walking stick for support, my father wandered like a shepherd among his blind, woolly flock, among the bleating headless rumps crowded around the drinking trough. He was still waiting, postponing the moment when he would have to move his tribe and go out into the night burdened with responsibility for that swarming, homeless Israel. . . .

The night behind the door was leaden — close, without a breeze. After a few steps it became impassable. One walked without moving forward as in a dream, and while one's feet stuck to the ground, one's thoughts continued to run forward endlessly, incessantly questioning, led astray by the dialectical byways of the night. The differential calculus of the night continued. At last, one's feet stopped moving, and one stood riveted to the spot, at the darkest, most intimate corner of the night, as in front of a privy, in dead silence, for long hours, with a feeling of blissful shame. Only thought, left to itself, slowly made an about turn, the complex anatomy of the brain unwound itself like a reel, and the abstract treatise of the summer night continued its venomous dialectic, turning logical somersaults, inventing new sophisticated questions to which there was no answer. Thus one debated with oneself through the speculative vastness of the night and entered, disembodied, into ultimate nothingness.

It was long after midnight when my father abruptly lifted his head from his pile of papers. He stood up, full of self-importance, with dilated eyes, listening intently.

"He is coming," he said with a radiant face, "open the door."

Almost before Theodore, the senior assistant, could open the glass door, which had been bolted for the night, a man had already squeezed himself in, loaded with bundles, black-haired, bearded, splendid, and smiling: the long awaited guest. Mr. Jacob, deeply moved, hurried to greet him, bowing, both his hands outstretched in greeting. They embraced. It seemed for a moment as if the black shining engine of a train had voicelessly driven up to the very door of the shop. A porter in a railwayman's hat came in carrying an enormous trunk on his back.

We never learned who this distinguished visitor really was. Theodore firmly maintained that he was Christian Seipel & Sons (Spinners and Mechanical Weavers) in person, but there was little evidence for it, and my mother did not subscribe to this theory. There was no doubt, though, that the man must have been a powerful demon, one of the pillars of the County Creditors' Union. A black, carefully trimmed beard surrounded his fat, shiny, and most dignified face. With Father's arm around him, he proceeded, bowing, toward the desk.

Unable to understand the conversation, which was in a foreign language, we nonetheless listened to it with respect, and watched the smiles, the closing of the eyes, the delicate and tender mutual self-congratulations. After the exchange of preliminary courtesies, the gentlemen proceeded to the crux of the matter. Ledgers and papers were spread out on the desk, a bottle of white wine was uncorked. With strong cigars in the corners of their mouths, with faces folded into grimaces of gruff contentment, the gentlemen exchanged short one-syllable code words, spasmodically pointing their fingers at an appropriate entry in the ledgers with a humorous flash of villainy in their eyes. Slowly the discussion became more heated; one could perceive a mounting, barely suppressed, excitement. They bit their lips, the cigars hung down, now bitter and cold, from mouths suddenly disappointed and hostile. They were trembling with inner irritation. My father was breathing through the nose, red flushes under his eyes, his hair bristling over his perspiring brow. The situation became inflammable. A moment came when both men got up from their chairs and stood almost blind with anger, breathing heavily and glaring from under their spectacles. Mother, frightened, began to pat Father imploringly on his back, wanting to prevent a catastrophe. At the sight of a lady, both gentlemen came to their senses, recalled the rules of etiquette, bowed, smiling, to one another, and sat down to a further spell of work.

At about two o'clock in the morning, Father banged shut the heavy cover of the main ledger. We looked anxiously into the faces of both men to discern who had won the battle. My father's apparent good humor seemed to be artificial and forced, while the black-bearded man was leaning back in his armchair, with legs crossed, and breathing kindness and optimism. With ostentatious generosity he began to distribute gratuities among the shop assistants.

Having tidied up the papers and invoices, the gentlemen now rose from behind the desk. Winking to the shop assistants with implied anticipation, they silently intimated that they were now ready for new initiatives. They suggested behind Mother's back that the time had come for a little celebration. This was empty talk, and the shop assistants knew what to make of it. That night did not lead anywhere. It had to end in the gutter, at a certain place by the blind wall of nothingness and secret shame. All the paths leading into the night turned back to the shop. All sorties attempted into the depth of it were doomed from the outset. The shop assistants winked back only from politeness.

The black-bearded man and my father, arm in arm, left the shop full of energy, followed by the tolerant looks of the young men. Immediately outside the door, darkness obliterated their heads at a stroke, and they plunged into the black waters of the night.

Who has ever plumbed the depths of a July night, who has ever measured how many fathoms of emptiness there are in which nothing happens? Having crossed that black infinity, the two men again stood in front of the door as if they had just left it, having regained their heads with yesterday's words still unused on their lips. Standing thus for a long time, they conversed in monotones, as if they had just returned from a distant expedition. They were now bound by the comradeship of alleged adventures and nighttime excesses. They pushed back their hats as drunks do and rocked on unsteady legs.

Avoiding the lighted front of the shop, they stealthily entered the porch of the house and began to walk quietly up the creaking steps to the first floor. They crept out onto the balcony and stood in front of Adela's window trying to look at the sleeping girl. They could not see her; she lay in shadow and sobbed unconsciously in her sleep, her mouth slightly open, her head thrown back and burning, fanatically engrossed in her dreams. They knocked at the black windowpanes and sang dirty songs. But Adela, a lethargic smile on her half-opened lips, was wandering, numb and hypnotized, on her distant roads, miles away, outside their reach.

Then, propping themselves up against the rail of the balcony, they yawned broadly and loudly in resignation and began to kick their feet against the balustrade. At some late and unknown hour of the night, they found their bodies again on two narrow beds, floating on high mountains of bedding. They swam on them side by side, racing one another in a gallop of snoring.

At some still more distant mile of sleep — had the flow of sleep joined their bodies, or had their dreams imperceptibly merged into one? — they felt that lying in each other's arms they were still fighting a difficult, unconscious duel. They were panting face to face in sterile effort. The black-bearded man lay on top of my father like the angel on top of Jacob. My father pressed against him with all the strength of his knees and, stiffly floating away into numbness, stole another short spell of fortifying sleep between one round of wrestling and another. So they fought: What for? For their good name? For God? For a contract? They grappled in mortal sweat, to their last ounce of strength, while the waves of sleep carried them away into ever more distant and stranger areas of the night.

IV

The next day my father walked with a slight limp. His face was radiant. At dawn a splendid phrase for his letter had come to him, a formulation he had been trying in vain to find for many days and nights. We never saw the black-bearded gentleman again. He left before daybreak with his trunk and bundles, without taking leave of us. That was the last night of the dead season. From that summer night onward seven long years of prosperity began for the shop.

SANATORIUM
UNDER THE SIGN
OF THE
HOURGLASS

I

The journey was long. The train, which ran only once a week on that forgotten branch line, carried no more than a few passengers. Never before had I seen such archaic coaches; withdrawn from other lines long before, they were spacious as living rooms, dark, and with many recesses. Corridors crossed the empty compartments at various angles; labyrinthine and cold, they exuded an air of strange and frightening neglect. I moved from coach to coach, looking for a comfortable corner. Drafts were everywhere: cold currents of air shooting through the interiors, piercing the whole train from end to end. Here and there a few people sat on the floor, surrounded by their bundles, not daring to occupy the empty seats. Besides, those high, convex oilcloth-covered seats were cold as ice and sticky with age. At the deserted stations no passengers boarded the train. Without a whistle, without a groan, the train would slowly start again, as if lost in meditation.

For a time I had the company of a man in a ragged railwayman's uniform — silent, engrossed in his thoughts. He pressed a handkerchief to his swollen, aching face. Later even he disappeared, having slipped out unobserved at some stop. He left behind him the mark of his body in the straw that lay on the floor, and a shabby black suitcase he had forgotten.

Wading in straw and rubbish, I walked shakily from coach to coach. The open doors of the compartments were swinging in the drafts. There was not a single passenger left on the train. At last, I met a conductor, in the black uniform of that line. He was wrapping a thick scarf around his neck and collecting his things — a lantern, an official logbook.

"We are nearly there, sir," he said, looking at me with washed-out eyes.

The train was coming slowly to a halt, without puffing, without rattling, as if, together with the last breath of steam, life were slowly escaping from it. We stopped. Everything was empty and still, with no station buildings in sight. The conductor showed me the direction of the Sanatorium. Carrying my suitcase, I started walking along a white narrow road toward the dark trees of a park. With some curiosity, I looked at the landscape. The road along which I was walking led up to the brow of a gentle hill, from which a wide expanse of country could be seen. The day was uniformly gray, extinguished, without contrasts. And perhaps under the influence of that heavy and colorless aura, the great basin of the valley, in which a vast wooded landscape was arranged like

theatrical scenery, seemed very dark. The rows of trees, one behind the other, ever grayer and more distant, descended the gentle slopes to the left and right. The whole landscape, somber and grave, seemed almost imperceptibly to float, to shift slightly like a sky full of billowing, stealthily moving clouds. The fluid strips and bands of forest seemed to rustle and grow with rustling like a tide that swells gradually toward the shore. The rising white road wound itself dramatically through the darkness of that woody terrain. I broke a twig from a roadside tree. The leaves were dark, almost black. It was a strangely charged blackness, deep and benevolent, like restful sleep. All the different shades of gray in the landscape derived from that one color. It was the color of a cloudy summer dusk in our part of the country, when the landscape has become saturated with water after a long period of rain and exudes a feeling of self-denial, a resigned and ultimate numbness that does not need the consolation of color.

It was completely dark among the trees of the parkland. I groped my way blindly on a carpet of soft needles. When the trees thinned, the planks of a footbridge resounded under my feet. Beyond it, against the blackness of the trees, loomed the gray walls of the many-windowed hotel that advertised itself as the Sanatorium. The double glass door of the entrance stood open. The little footbridge, with shaky handrails made of birch branches, led straight to it.

In the hallway there was semidarkness and a solemn silence. I moved on tiptoe from door to door, trying to see the numbers on them. Rounding a corner, I at last met a chambermaid. She had run out of a room, as if having torn herself from someone's importuning arms, and was breathless and excited. She could hardly understand what I was saying. I had to repeat it. She was fidgeting helplessly.

Had my telegram reached them? She spread her arms, her eyes moved sideways. She was only awaiting an opportunity to leap back behind the half-opened door, at which she kept squinting.

"I have come a long way. I booked a room here by telegram," I said with some impatience. "Whom shall I see about it?"

She did not know. "Perhaps you could wait in the restaurant," she babbled. "Everybody is asleep just now. When the doctor gets up, I shall announce you."

"They are asleep? But it is daytime, not night."

"Here everybody is asleep all the time. Didn't you know?" she said, looking at me with interest now. "Besides, it is never night here," she added coyly.

She had obviously given up the idea of escape, for she was now picking fussily at the lace of her apron. I left her there and entered the half-lighted restaurant. There were some tables, and a large buffet ran the length of one wall. I was now feeling a little hungry and was pleased to see some pastries and a cake on the buffet.

I placed my suitcase on one of the tables. They were all unoccupied. I clapped my hands. No response. I looked into the next room, which was larger and brighter. That room had a wide window or loggia overlooking the landscape I already knew, which, framed by the window, seemed like a constant reminder of mourning, suggestive of deep sorrow and resignation. On some of the tables stood the remains of recent meals, uncorked bottles, half-empty glasses. Here and there lay the tips, not yet picked up by the waiters. I returned to the buffet and looked at the pastries and cake. They looked most appetizing. I wondered whether I should help myself; I suddenly felt extremely greedy. There was a particular kind of apple flan that made my mouth water. I was about to lift a piece of it with a silver knife when I felt somebody behind me. The chambermaid had entered the room in her soft slippers and was touching my back lightly.

"The doctor will see you now," she said looking at her fingernails.

She stood facing me and, conscious of the magnetism of her wriggling hips, did not turn away. She provoked me, increasing and decreasing the distance between our bodies as, having left the restaurant, we passed many numbered doors. The passage became ever darker. In almost complete darkness, she brushed against me fleetingly.

"Here is the doctor's door," she whispered. "Please go in."

Dr. Gotard was standing in the middle of the room to receive me. He was a short, broad-shouldered man with a dark beard.

"We received your telegram yesterday," he said. "We sent our carriage to the station, but you must have arrived by another train. Unfortunately, the railway connections are not very good. Are you well?"

"Is my father alive?" I asked, staring anxiously into his calm face.

"Yes, of course," he answered, calmly meeting my questioning eyes. "That is, within the limits imposed by the situation," he added,

half closing his eyes. "You know as well as I that from the point of view of your home, from the perspective of your own country, your father is dead. This cannot be entirely remedied. That death throws a certain shadow on his existence here."

"But does Father himself know it, does he guess?" I asked him in a whisper.

He shook his head with deep conviction. "Don't worry," he said in a low voice. "None of our patients know it, or can guess. The whole secret of the operation," he added, ready to demonstrate its mechanism on his fingers, "is that we have put back the clock. Here we are always late by a certain interval of time of which we cannot define the length. The whole thing is a matter of simple relativity. Here your father's death, the death that has already struck him in your country, has not occurred yet."

"In that case," I said, "my father must be on his deathbed or about to die."

"You don't understand me," he said in a tone of tolerant impatience. "Here we reactivate time past, with all its possibilities, therefore also including the possibility of a recovery." He looked at me with a smile, stroking his beard. "But now you probably want to see your father. According to your request, we have reserved for you the other bed in your father's room. I shall take you there."

When we were out in the dark passage, Dr. Gotard spoke in a whisper. I noticed that he was wearing felt slippers, like the chambermaid. "We allow our patients to sleep long hours to spare their vitality. Besides, there is nothing better to do."

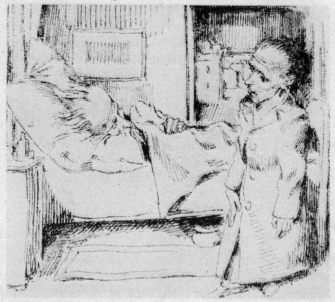

At last, we stopped in front of one of the doors, and he put a finger to his lips. "Enter quietly. Your father is asleep. Settle down to sleep, too. This is the best thing for you to do. Goodbye for now."

"Goodbye," I whispered, my heart beating fast.

I pressed the handle, and the door opened, like unresisting lips that part in sleep. I went in. The room was almost empty, gray and bare. Under a small window, my father was lying on an ordinary wooden bed, covered by a pile of bedding, fast asleep. His breathing extracted layers of snoring from the depths of his breast. The whole room seemed to be lined with snores from floor to ceiling, and yet new layers were being added all the time. With deep emotion, I looked at Father's thin, emaciated face, now completely engrossed in the activity of snoring — a remote, trancelike face, which, having left its earthly aspect, was confessing its existence somewhere on a distant shore by solemnly telling its minutes.

There was no second bed in the room. Piercingly cold air blew in through the window. The stove had not been lighted.

They don't seem to care much for patients here, I thought. To expose such a sick man to such drafts! And no one seems to do any cleaning here, either. A thick layer of dust covered the floor and the bedside table, on which stood medicine bottles and a cup of cold coffee. Stacks of pastries in the restaurant, yet they give the patients black coffee instead of anything more nourishing! But perhaps this is a detail compared with the benefits of having the clock put back.

I slowly undressed and climbed onto Father's bed. He did not wake up, but his snoring, having probably been pitched too high, fell an octave lower, forsaking its high declamatory tone. It became, as it were, more private, for his own use. I tucked Father in under his eiderdown, to protect him as much as possible from the drafts in the room. Soon I fell asleep by his side.

II

The room was in twilight when I woke up. Father was dressed and sitting at the table drinking tea, dunking sugar-coated biscuits in it. He was wearing a black suit of English cloth, which he had had made only the

118

previous summer. His tie was rather loose.

Seeing that I was awake, he said with a pleasant smile on his pale face, "I am extremely pleased that you have come, Joseph. It was a real surprise! I feel so lonely here. But I suppose one should not complain in my situation. I have been through worse things, and if one were to itemize them all — but never mind. Imagine, on my very first day here they served an excellent fillet of beef with mushrooms. It was a hell of a piece of meat, Joseph. I must warn you most emphatically — beware if they should ever serve you fillet of beef! I can still feel the fire in my stomach. And the diarrhea — I could hardly cope with it. But I must tell you a piece of news," he continued. "Don't laugh. I have rented premises for a shop here. Yes, I have. And I congratulate myself for having had that bright idea. I have been bored most terribly, I must say. You cannot imagine the boredom. And so I at least have a pleasant occupation. Don't imagine anything grand. Nothing of the kind. A much more modest place than our old store. It is a booth compared with the previous one. Back home I would be ashamed of such a stall, but here, where we have had to give up so many of our pretensions — don't you agree, Joseph?" He laughed bitterly. "And so one manages somehow to live."

The wrong word — I was embarrassed by Father's confusion when he realized that he had used it.

"I see you are sleepy," he continued after a while. "Go back to sleep, and then you can visit me in the shop if you want. I am going there now to see how things are. You cannot imagine how difficult it has been to get credit, how mistrustful they are here of old merchants, of merchants with a reputable past. Do you recall the optician's shop in the market square? Well, our shop is right next door to it. There is still no sign over it, but you will find your way, I am sure. You can't miss it."

"Are you going out without a coat?" I asked anxiously.

"They have forgotten to pack it. Imagine, I could not find it in my trunk. But I don't really need it. That mild climate, that sweet air — "

"Please take my coat, Father," I insisted. "You must."

But Father was already putting on his hat. He waved to me and slipped out of the room.

I did not feel sleepy any more. I felt rested and hungry. With pleasant anticipation I thought of the buffet. I dressed, wondering how many pastries to sample. I decided to start with the apple flan but did not forget the sponge cake with orange peel, which had caught my eye, too. I stood in front of the mirror to fix my tie, but the surface was like bottle glass: it secreted my reflection somewhere in its depth, and only an opaque blur was visible. I tried in vain to adjust the distance — approaching the mirror, then retreating from it — but no reflection would emerge from the silvery, fluid mist. I must ask for another looking glass, I thought, and left the room.

The corridor was completely dark. In one corner a tiny gas lamp flickered with a bluish flame, intensifying the impression of solemn silence. In that labyrinth of rooms, archways, and niches, I had difficulty remembering which door led to the restaurant.

I'll go out, I thought with sudden decision. I'll eat in the town.

There must be a good café somewhere.

Beyond the gate, I plunged into the heavy, damp, sweet air of that peculiar climate. The grayness of the aura had become somewhat deeper: now it seemed to me that I was seeing daylight through mourning crêpe.

I feasted my eyes on the velvety, succulent blackness of the darkest spots, on passages of dull grays and ashen, muted tones — that nocturne of a landscape. Waves of air fluttered softly around my face. They smelled of the sickly sweetness of stale rainwater.

And again that perpetual rustle of black forests — dull chords disturbing space beyond the limits of audibility! I was in the backyard of the Sanatorium. I turned to look at the rear of the main building, which was shaped like a horseshoe around a courtyard. All the windows were shuttered in black. The Sanatorium was in deep sleep. I went out by a gate in an iron fence. Nearby stood a dog kennel of extraordinary size, empty. Again I was engulfed and embraced by the black trees. Then it became somewhat lighter, and I saw outlines of houses between the trees. A few more steps and I found myself in a large town square.

What a strange, misleading resemblance it bore to the central square of our native city! How similar, in fact, are all the market squares in the world! Almost identical houses and shops!

The sidewalks were nearly empty. The mournful semidarkness of an undefined time descended from a sky of an indeterminable grayness. I could easily read all the shop signs and posters, yet it would not have surprised me to learn that it was the middle of the night. Only some of the shops were open. Others, their iron shutters pulled halfway down, were being hurriedly closed. A heady, rich, and inebriating air seemed to obscure some parts of the view, to wash away like a wet sponge some of the houses, a street lamp, a section of signboard. At times it was difficult to keep one's eyes open, overcome as one was by a strange indolence or sleepiness. I began to look for the optician's shop that my father had mentioned. He had spoken of it as of something I knew, and he seemed to assume that I was familiar with local conditions. Didn't he remember that I had just come here for the first time? No doubt his mind was confused. Yet what could one expect of Father, who was only half real, who lived a relative and conditional life, circumscribed by so many

121

limitations! I cannot deny that much goodwill was needed to believe in his kind of existence. What he experienced was a pitiful substitute for life, depending on the indulgence of others, on a *consensus omnium* from which he drew his faint strength. It was clear that only by the solidarity of forbearance, by a communal averting of eyes from the obvious and shocking shortcomings of his condition, could this pitiful semblance of life maintain itself, for however short a moment, within the tissue of reality. The slightest doubt could undermine it, the faintest breeze of skepticism destroy it. Could Dr. Gotard's Sanatorium provide for Father this hothouse atmosphere of friendly indulgence and guard him from the cold winds of sober analysis? It was astonishing that in this insecure and questionable state of affairs, Father was capable of behaving so admirably.

I was glad when I saw a shop window full of cakes and pastries. My appetite revived. I opened the glass door, with the inscription "Ices" on it and entered the dark interior. It smelled of coffee and vanilla. From the depths of the shop a girl appeared, her face misted over by dusk, and took my order. At last, after waiting so long, I could eat my fill of excellent doughnuts, which I dipped in my coffee. Surrounded by the dancing arabesques of dusk, I devoured pastries one after another, feeling darkness creep under my eyelids and stealthily fill me with its warm pulsations, its thousand delicate touches. In the end, only the window shone, like a gray rectangle, in the otherwise complete darkness. I knocked with my spoon on the tabletop, but in vain; no one appeared to take money for my refreshment. I left a silver coin on the table and walked out into the street.

In the bookshop next door, the light was still on. The shop assistants were busy sorting books. I asked for my father's shop. "It is next door to ours," one of them explained. A helpful boy even went with me to the door, to show me the way.

Father's shop had a glass pane in the door; the display window was not ready and was covered with a gray paper. On entering, I was astonished to see that the shop was full of customers. My father was standing behind the counter and adding a long row of figures on an invoice, repeatedly licking his pencil. The man for whom the invoice was being prepared was leaning over the counter and moving his index finger down the column of figures, counting softly. The rest of the customers looked on in silence.

My father gave me a look from over his spectacles and, marking his place on the invoice, said, "There is a letter for you. It is on the desk among all the papers." He went back to his sums. Meanwhile, the shop assistants were taking pieces of cloth bought by the customers, wrapping them in paper, and tying them with string. The shelves were only half filled with cloth; some of them were still empty.

"Why don't you sit down, Father?" I asked softly, going behind the counter. "You don't take enough care of yourself, although you are very sick."

Father lifted his hand, as if wanting to reject my pleas, and did not stop counting. He looked very pale. It was obvious that only the excitement of his feverish activity sustained him and postponed the moment of complete collapse.

I went up to the desk and found not a letter but a parcel. A few days earlier, I had written to a bookshop about a pornographic book, and here it was already. They had found my address, or rather, Father's address, although he had only just opened a new shop here that had neither a name nor a signboard! What amazing efficiency in collecting information, what astounding delivery methods! And what incredible speed!

"You may read it in the office at the back," said my father, looking at me with displeasure. "As you can see, there is no room here."

The room behind the shop was still empty. Through a glass door some light filtered in from the shop. On the walls the shop assistants' overcoats hung from hooks. I opened the parcel and, by the faint light from the door, read the enclosed letter.

The letter informed me that the book I had ordered was unfortunately out of stock. They would look out for it, although the result of the search was uncertain; meanwhile, they were sending me, without obligation, a certain object, which, they were sure, would interest me. There followed a complicated description of a folding telescope with great refractive power and many other virtues. Interested, I took the instrument out of the wrapping. It was made of black oilcloth or canvas and was folded into the shape of a flattened accordion. I have always had a weakness for telescopes. I began to unfold the pleats of the instrument.

Stiffened with thin rods, it rose under my fingers until it almost filled the room; a kind of enormous bellows, a labyrinth of black chambers, a long complex of camera obscuras, one within another. It looked, too, like a long-bodied model automobile made of patent leather, a theatrical prop, its lightweight paper and stiff canvas imitating the bulkiness of reality. I looked into the black funnel of the instrument and saw deep inside the vague outline of the back of the Sanatorium. Intrigued, I put my head deeper into the rear chamber of the apparatus. I could now see in my field of vision the maid walking along the darkened corridor of the Sanatorium, carrying a tray. She turned round and smiled. "Can she see me?" I asked myself. An overwhelming drowsiness misted my eyes. I was sitting, as it were, in the rear chamber of the telescope as if in the back seat of a limousine. A light touch on a lever and the apparatus began to rustle like a paper butterfly; I felt that it was moving and turning toward the door.

Like a large black caterpillar, the telescope crept into the lighted shop — an enormous paper arthropod with two imitation headlights on the front. The customers clustered together, retreating before this blind paper dragon; the shop assistants flung open the door to the street, and I rode slowly in my paper car amid rows of onlookers, who followed with scandalized eyes my truly outrageous exit.

III

That is how one lives in this town, and how time goes by. The greater part of the day is spent in sleeping — and not only in bed. No one is very particular when it comes to sleep. At any place, at any time, one is ready for a quiet snooze: with one's head propped on a restaurant table, in a horse-drawn cab, even standing up when, out for a walk, one looks into the hall of an apartment house for a moment and succumbs to the irrepressible need for sleep.

Waking up, still dazed and shaky, one continues the interrupted conversation or the wearisome walk, carries on complicated discussions without beginning or end. In this way, whole chunks of time are casually lost somewhere; control over the continuity of the day is loosened until it finally ceases to matter; and the framework of uninterrupted chronology that one has been disciplined to notice every day is given up without regret. The compulsive readiness to account for the passage of time, the scrupulous penny-wise habit of reporting on the used-up hours — the pride and ambition of our economic system — are forsaken. Those cardinal virtues, which in the past one never dared to question, have long ago been abandoned.

A few examples will illustrate this state of affairs. At a certain time of day or night — a hardly perceptible difference in the color of the sky allows one to tell which it is — I wake up in twilight at the railings of the footbridge leading to the Sanatorium. Overpowered by sleep, I must have wandered unconsciously for a long time all over the town before, mortally tired, I dragged myself to the bridge. I cannot say whether Dr. Gotard accompanied me on that walk, but now he stands in front of me, finishing a long tirade and drawing conclusions. Carried away by his own eloquence, he slips his hand under my arm and leads me somewhere. I walk on, with him, and even before we have crossed the bridge, I am asleep again. Through my closed eyelids I can vaguely see the Doctor's expressive gestures, the smile under his black beard, and I try to understand, without success, his ultimate point — which he must have triumphantly revealed, for he now stands with arms outstretched. We have been walking side by side for I don't know how long, engrossed in a conversation at cross purposes, when all of a sudden I wake up com-

pletely. Dr. Gotard has gone; it is quite dark, but only because my eyes are shut. When I open them, I find that I am in our room and don't know how I got there.

An even more dramatic example: At lunchtime, I enter a restaurant in town, which is full and very noisy. Whom do I meet in the middle of it, at a table sagging under the weight of dishes? My father. All eyes are on him, while he, animated, almost ecstatic with pleasure, his diamond tiepin shining, turns in all directions, making fulsome conversation with everybody at once. With false bravado, which I observe with the greatest misgivings, he keeps ordering new dishes, which are then stacked on the table. He gathers them around him with glee, although he has not even finished the first course. Smacking his lips, chewing and speaking at the same time, he mimes his great satisfaction with this feast and follows with adoring eyes Adam, the waiter, to whom, with an ingratiating smile, he gives more orders. And when the waiter, waving his napkin, rushes to get them, Father turns to the company and calls them to witness the irresistible charm of Adam, the Ganymede.

"A boy in a million," Father exclaims with a happy smile, half closing his eyes, "a ministering angel! You must agree, gentlemen, that he is a charmer!"

I leave in disgust, unnoticed by Father. Had he been put there by the management of the restaurant in order to amuse the guests, he could not behave in a more ostentatious way. My head heavy with drowsiness, I stumble through the streets toward the Sanatorium. On a pillar box I rest my head and take a short siesta. At last, groping in darkness, I find the gate and go in. Our room is dark. I press the light switch, but there is no current. A cold draft comes from the window. The bed creaks in the darkness.

My father lifts his head from the pillows and says, "Ah, Joseph, Joseph! I have been lying here for two days without any attention. The bells are out of order, no one has been to see me, and my own son has left me, a very sick man, to run after girls in the town. Look how my heart is thumping!"

How do I reconcile all this? Has Father been sitting in the restaurant, driven there by an unhealthy greed, or has he been lying in bed feeling very ill? Are there two fathers? Nothing of the kind. The problem is the quick decomposition of time no longer watched with incessant vigilance.

We all know that time, this undisciplined element, holds itself within bounds but precariously, thanks to unceasing cultivation, meticulous care, and a continuous regulation and correction of its excesses. Free of this vigilance, it immediately begins to do tricks, run wild, play irresponsible practical jokes, and indulge in crazy clowning. The incongruity of our private times becomes evident. My father's time and my own no longer coincide.

Incidentally, the accusation that my father has made is completely groundless. I have not been chasing after girls. Swaying like a drunkard from one bout of sleep to another, I can hardly pay attention, even in my more wakeful moments, to the local ladies.

Moreover, the chronic darkness in the streets does not allow me to see faces clearly. What I have been able to observe — being a young man who still has a certain amount of interest in such things — is the peculiar

way in which these girls walk.

Heedless of obstacles, obeying only some inner rhythm, each one walks in an inexorably straight line, as if along a thread that she seems to unwind from an invisible skein. This linear trot is full of mincing accuracy and measured grace. Each girl seems to carry inside her an individual rule, wound tight like a spring.

Walking thus, straight ahead, with concentration and dignity, they seem to have only one worry — not to break the rule, not to make any mistake, not to stray either to the right or to the left. And then it becomes clear to me that what they so conscientiously carry within themselves is an *idée fixe* of their own excellence, which the strength of their conviction almost transforms into reality. It is risked anticipation, without any guarantee; an untouchable dogma, held high, impervious to doubt.

What imperfections and blemishes, what *retroussé* or flat noses, what freckles or spots are smuggled under the bold flag of that fiction! There is no ugliness or vulgarity that cannot be lifted up to a fictional heaven of perfection by the flight of such a belief.

Sanctified by it, bodies become distinctly more beautiful, and feet, already shapely and graceful in their spotless footwear, speak eloquently, their fluid, shiny pacing monologue explaining the greatness of an idea that the closed faces are too proud to express. The girls keep their hands in the pockets of their short, tight jackets. In the cafés and in the theater, they cross their legs, uncovered to the knee, and hold them in provocative silence.

So much for one of the peculiarities of this town. I have already mentioned the black vegetation of the region. A certain kind of black fern deserves special mention: enormous bunches of it in vases are in the windows of every apartment here, and every public place. The fern is

almost the symbol of mourning, the town's funereal crest.

IV

Conditions in the Sanatorium are becoming daily more insufferable. It has to be admitted that we have fallen into a trap. Since my arrival, when a semblance of hospitable care was displayed for the newcomer, the management of the Sanatorium has not taken the trouble to give us even the illusion of any kind of professional supervision. We are simply left to our own devices. Nobody caters to our needs. I have noticed, for instance, that the wires of the electric bells have been cut just behind the doors and lead nowhere. There is no service. The corridors are dark and silent by day and by night. I have a strong suspicion that we are the only guests in this Sanatorium and that the mysterious or discreet looks with which the chambermaid closes the doors of the rooms on entering or leaving are simply mystification.

I sometimes feel a strong desire to open each door wide and leave it ajar, so that the miserable intrigue in which we have got ourselves involved can be exposed.

And yet I am not quite convinced that my suspicions are justified. Sometimes, late at night, I meet Dr. Gotard in a corridor, hurrying somewhere in a white coverall, with an enema bottle in his hand, preceded by the chambermaid. It would be difficult to stop him then and demand an explanation.

Were it not for the restaurant and pastry shop in town, one might starve to death. So far, I have not succeeded in getting a second bed for our room. There is no question of the sheets being changed.

One has to admit that the general neglect of civilized habits has affected both of us, too. To get into bed dressed and with shoes on was once, for me — a civilized person — unthinkable. Yet now, when I return home late, sleep-drunk, the room is in semidarkness and the curtains at the window billow in a cold breeze. Half dazed, I tumble onto the bed and bury myself in the eiderdown. Thus I sleep for irregular stretches of time, for days or weeks, wandering through empty landscapes of sleep, always on the way, always on the steep roads of respiration, sometimes sliding lightly and gracefully from gentle slopes, then climbing laboriously up the cliffs of snoring. At their summit I embrace the horizons of the rocky and empty desert of sleep. At some point, somewhere on the sharp turn of a snore, I wake up half conscious and feel the body of my father at the foot of the bed. He lies there curled up, small as a kitten. I fall asleep again, with my mouth open, and the vast panorama of mountain landscape glides past me majestically.

In the shop, my father displays an energetic activity, transacting business and straining all his capacities to attract customers. His cheeks are flushed with animation, his eyes shine. In the Sanatorium he is very sick, as sick as during his last weeks at home. It is obvious that the end must be imminent. In a weak voice he addresses me: "You should look into the store more often, Joseph. The shop assistants are robbing us. You can see that I am no longer equal to the task. I have been lying here sick for weeks, and the shop is being neglected, left to run itself. Was there any mail from home?"

I begin to regret this whole undertaking. Perhaps we were misled by skillful advertising when we decided to send Father here. Time put back — it sounded good, but what does it come to in reality? Does anyone here get time at its full value, a true time, time cut off from a fresh bolt of cloth, smelling of newness and dye? Quite the contrary. It is used-up time, worn out by other people, a shabby time full of holes, like a sieve.

No wonder. It is time, as it were, regurgitated — if I may be forgiven this expression: secondhand time. God help us all!

And then there is the matter of the highly improper manipulation of time. The shameful tricks, the penetration of time's mechanism from behind, the hazardous fingering of its wicked secrets! Sometimes one feels like banging the table and exclaiming, "Enough of this! Keep off time, time is untouchable, one must not provoke it! Isn't it enough for you to have space? Space is for human beings, you can swing about in space, turn somersaults, fall down, jump from star to star. But for goodness' sake, don't tamper with time!"

On the other hand, can I be expected to give notice to Dr. Gotard? However miserable Father's existence, I am able to see him, to be with him, to talk to him. In fact, I should be infinitely grateful to Dr. Gotard.

Several times, I have wanted to speak openly to Dr. Gotard, but he is elusive. He has just gone to the restaurant, says the chambermaid. I turn to go there, when she runs after me to say that she was wrong, that Dr. Gotard is in the operating theater. Hurrying upstairs, I wonder what kind of operations can be performed here; I enter the anteroom and am told to wait. Dr. Gotard will be with me in a moment, he has just finished the operation, he is washing his hands. I can almost visualize him: short, taking long steps, his coat open, hurrying through a succession of hospital wards. After a while, what am I told? Dr. Gotard had not been there at all, no operation has been performed there for many years. Dr. Gotard is asleep in his room, his black beard sticking up into the air. The room fills with his snores as if with clouds that lift him in his bed, ever higher and higher — a great pathetic ascension on waves of snores and voluminous bedding.

Even stranger things happen here — things that I try to conceal from myself and that are quite fantastic in their absurdity. Whenever I leave our room, I have the impression that someone who has been standing behind the door moves quickly away and turns a corner. Or somebody seems to be walking in front of me, not looking back. It is not a nurse. I know who it is! "Mother!" I exclaim, in a voice trembling with excitement, and my mother turns her face to me and looks at me for a moment with a pleading smile. Where am I? What is happening here? What maze have I become entangled in?

V

I don't know why — it may be the time of year — but the days are growing more severe in color, darker and blacker. It seems as if one were looking at the world through black glasses.

The landscape is now like the bottom of an enormous aquarium full of watery ink. Trees, people, and houses merge, swaying like underwater plants against the background of the inky deep.

Packs of black dogs are often seen in the vicinity of the Sanatorium. Of all shapes and sizes, they run at dusk along the roads and paths, engrossed in their own affairs, silent, tense, and alert.

They run in twos and threes, with outstretched necks, their ears pricked up, whining softly in plaintive tones that escape from their throats as if against their will — signals of the highest nervousness. Absorbed in running, hurrying, always on their way somewhere, always pursuing some mysterious goal, they hardly notice the passersby. Occasionally one shoots out a glance while running past, and then the black and intelligent eyes are full of a rage contained only by haste. At times the dogs even rush at one's feet, succumbing to their anger, with heads held low and ominous snarls, but soon think better of it and turn away.

Nothing is to be done about this plague of dogs, but why does the management of the Sanatorium keep an enormous Alsatian on a chain — a terror of a beast, a werewolf of truly demoniacal ferocity? I shiver with fear whenever I pass his kennel, by which he stands immobile on his short chain, a halo of matted hair bristling around his head, bewhiskered and bearded, his powerful jaws displaying the whole apparatus of his long teeth. He does not bark, but his wild face contorts at the sight of a human being. He stiffens with an expression of boundless fury and, slowly raising his horrible muzzle, breaks into a low, fervent, convulsive howl that comes from the very depths of his hatred — a howl of despair and lament at his temporary impotence.

My father walks past the beast with indifference whenever we go out together. As for myself, I am deeply shaken when confronted by the dog's impotent hatred. I am now some two heads taller than Father who, small and thin, trots at my side with the mincing gait of a very old man.

Approaching the city square one day, we noticed an extraordinary commotion. Crowds of people filled the streets. We heard the incredible news that an enemy army had entered the town.

In consternation, people exchanged alarmist and contradictory news that was hard to credit. A war not preceded by diplomatic activity? A war amid blissful peace? A war against whom and for what reason? We were told that the enemy incursion gave heart to a group of discontented townspeople, who have come out in the open, armed, to terrorize the peaceful inhabitants. We noticed, in fact, a group of these activists, in black civilian clothing with white straps across their breasts, advancing in silence, their guns at the ready. The crowd fell back onto the pavements, as they marched by, flashing from under their hats ironical dark looks, in which there was a touch of superiority, a glimmer of malicious and perverse enjoyment, as if they could hardly stop themselves from bursting into laughter. Some of them were recognized by the crowd, but the exclamations of relief were at once stilled by the sight of rifle barrels. They passed by, not challenging anybody. All the streets filled at once with a frightened, grimly silent crowd. A dull hubbub floated over the city. We seemed to hear a distant rumble of artillery and the rattle of gun carriages.

"I must get to the shop," said my father, pale but determined. "You need not come with me," he added. "You will be in my way. Go back to the Sanatorium."

The pull of cowardice made me obey him. I saw my father trying to squeeze himself through the compact wall of bodies in the crowd and lost sight of him.

I broke into a run along side streets and alleys, and hurried toward the upper part of town. I realized that by going uphill I might be able to avoid the center, now packed solid by people.

Farther up, the crowd thinned and at last completely disappeared. I walked quietly along empty streets to the municipal park. Street lamps were lighted there and burned with a dark bluish flame, the color of asphodels, the flowers of mourning. Each light was surrounded by a swarm of dancing June bugs, heavy as bullets, carried on their slanting flight by vibrating wings. The fallen were struggling clumsily in the sand, their backs arched, hunched beneath the hard shields under which they were trying to fold the delicate membranes of their wings. On grassy plots and paths people were walking along, engrossed in carefree conversation.

The trees at the far end of the park drooped into the courtyards of houses that were built on lower ground on the other side of the park wall. I strolled along that wall on the park side, where it reached only to my breast; on the other side, it fell in escarpments to the level of courtyards. In one place, a ramp of firm soil rose from the courtyards to the top of the wall. There I crossed the wall without difficulty and squeezed between houses into a street. As I had expected, I found myself almost facing the Sanatorium; its back was outlined clearly in a black frame of trees. As usual, I opened the gate in the iron fence and saw from a distance the watchdog at his post. As usual, I shivered with aversion and wished to pass by him as quickly as possible, so as not to have to listen to his howl of hatred; but I suddenly noticed that he was unchained and was circling toward the courtyard, barking hollowly and trying to cut me off.

Rigid with fright, I retreated and, instinctively looking for shelter, crept into a small arbor, sure that all my efforts to evade the beast would be in vain. The shaggy animal was leaping toward me, his muzzle already pushing into the arbor. I was trapped. Horror-struck, I then saw that the dog was on a long chain that he had unwound to its full length, and that the inside of the arbor was beyond the reach of his claws. Sick

with fear, I was too weak to feel any relief. Reeling, almost fainting, I raised my eyes. I had never before seen the beast from so near, and only now did I see him clearly. How great is the power of prejudice! How powerful the hold of fear! How blind had I been! It was not a dog, it was a man. A chained man, whom, by a simplifying metaphoric wholesale error, I had taken for a dog. I don't want to be misunderstood. He was a dog, certainly, but a dog in human shape. The quality of a dog is an inner quality and can be manifested as well in human as in animal shape. He who was standing in front of me in the entrance to the arbor, his jaws wide open, his teeth bared in a terrible growl, was a man of middle height, with a black beard. His face was yellow, bony; his eyes were black, evil, and unhappy. Judging by his black suit and the shape of his beard, one might take him for an intellectual or a scholar. He might have been Dr. Gotard's unsuccessful elder brother. But that first impression was false. The large hands stained with glue, the two brutal and cynical furrows running down from his nostrils and disappearing into his beard, the vulgar horizontal wrinkles on the low forehead quickly dispelled that first impression. He looked more like a bookbinder, a tub-thumper, a vocal party member — a violent man, given to dark, sudden passions. And it was this — the passionate depth, the convulsive bristling of all his fibers, the mad fury of his barking when the end of a stick was pointed at him — that made him a hundred per cent dog.

If I tried to escape through the back of the arbor, I thought, I would completely elude his reach and could walk along a side path to the gate of the Sanatorium. I was about to put my leg over the railing when I suddenly stopped. I felt it would be too cruel simply to go away and leave the dog behind, possessed by his helpless and boundless fury. I could imagine his terrible disappointment, his inexpressible pain as I escaped from his trap, free once and for all from his clutches. I decided to stay.

I stepped forward and said quietly, "Please calm down. I shall unchain you."

His face, distorted by spasms of growling, became whole again, smooth and almost human. I went up to him without fear and unfastened the buckle of his collar. We walked side by side. The bookbinder was wearing a decent black suit but had bare feet. I tried to talk to him, but a

137

confused babble was all I heard in reply. Only his eyes, black and eloquent, expressed a wild spurt of gratitude, of submission, which filled me with awe. Whenever he stumbled on a stone or a clod of earth, the shock made his face shrivel and contract with fear, and that expression was followed by one of rage. I would then bring him to order with a harsh comradely rebuke. I even patted him on the back. An astonished, suspicious, unbelieving smile tried to form on his face. Ah, how hard to bear was this terrible friendship! How frightening was this uncanny sympathy! How could I get rid of this man striding along with me, his eyes expressing his total submission, following the slightest changes in my face? I could not show impatience.

I pulled out my wallet and said in a matter-of-fact tone, "You

probably need some money. I will lend you some with pleasure." But at the sight of my wallet his look became so unexpectedly wild that I put it away again as quickly as I could. For quite some time afterward, he could not calm himself and his features continued to be distorted by more spasms of growling. No, I could not stand this any longer. Anything, but not this. Matters were already confused and entangled enough.

I then noticed the glare of fire over the town: my father was somewhere in the thick of a revolution or in a burning shop. Dr. Gotard was unavailable. And to cap it all, my mother had appeared, incognito, on that mysterious errand! These were the elements of some great and obscure intrigue, which was hemming me in. I must escape, I thought, escape at any cost. Anywhere. I must drop this horrible friendship with a bookbinder who smells of dog and who is watching me all the time. We were now standing in front of the Sanatorium.

"Come to my room, please," I said with a polite gesture. Civilized gestures fascinated him, soothed his wildness. I let him enter my room first and gave him a chair.

"I'll go to the restaurant and get some brandy," I said.

He got up, terrified, and wanted to follow me.

I calmed his fears with gentle firmness. "You will sit here and wait for me," I said in a deep, sonorous voice, which concealed fear. He sat down again with a tentative smile.

I went out and walked slowly along the corridor, then downstairs and across the hall leading to the entrance door; I passed the gate, strode across the courtyard, banged the iron gate shut, and only then began to run, breathlessly, my heart thumping, my temples throbbing, along the dark avenue leading to the railway station.

Images raced through my head, each more horrible than the next. The impatience of the monster dog; his fear and despair when he realized that I had cheated him; another attack of fury, another bout of rage breaking out with unchecked force. My father's return to the Sanatorium, his unsuspecting knock at the door, and his confrontation with the terrible beast.

Luckily, in fact, Father was no longer alive; he could not really be reached, I thought with relief, and saw in front of me the black row of railway carriages ready to depart.

I got into one of them, and the train, as if it had been waiting for me, slowly started to move, without a whistle.

Through the window the great valley, filled with dark rustling forests — against which the walls of the Sanatorium seemed white — moved and turned slowly once again. Farewell, Father. Farewell, town that I shall never see again.

Since then, I have travelled continuously. I have made my home in that train, and everybody puts up with me as I wander from coach to coach. The compartments, enormous as rooms, are full of rubbish and straw, and cold drafts pierce them on gray, colorless days.

My suit became torn and ragged. I have been given the shabby uniform of a railwayman. My face is bandaged with a dirty rag, because one of my cheeks is swollen. I sit on the straw, dozing, and when hungry, I stand in the corridor outside a second-class compartment and sing. People throw small coins into my hat: a black railwayman's hat, its visor half torn away.

DODO

He usually visited us on Saturday afternoons wearing a dark suit, a white piqué waistcoat, and a bowler hat that he had to have specially made to fit his head. He would stay for a quarter of an hour or so and sip a drink of raspberry syrup with soda, his chin propped on the bone handle of a walking stick planted between his knees, or else he would quietly contemplate the blue smoke of his cigarette.

Other relatives usually called on us at the same time, and then, as the conversation became general, Dodo withdrew and assumed the passive role of an extra. He would not say a word during these animated meetings, but his expressive eyes under his magnificent eyebrows would rest in turn on each person, while his jaw dropped and his face became elongated, unable to control its muscles in the act of passionate listening.

Dodo spoke only when spoken to — and then he answered in monosyllables, grudgingly, looking away — and only if the questions were easy ones dealing with simple matters. Sometimes he succeeded in keeping the conversation going beyond these elementary questions by resorting to a stock of expressive gestures and grimaces that were most useful because they could be interpreted in many different ways, filling the gaps in articulate talk and creating an impression of sensible response. This, however, was an illusion that was quickly dispelled; the conversation would break down completely; and while the interlocutor's gaze wandered slowly and pensively away from Dodo, he, left to himself, reverted once more to his proper role as an outsider, a passive observer of other people's social intercourse.

How could one talk to him when, to the question whether he had been in the country with his mother, he would answer softly: "I don't know." And this was the sad and embarrassing truth, for Dodo's mind did not register anything but the present.

During his childhood, a long time before, Dodo had suffered a serious brain disease during which he had been unconscious for many months, more dead than alive. When his condition had finally improved, it became obvious that he had been withdrawn from circulation and that he no longer belonged to the community of sensible people. His education had to be private, for the sake of form, and taken in tiny doses. The demands of convention, harsh and unyielding where other people were concerned, lost their sternness and gave way to tolerance with regard to Dodo.

A zone of special privilege was created around Dodo for his own protection, a no-man's-land unaffected by the pressures of life. Everyone outside it was subjected to the buffeting of events, waded in them noisily, let himself be carried away, absorbed, and engrossed; within the zone there was calm and stillness, a caesura in the general tumult.

Thus Dodo lived and grew, and his exceptional destiny grew together with him, taken for granted, without protest from anyone.

Dodo was never given a new suit; he always wore the cast-off clothes of his elder brother. While the life of his peers was divided into phases and periods, marked by notable events, sublime and symbolic moments — birthdays, exams, engagements, promotions — his life passed in a level monotony, undisturbed by anything pleasant or painful, and his future, too, appeared as a completely straight, smooth path without surprises.

It would be wrong to think that Dodo protested inwardly against such a state of affairs. He accepted it with simplicity and without astonishment as a life that was suited to him. He managed his existence and arranged details of it within the confines of that eventless monotony with sober and dignified optimism.

Every morning he went for a walk along three streets and, having come to the end of the third, he returned the same way. Clad in an elegantly cut but rather shabby suit passed on by his brother, he proceeded with unhurried dignity, holding his walking stick behind his back. He might have been a gentleman walking about the city for pleasure. This lack of haste, of any direction or purpose, sometimes became quite embarrassing, for Dodo was inclined to stand gaping in front of shops, outside workshops where people were hard at work, and even joined groups of people engaged in conversation.

His face matured early, and, strange to say, while experience and the trials of living spared the empty inviolability, the strange marginality of his life, his features reflected experiences that had passed him by, elements in a biography never to be fulfilled; these experiences, although completely illusory, modeled and sculpted his face into the mask of a great tragedian, which expressed the wisdom and sadness of existence. His eyebrows were arched magnificently, shadowing his large, sad, darkly circled eyes. On both sides of his nose two furrows, marks of spurious suffering and wisdom, ran toward the corners of his lips. The small full mouth was shut tight in pain, and a coquettishly pointed beard on a protruding Bourbon chin gave him the appearance of an elderly *bon viveur*.

It was inevitable that Dodo's privileged strangeness should be detected by the lurking and always hungry malice of the human race.

Thus, with increased frequency, Dodo would get company on his morning walks: one of the penalties of not being an ordinary person was that these companions were of a special kind, and not colleagues sharing communal interests. They were individuals of much younger years who clung to the dignified and serious Dodo; the conversations they conducted were in a gay and bantering tone that might have been agreeable to Dodo.

As he walked, towering by a head over that merry and carefree gang, he looked like a peripatetic philosopher surrounded by his disciples, and his face, under its mask of seriousness and sadness, broke into frivolous smiles that fought against its usually tragic expression.

Dodo now began to return late from his morning walks, to come home with tousled hair, his clothes in some disarray, but animated and inclined to tease Caroline, a poor cousin given a home by Aunt Retitia.

Fully aware of the fact that the company he was keeping was perhaps of no great consequence, Dodo maintained at home a complete silence on the subject.

Very occasionally, events occurred in his monotonous life that stood out by their importance. Once, having left in the morning, Dodo did not return to lunch. Nor did he return to supper, nor to lunch the following day. Aunt Retitia was in despair. But in the evening of the second day he returned somewhat the worse for wear, his bowler hat crushed and awry, but otherwise in good health and full of spiritual calm.

It was difficult to reconstruct the history of that escapade, as Dodo kept completely silent about it. Most probably, having extended the course of his daily walk, he had wandered off to an unfamiliar area of the city, perhaps helped in it by the young peripatetics, who were not averse to exposing Dodo to new and unfamiliar conditions of life.

Maybe it was one of the occasions when Dodo's poor, overburdened memory had a day off, and he forgot his address and even his name, details he somehow usually managed to remember, but we never did learn the details of his adventure.

When Dodo's elder brother went abroad, the family shrunk to four members. Apart from Uncle Jerome and Aunt Retitia, there was only Caroline, who played the part of lady housekeeper in that patrician establishment.

Uncle Jerome had been confined to his room for many years. From the moment when Providence gently eased from his hand the steering of the battered ship of his life, he had led the existence of a pensioner in the narrow space allotted to him between the hallway and the dark alcove of his apartment.

In a long housecoat reaching down to his ankles, he used to sit in the darkest corner of the alcove, his facial hair growing daily longer. A beard the color of pepper, with long strands of hair almost completely white at the ends, surrounded his face and spread halfway up his cheeks, leaving free only a hawk's nose and eyes, rolling their whites under the shadow of shaggy eyebrows.

In this windowless room — a narrow prison in which, like a large cat, he was condemned to walk up and down in front of the glass door leading to the drawing room — stood two enormous oak beds, Uncle's and Aunt's nightly abode. The whole back wall of the room was covered with a large tapestry, the indistinct woven figures of which loomed through the darkness. When one's eyes became accustomed to the dark, one could see on it, among bamboos and palms, an enormous lion, powerful and forbidding as a prophet, majestic as a patriarch.

Sitting back to back, the lion and Uncle Jerome felt each other's presence and loathed it. Without looking, they growled at each other, bared their evil teeth, and muttered threats. Sometimes the lion in an excess of irritation would rise on his forelegs, his mane bristling, and fill the overcast tapestry sky with his roaring. Sometimes Uncle Jerome would tower over the lion and deliver a prophetic tirade, frowning under the weight of the great words, his beard waving in inspiration. Then the lion would narrow his eyes in pain and, slowly turning his head, cringe under the lash of divine words.

The lion and Jerome transformed the dark alcove in my uncle's apartment into a perpetual battlefield.

Uncle Jerome and Dodo lived in the small apartment independently from each other, in two different dimensions that never coincided. Their eyes, whenever they met, wandered on without focusing, like the eyes of animals of two unrelated and distant species that are incapable of retaining the picture of anything unfamiliar.

They never spoke to each other.

At table, Aunt Retitia, sitting between her husband and her son, formed a buffer between two worlds, an isthmus between two oceans of madness.

Uncle Jerome ate jerkily, his long beard dipping into his plate. When the kitchen door creaked, he half rose from his chair and grabbed his plate of soup, ready to flee with it to the alcove should a stranger enter the room. Aunt Retitia would reassure him, saying:

"Don't be afraid, no one is there; it is only the maid."

Then Dodo would cast an angry and indignant look at his frightened father and mumble to himself with great displeasure: "He's off his head."

Before Uncle Jerome accepted absolution from the complex and difficult affairs of life and got permission to retreat into his refuge in the alcove, he was a man of quite a different stamp. Those who knew him in his youth said that his reckless temperament knew no restraints, considerations, or scruples. With great satisfaction he spoke to mortally sick people about the death that awaited them. Visits of condolence provided him with an opportunity for sharply criticizing the life of the deceased, still being mourned by his family. About the unpleasant or intimate incidents in people's private lives that they wanted to conceal, he spoke to them loudly and with sarcasm. Then one night he returned from a business trip completely transformed and, shaking with fear, tried to hide under his bed. A few days later news was spread in the family that Uncle Jerome had given up all the complicated, dubious, and risky business affairs that had threatened to submerge him, had abdicated, and had begun a new life, regulated by strict, although to us somewhat obscure, principles.

On Sunday afternoons when we were usually invited by Aunt Retitia to a small family tea party, Uncle Jerome did not recognize us. Sitting in the alcove, he looked through the glass door at the company with wild and frightened eyes. Sometimes, however, he unexpectedly left his hermitage, still in his long housecoat, his beard waving round his face, and, spreading his hands as if he wanted to separate us, he would say:

"And now, I beg you, all you that are here, disperse, run along, but quietly, stealthily, on tiptoe . . ."

Then, waving his finger mysteriously at us, he would add in a low voice:

"Everybody is talking about it: Dee-da . . ."

My aunt would push him gently back to the alcove, but he would turn at the door and grimly, with raised finger, repeat: "Dee-da."

Dodo's understanding was a little slow, and he needed a few moments of silence and concentration before a situation became clear to

him. When it did, his eyes wandered from one person to another, as if to make sure that something very funny had really happened. He then burst into noisy laughter, and, with great satisfaction, shaking his head in derision, he repeated amid the bursts of laughter: "He's off his head!"

Night fell on Aunt Retitia's house. The servant girl went to bed in the kitchen; bubbles of night air floated from the garden and burst against the window. Aunt Retitia slept in the depths of her large bed; on the other, Uncle Jerome sat upright among the bedclothes, like a tawny owl, his eyes shining in the darkness, his beard flowing over his knees, which were drawn up to his chin.

He slowly climbed down from his bed and walked on tiptoe to my aunt's bed. He stood over the sleeping woman, like a cat ready to leap, eyebrows and beard abristle. The lion on the wall tapestry gave a short yawn and turned his head away. My aunt, awakened, was alarmed by that head with its shining eyes and spitting mouth.

"Go back to bed at once," she said, shooing him away as one would shoo a hen.

Jerome retreated spitting and looking back with nervous movements of his head.

In the next room Dodo lay on his bed. Dodo never slept. The center of sleep in his diseased brain did not function correctly, so he wriggled and tossed and turned from side to side all night long.

The mattress groaned. Dodo sighed heavily, wheezed, sat up, lay down again.

His unlived life worried him, tortured him, turning round and round inside him like an animal in a cage. In Dodo's body, the body of a half-wit, somebody was growing old, although he had not lived; somebody was maturing to a death that had no meaning at all.

Then suddenly, he sobbed loudly in the darkness.

Aunt Retitia leapt from her bed.

"What is it, Dodo, are you in pain?"

Dodo turned to her amazed.

"Who?" he asked.

"Why are you sobbing?" asked my aunt.

"It is not I, it's he . . ."

"Which he?"

"The one inside . . ."

"Who is he?"

Dodo waved his hand resignedly.

"Eh . . ." he said and turned on his other side.

Aunt Retitia returned to bed on tiptoe. As she passed Uncle Jerome's bed, he waved a threatening finger at her.

"Everybody is talking about it: Dee-da . . ."

EDDIE

I

On the same floor as our family, in a long and narrow wing of the house overlooking the courtyard, Eddie lives with his.

Eddie has long ago stopped being a small boy. Eddie is a grown-up man with a full, manly voice who sometimes sings arias from operas.

Eddie is inclined to obesity, not to its spongelike and flabby form, but rather to the athletic and muscular variety. His shoulders are strong and powerful like a bear's, but what of it? He has no use of his legs, which are completely degenerate and shapeless. Looking at his legs, it is difficult to determine the reason for his strange infirmity. It looks as if his legs had too many joints between the knee and the ankle; at least two more joints than normal legs. No wonder that they bend pitifully at those supernumerary joints, not only to the side but also forward and indeed in all possible directions.

Thus, Eddie can move only with the help of two crutches, which are remarkably well made and polished to resemble mahogany. On these he walks downstairs every day to buy a newspaper: this is his only walk and his only diversion. It is painful to look at his progress down the stairs. His legs sway irregularly to one side, then back, bending in unexpected places; and his feet, like horses' hooves, small but thick, knock like sticks on the wooden planks. But having reached street level, Eddie unexpectedly changes. He straightens himself up, pushes out his chest grandly, and makes his body swing. Taking his weight on his crutches as if on parallel bars, he throws his legs far to the front. When they hit the ground with an uneven thud, Eddie moves the crutches forward and with a new impetus swings his body again. With these forward swings, he conquers space. Often, maneuvering his crutches in the courtyard, he can, with the excess of strength gathered during long hours of rest, demonstrate with truly magnificent gusto this heroic method of locomotion, to the amazement of servant girls from the first and the second floors. The back of his neck swells, two folds of flesh form under his chin, and on his face held aslant appears a grimace of pain when he clenches his teeth in effort. Eddie does no work, as if fate, having saddled him with the burden of infirmity, had in exchange freed him from that curse of Adam's breed. In the shadow of his disability Eddie exploits to the full his exceptional right to idleness and deep at heart is not displeased at that private transaction, individually negotiated with fate.

Nonetheless, we have often wondered how such a young man in his twenties can fill his time. The reading of the newspaper provides a lot of work, for Eddie is a careful reader. No advertisement or announcement in small print escapes his notice. And when he finally gets to the last page of the journal, he is not condemned to boredom for the rest of the day — not at all. Only then does Eddie get down to the hobby to which he looks forward with pleasure. In the afternoon, when other people take a short siesta, Eddie gets out his large, fat scrapbooks, spreads them on the table under the window, prepares glue, sets out a brush and a pair of scissors, and begins the pleasant and rewarding job of cutting out the most interesting articles and pasting them in, according to a certain rigid system. The crutches are at his side, prepared for any eventuality, standing propped against the windowsill, but Eddie does not need them, for everything is within his reach. Thus busily occupied, he fills the few hours until teatime.

Every third day Eddie shaves himself. He likes this activity and all the paraphernalia associated with it: hot water, shaving soap, and the smooth, gentle cutthroat razor. While mixing soap with water and stropping the razor on a leather strap, Eddie sings. His voice is not trained, nor is it very tuneful, so he sings loudly without any pretensions, and Adela maintains that his voice is pleasant.

However, Eddie's home life is not entirely harmonious. Unfortunately there seems to be a very serious conflict between him and his parents, the reason and background to which we do not know. We shan't repeat the gossip or hearsay; we shall limit ourselves to facts empirically confirmed.

It is usually toward the evening during the warm season, when Eddie's window is open, that we hear the echoes of these altercations. We hear, to be precise, only one half of the dialogue, Eddie's part, because the replies of his antagonists, hidden in the farther parts of the flat, cannot reach our ears.

It is difficult, therefore, to guess what Eddie is accused of, but from the tone of his retorts one can only deduce that he is cut to the quick, almost at his wits' ends. His words are violent and injudicious, obviously dictated by great agitation, but his tone, although indignant, is rather whining and miserable.

"Yes, indeed," he calls in a plaintive voice, " and so what? . . . What time yesterday? . . . It is not true! . . . And what if it were? . . . Then Dad is lying!"

And so it continues for whole stretches of time, diversified only by outbursts of Eddie's anger and by his attempts to tear out his reddish hair in helpless fury.

But sometimes — and this is the climax of these scenes that gives them a specific appeal — there follows what we have been waiting for with bated breath. In the depth of the flat there is a loud crash, a door is opened with a bang, pieces of furniture are thrown to the floor, and lastly Eddie emits a heartrending scream.

We listen to it shaken and embarrassed, but also morbidly excited at the thought of the savage and fantastic violence being wrought on an athletic full-blooded youth, however crippled in his legs.

II

At dusk, when the washing up after an early supper is finished, Adela usually sits on one of the balconies overlooking the courtyard, not far from Eddie's window. Two long balconies in the form of a squared horseshoe overlook the courtyard, one on the first floor and one on the second floor. In the cracks of their wooden planks bits of grass are growing, and from one crack even a small acacia tree waves high above the courtyard.

Apart from Adela, one or two neighbors sit on these balconies in front of their doors sprawled on chairs or squatting on stools, wilting faintly in the dusk; they rest after the toil of their day, mute as tied-up sacks, waiting for the night to untie them gently.

Down below, the courtyard quickly fills with darkness, but the air above it does not yet relinquish its light and seems to become steadily lighter as everything below gradually turns pitch dark: it shimmers and trembles from the sudden, furtive flights of bats.

Down below, the quick and silent work of night now begins in earnest. Greedy ants swarm everywhere, decomposing into atoms the substance of things, eating them down to their white bones, to their ribs and skeletons, which phosphoresce in the nightmare of this sad battlefield. White papers, in tatters on the rubbish heap, survive longest, like undigested rays of brightness in the worm-ridden darkness, and cannot completely dissolve. At times they seem engulfed by darkness, then they emerge again, but in the end it is impossible to say whether one sees anything or whether these are illusions that begin their nightly ravings; in the end people sit in their own aura under stars projected by their own pulsating brains, by the phantoms of hallucinations.

And then thin veins of breezes rise from the bottom of the courtyard, hesitant and uncertain, streaks of freshness, which line like silk the folds of summer nights. And while the first shimmering stars appear in the sky, the summer night emerges with a sigh — deep, full of starry dust and the distant croaking of frogs.

Without putting on the light, Adela goes to bed and sinks into the tired bedding of the previous night; hardly has she closed her eyes when the race on all floors and in all apartments of the house begins.

Only for the uninitiated is the summer night a time of rest and forgetfulness. Once the activities of the day have finished and the tired brains long for sleep, the confused to-ing and fro-ing, the enormous tangled hubbub of a July night begins. All the apartments of the house, all rooms and alcoves, are full of noise, of wanderings, enterings and leavings. In all windows lamps with milky shades can be seen, even passages are brightly lighted and doors never stop being opened and shut. A great, disorderly, half-ironical conversation is conducted with constant misunderstandings in all the chambers of the human hive. On the second floor people misunderstand what those from the first floor have said and send emissaries with urgent instructions. Couriers run through all the apartments, upstairs and downstairs, forget their instructions on their way and are repeatedly called back. And there is always something to add, nothing is ever fully explained, and all that bustle among the laughter and the jokes leads to nothing.

The back rooms, which do not participate in this great muddle of the night, have their separate time, measured by the ticking of clocks, by monologues of silence, by the deep breathing of the sleepers. Enormous wet-nurses swollen with milk sleep there, clinging greedily to the lap of night, their cheeks burning in ecstasy. Small babies wander with closed eyelids on the surface of their nurses' sleep, crawl delicately like ferreting animals over the blue map of veins on the white plains of their breasts, searching with blind faces the warm opening, the entry into the depths of sleep, and find at last with their tender lips the source of sleep: the trusted nipple filled with sweet forgetfulness.

And those in their beds who have already caught sleep will not let go of it; they fight with it as with an angel that is trying to escape until they conquer it and press it to the pillow. Then they snore intermittently as if quarreling and reminding themselves of the angry history of their hatreds. And when the grumbles and recriminations have ceased and the struggle with sleep is over and every room in turn has sunk into stillness and nonexistence, Leon the shop assistant climbs blindly and slowly up the stairs, his boots in his hand, and in darkness tries to find the keyhole of the door. He returns thus nightly from the brothel, with bloodshot eyes, shaken by hiccups and with a thread of saliva trailing down his half-opened lips.

In Mr. Jacob's room a lamp is alight on the table, over which he sits hunched, writing a long letter to Christian Seipel & Sons, Spinners and

Mechanical Weavers. On the floor lies a whole stack of papers covered with his writing, but the end of the letter is not yet in sight. Every now and then he rises from the table and runs round the room, his hands in his windswept hair, and as he circles thus, he occasionally climbs a wall, flies along the wallpaper like a large gnat blindly hitting the arabesques of design, and descends again to the floor to continue his inspired circling.

Adela is fast asleep, her mouth half open, her face relaxed and absent; but her closed lids are transparent, and on their thin parchment the night is writing its pact with the devil, half text, half picture, full of erasures, corrections, and scribbles.

Eddie stands undressed in his room and exercises with dumbbells. He needs a lot of strength in his shoulders, twice as much as a normal man, for shoulders replace his useless legs, and, therefore, he exercises every night, zealously and in secret.

Adela is flowing backward into oblivion and cannot shout or call, nor can she stop Eddie from trying to climb out of his window.

Eddie crawls out onto the balcony without his crutches, and one wonders if his stumps would carry him. But Eddie is not attempting to walk. Like a large white dog, he approaches in four-legged squat jumps, in great shuffling leaps on the resounding planks of the balcony, until he has reached Adela's window. Every night, grimacing with pain, he presses his white, fat face to the windowpane shining in the moonlight, and plaintively and eagerly he tells her, crying, that his crutches have been locked in a cupboard for the night and that now he must run about like a dog, on all fours.

But Adela is completely limp, completely surrendered to the deep rhythm of sleep. She has no strength even to pull up the blanket over her bare thighs and cannot prevent the columns of bedbugs from wandering over her body. These light and thin, leaflike insects run over her so delicately that she does not feel their touch. They are flat receptacles for blood, reddish blood bags without eyes or faces, now on the march in whole clans on a migration of the species subdivided into generations and tribes. They run up from her feet in scores, a never-ending procession; they are larger now, as large as moths, flat red vampires without heads, lightweight as if cut out of paper, on legs more delicate than the web of spiders.

And when the last laggard bedbugs have come and gone, with an enormous one bringing up the rear, complete silence comes at last. Deep sleep fills the empty passages and apartments, while the rooms slowly begin to absorb the grayness of the hours before dawn.

In all the beds people lie with their knees drawn up, with faces violently thrown to one side, in deep concentration, immersed in sleep and given to it wholly.

And the process of sleeping is, in fact, one great story, divided into chapters and sections, into parts distributed among sleepers. When one of them stops and grows silent, another takes up his cue so that the story can proceed in broad, epic zigzags while they all lie in the separate rooms of that house, motionless and inert like poppy seed within the partitions of a large, dried-up poppy.

THE OLD AGE PENSIONER

I am an old-age pensioner in the true and full meaning of the word, very far advanced in that estate, an old pensioner of high proof.

It may be that I have even exceeded the definite and allotted limits of my new status. I don't wish to hide it. There is nothing extraordinary about it. Why cast wondering looks and stare at me with hypocritical respect and solemn seriousness that conceal a lot of secret pleasure at one's neighbor's misfortune? How little elementary tact most people have! Facts of this kind should be accepted with a certain nonchalance. One must take these things as they come, just as I have accepted them lightly and without care. Perhaps this is why I am a little shaky on my feet and must put one before the other slowly and cautiously and watch where I go. It is so easy to stray under such circumstances. The reader will understand that I cannot be too explicit. My form of existence depends to a large degree on conjecture and requires a fair amount of goodwill. I will now have to appeal to this goodwill frequently by discreet winks, which don't come easily to me because of the stiffening of my facial muscles unused to mimic expressions. On the whole I don't force myself on anyone. I don't want to dissolve in gratitude for the sanctuary kindly provided for me by anyone's quick understanding. I acknowledge kindness without emotion, coolly and with complete indifference. I don't like to receive, along with the bonus of understanding, a heavy account for gratitude. The best thing is to treat me offhandedly, with a dose of healthy ruthlessness, with camaraderie and a sense of humor. In this respect, my good simpleminded colleagues from the office, all younger than myself, have found the proper tone.

I sometimes call at the office by force of habit, around the first of each month, and stand quietly at the counter waiting to be noticed. The following scene then takes place: At a given time, the head of the office, Mr. Filer, puts away his pen, winks at his subordinates, and says suddenly, looking past me into space, his hand cupping his ear:

"If my hearing doesn't deceive me, it must be you, Councilor, somewhere among us!"

His eyes, looking over my head into emptiness, begin to squint as he says this, and a humorous smile lights his face.

"I heard a voice somewhere and I at once thought it must be you, dear Councilor!" he exclaims loudly, articulating distinctly as if he were speaking to a deaf person. "Please do make a sign, disturb the air at least in the place where you are floating!"

"Don't pull my leg, Mr. Filer," I say softly, "I have come to collect my pension."

"Your pension?" Mr. Filer exclaims, again squinting into the air. "Did you say your pension? You can't be serious, dear Councilor. Your name has been removed from the list of pensioners. Do you still expect to receive a pension, dear Councilor?"

Thus they joke with me, in a warm, sympathetic, and humane way. That roughness, that direct jocularity, gives me a certain comfort. I leave the place more cheerful and hurry home quickly, in order to take with me indoors some of the pleasant warmth before it all evaporates.

But as to other people . . . An insistent questioning, never voiced aloud, which I can read in their eyes. It is difficult to avoid it. Supposing things are as they suspect — why immediately make these long faces, put on these solemn expressions, fall into uninvited silences, be both embarrassed and overcautious? Anything in order not to mention my condition . . . How well can I see through that game! It is no more than a kind of sybaritic self-indulgence and delight at their being different, a complete detachment from my condition, masked with hypocrisy. They exchange telltale looks but don't speak, and allow the thing to grow bigger in silence. Perhaps my condition is not quite as it should be. Perhaps it is even due to a small basic disability? Goodness gracious, so what? Is this a reason for that quick and frightened eagerness to please? Sometimes I want to burst out laughing when I see the recognition they show me, a kind of deference. Why do they insist so, why stress it, and why does doing it give them the profound satisfaction, which they try to conceal behind a mask of scared devotion?

Let's assume that I am a passenger of light weight, even of excessively light weight; let's assume that I am embarrassed by certain questions such as how old I am, when is my birthday, and so on — is that a reason for incessantly touching upon these subjects as if they were very relevant? Not that I am in the least ashamed of my condition. Not at all. But I cannot bear the exaggeration with which they magnify the importance of a certain fact, a certain difference, no bigger really than a hair's breadth. I am amused by the false theatricality and the solemn pathos that surrounds this matter, by the tragic costumes and gloomy pomp that drape this fact. While in reality? . . . Nothing pathetic at all, nothing more natural and commonplace. Lightness, independence, irresponsibility . . . And an increased ear for music, a most extraordinary musicality of one's limbs, as it were. It is impossible to pass by a barrel organ and not dance to it. Not because you feel happy, but because you don't care, and the tune has its own will, its own stubborn rhythm. So you give in. "Maggie, Maggie, treasure of my soul . . ." You are too light, too agile to protest; and besides, why protest against such an unpretentious and enticing proposal? Therefore I dance, or rather trot, in time with the tune, with the tiny steps of an old-age pensioner, and from time to time I give a little skip. Few people notice it, they are too busy rushing about their daily affairs.

I am anxious to avoid one thing: that the reader should have exaggerated ideas about my situation. I must warn him against it both in the positive and negative sense. No sentimentality please. It is a condition like any other, and therefore capable of being understood and treated naturally. Any strangeness disappears once you have crossed to the other side. You sober up — this is what is characteristic of my situation: you are unburdened, feel light, empty, irresponsible, without respect for class, for personal ties, for conventions. Nothing holds me and nothing fetters me. I am boundlessly free. The strange indifference with which I move lightly through all the dimensions of being should be pleasurable in itself. But . . . that lack of anchorage, the would-be careless animation and lightheartedness — but I must not complain. . . . There is a saying: gather no moss. That is exactly it: I stopped gathering moss a long time ago.

From the window of my room, which is high up, I have a bird's-eye view of the city, its walls, its roofs and chimneys in the gray light of a fall dawn — the whole, densely built-up panorama just unwrapped from the night, palely lighted at the yellow horizon, cut into light strips by the black scissors of cawing crows. I feel: this is life. Everyone is stuck within himself, within the day to which he wakes up, the hour which belongs to him, or the moment. Somewhere in the semidarkness of a kitchen coffee is brewing, the cook is not there, the dirty glare of a flame dances on the floor. Time deceived by silence flows backward for a while, retreats, and in these uncounted moments night returns and swells the undulating fur of a cat. Kathy from the first floor yawns and stretches languorously for long minutes before she opens the windows and starts sweeping and dusting. The night air, saturated with sleep and snoring, lazily wafts toward the window, gets out, and slowly enters the dun and smoky grayness of the day. Kathy dips her hands reluctantly into the dough of bedding, warm and sour from sleep. At last, with a shiver, with eyes full of night, she shakes from the window a large, heavy feather bed, and scatters over the city particles of feathers, stars of down, the lazy seed of night dreams.

At such a time I would dream of being a baker who delivers bread, a fitter from the electric company, or an insurance man collecting the weekly installments. Or at least a chimney sweep. In the morning, at dawn, I would enter some half-opened gateway, still lighted by the watchman's lantern. I would put two fingers to my hat, crack a joke, and

160

enter the labyrinth to leave late in the evening, at the other end of the city. I would spend all day going from apartment to apartment, conducting one never-ending conversation from one end of the city to the other, divided into parts among the householders; I would ask something in one apartment and receive a reply in another, make a joke in one place and collect the fruits of laughter in the third or fourth. Among the banging of doors I would squeeze through narrow passages, through bedrooms full of furniture, I would upset chamberpots, walk into squeaking perambulators in which babies cry, pick up rattles dropped by infants. I would stop for longer than necessary in kitchens and hallways, where servant girls were tidying up. The girls, busy, would stretch their young legs, tauten their high insteps, play with their cheap shining shoes, or clack around in loose slippers.

Such are my dreams during the irresponsible, extramarginal hours. I don't deny them, although I see their lack of sense. Everybody should be aware of his condition and know how to accept it.

For us, old-age pensioners, fall is on the whole a dangerous season. He who knows how difficult it is for us to achieve any stability at all, how difficult it is to avoid distraction or destruction by one's own hand, will understand that fall, its winds, disturbances, and atmospheric confusions do not favor our existence, which is precarious anyway.

There are, however, some days during fall that are calm, contemplative, and kind to us. Days sometimes occur without sun, but warm, misty, and amber-colored on their edges. In the gap between the houses, a view suddenly opens on a stretch of sky moving low, ever lower, toward the last windswept yellowness of the distant horizon. The perspectives opening into the depth of day seem like the archives of the calendar, the cross-section of days, the endless files of time, floating in tiers into a bright eternity. The tiers order themselves in the fawn sky, while the present moment remains in the foreground and only a few people ever lift their eyes to the distant shelves of this illusory calendar. Eyes on the ground, everybody rushes somewhere, impatiently avoiding others; the street is cut by the invisible paths of these comings and goings, meetings and avoidings. But in the gap between the houses, where one can see the lower part of the city and its whole architectural panorama, lighted from the back by a streak of sun, there is a gap in the hubbub. On a small square, wood is being cut for the city school. Cords of healthy, crisp timber are piled high and melt slowly, one log after another, under the saws and axes of workmen. Ah, timber, trustworthy, honest, true matter of reality, bright and completely decent, the embodiment of the decency and prose of life! However deep you look into its core, you cannot find anything that is not apparent on its evenly smiling surface, shining with that warm, assured glow of its fibrous pulp woven in a likeness of the human body. In each fresh section of a cut log a new face appears, always smiling and golden. Oh the strange complexion of timber, warm without exaltation, completely sound, fragrant, and pleasant!

The sawing of wood is a truly sacramental function, symbolic and dignified. I could stand for hours on a late afternoon watching the melodious play of saws, the rhythmical work of axes. Here is a tradition as old as the human race. In that bright gap of the day, in that hiatus of time opened onto a yellow and wilting eternity, beech logs have been sawed since Noah's day, with the same patriarchal and eternal movements, the same strokes and the same bent backs. The workmen stand up to their armpits in the golden shavings and slowly cut into the logs and cords of wood; covered with sawdust, with a tiny spark of light in their eyes, they cut ever deeper into the warm healthy pulp, into the solid mass; with each stroke a reflection sparks in their eyes, as if they were looking for something in the core of the timber: a golden salamander, a screaming fiery creature, that burrows deeper and deeper under their cutting. Perhaps they are simply dividing time into small splinters of wood. They husband time, they fill the cellars with an evenly sawed future for the winter months.

Oh, to endure that critical period, those few weeks, until the morning frosts begin and winter starts in earnest. How I like the prelude to winter, still without snow but with the smell of frost and smoke in the air. I remember Sunday afternoons in the late fall. Let us assume that it has been raining for a whole week, that a long downpour has saturated the earth with water, and that now the surface begins to dry out, exuding a hearty, healthy cold. The week-old sky with a cover of tattered clouds has been raked up, like mud, to one side of the firmament, where it looms dark in a folded compressed heap, while from the west the hale, healthy colors of a fall evening begin to spread and slowly fill the cloudy landscape. And while the sky clears gradually from the west and becomes translucent, servant girls walk out in their Sunday best, in threes, in fours, holding hands. They walk in the empty, Sunday-clean and drying street between the suburban houses bright in the tartness of the air which now turns crimson before dusk; rosy and round-faced from the cold, they walk with elastic steps in their new, too tight shoes. A pleasant, touching memory, brought up from a dark corner of the mind!

Recently, I have been calling almost daily at the office. It sometimes happens that someone is sick and they allow me to work in his place. Or somebody has something urgent to do in town and lets me deputize for him. Unfortunately, this is not regular work. It is pleasant to have, even for a few hours, a chair of one's own with a leather cushion, one's own rulers, pencils, and pens. It is pleasant to run into or even be rebuked by one's fellow workers. Someone addresses you, makes a joke, pulls your leg, and you blossom forth for a moment. You rub against somebody, attach your homelessness and nothingness to something alive and warm. The other person walks away and does not feel your burden, does not notice that he is carrying you on his shoulders, that like a parasite you cling momentarily to his life. . . .

But since the appointment of a new head of department, even this has come to an end.

Quite often now, if the weather is good, I sit out on a bench in a small square that faces the city school. From the street nearby comes the sound of wood being cut. Girls and young women return from the market. Some have serious and regular eyebrows and walk looking sternly from under them, slim and glum — angels with basketfuls of vegetables and meat. Sometimes they stop in front of shops and look at their reflections in the shop window. Then they walk away turning their heads, casting a proud and mustering eye on the backs of their shoes. At ten o'clock the beadle appears at the school gate and fills the street with the shrill ringing of his bell. Then the inside of the school seems to swell with a violent tumult that almost wrecks the building. Fugitives from the general commotion, small ragamuffins appear in the gateway, rush screaming down the stone steps and, finding themselves free, undertake some crazy leaps, and, between two mad looks of their rolling eyes, they throw themselves blindly into improvised games. Sometimes they venture up to my bench in their lunatic chases, throwing over their shoulders some obscure abuse at me. Their faces seem to come off their hinges in the violent grimaces that they make at me. Like a pack of busy monkeys, in a self-parody of clowning, this bunch of children run past me, gesticulating with a hellish noise. I can see their upturned, unformed, running noses, their mouths torn by shouting, their cheeks covered with spots, their small tight fists. Sometimes they stop near me. Strange to say, they treat me as if I were their age. True, I have been growing smaller for a long time. My face, wilted and flabby, has assumed the appearance of a child's face. I am slightly embarrassed when they address me as "thou." When one day one of them suddenly struck me across my chest, I rolled under the bench. I was not offended. They pulled me out, enchanted by this rather unexpected but refreshing behavior. The fact that I take no offense however violent and impetuous their conduct has gradually won me a measure of popularity. From then on, I have carried a supply of stones, buttons, empty cotton reels, and pieces of rubber in my pockets. This has enormously facilitated exchanges of ideas and made a natural bridge for starting friendships. Moreover, engrossed in factual interests, they pay less attention to me as a person. Under the cover of the arsenal produced from my pockets, I need not fear any more that their curiosity and inquisitiveness will be directed at me.

One day I decided to translate into action a certain idea that had been worrying me more and more insistently.

The day was mild, dreamy, and calm — one of those late fall days when the year, having exhausted all the colors and nuances of that season, seems to revert to the springtime pages of the calendar. The sunless sky had settled itself into colored streaks, gentle strips of cobalt, verdigris, and celadon, framed at the edges with whiteness as clear as water — the colors of April, inexpressible and long forgotten. I had put on my best suit and went out not without some misgivings. I walked quickly, effortlessly in the calm aura of the day, straying neither to the left nor right. Breathless, I ran up the stone steps. *Alea iacta est*, I said to myself, knocking at the door of the office. I stood in a modest posture in front of the headmaster's desk, as befitted my new role. I was slightly embarrassed.

The headmaster produced from a glass-topped box a cockchafer on a pin and lifting it aslant to his eye, looked at it against the light. His fingers were stained with ink, the nails were short and cut straight. He looked at me from behind his glasses.

"So you wish to enroll in the first form, Councilor?" he said. "This is praiseworthy and admirable. I understand that you would like to refresh your education from the foundations, from the beginnings. I always repeat: grammar and the tables are the foundations of all learning. Of course, we cannot consider you, Councilor, as a schoolboy to whom compulsory education applies. Rather as a volunteer, a veteran of the alphabet, to coin a phrase, who after long years of wandering has called again at the haven of the school, who has brought his distressed ship to a safe port, as it were. Yes, yes, Councilor, very few people show us gratitude and recognition for our work, and few return to us after a lifetime of toil and settle down here permanently as a voluntary, life pupil. You shall enjoy special privileges, Councilor, I have always thought — "

"Excuse me," I interrupted, "but I should like to say that, as far as special privileges are concerned, I would like to renounce them completely. . . . I don't want any. On the contrary, I should not like to be treated differently in any way; I wish to merge completely, to disappear in the gray mass of the class. My plan would fail if I were to be privileged. Even with regard to corporal punishment," here I lifted my finger, "and I completely recognize its beneficial and educational importance — I insist that no exception should be made for me."

"Most praiseworthy, most thoughtful," said the headmaster with respect. "Come to think of it, your education might reveal certain gaps through the long years of nonusage. We all have in this respect some optimistic illusions, which can easily be dispelled. Do you remember, for instance, how much is five times seven?"

"Five times seven," I repeated embarrassed, feeling confusion flowing in a warm and blissful wave to my head, creating a mist that obscured the clarity of my thoughts. Enchanted by my own ignorance, I began to stammer and repeat over and over again: "Five times seven, five times seven . . . ," enormously pleased that I was really reverting to childlike ignorance.

"There you are," said the headmaster, "it is high time for you to enroll in school once more."

Then, taking me by the hand, he led me to the form where a class was being held.

Again, as half a century ago, I found myself in the tumult of a room swarming and dark from a multitude of mobile heads. I stood, very small, in the center, holding the tail of the headmaster's coat, while fifty pairs of young eyes looked at me with the indifferent, cruel matter-of-factness of young animals confronted with a specimen of the same race. From all sides faces were made at me, grimaces of instant token enmity, tongues stuck out. I did not react to these provocations, remembering the good upbringing I had once received. Looking round the mobile, awkwardly grimacing faces, I recalled the same situation fifty years before. At that time I had stood next to my mother, while she talked to the lady teacher. Now, instead of my mother, it was the headmaster whispering something into the ear of the instructor, who was nodding his head and staring at me attentively.

"He is an orphan," the instructor said at last to the class, "he has no father or mother, so don't be unkind to him."

Tears came to my eyes after that short address, real tears of emotion, and the headmaster, himself moved, placed me on the bench nearest the rostrum.

A new life thus began for me. The school at once absorbed me completely. Never in my earlier life had I been so engrossed in a thousand affairs, intrigues, and interests. I lived a life of incessant excitement. Over my head the lines of multiple and complicated messages were crossing. I was on the receiving end of signals, telegrams, signs of understanding. I was hissed at, winked at, and reminded in all manner of ways about a hundred promises which I had sworn to fulfill. I could hardly wait for the end of the lesson, during which out of inborn decency I sustained with stoicism all attacks and tried not to miss a single one of the instructor's words. But hardly had the bell been rung than the whole shouting gang fell upon me, surrounding me with an elemental impetus, and almost tearing me to pieces. They came from behind, or, stamping across the benches, they jumped over my head and turned somersaults over me. Each of them shouted his demands into my ears. I became the center of all interests, and the most important transactions, the most complicated and doubtful deals, could not take place without my participation. In the street, I walked surrounded by a noisy, violently gesticulating gang. Dogs passed us at a distance, with tails between their legs, cats jumped onto roofs when they saw us approaching, and lonely small boys, met in the street, with passive fatalism hunched their heads between their shoulders, preparing for the worst.

Tuition at school had lost none of the charm of novelty, as, for instance, the art of spelling. The instructor appealed to our ignorance very skillfully and cunningly, he drew it forth until he reached that tabula rasa on which the seeds of all teaching must fall. Having thus eradicated all our prejudices and habits, he taught us from the very start. With difficulty and with concentration we melodiously spelled and divided words into syllables, sniffing in the intervals and pointing with our fingers at each new letter in our book. My primer had the same traces of my index finger, thicker at the more difficult letters, as the primers of my schoolmates.

One day, I cannot remember why, the headmaster entered the room and in the sudden silence pointed his finger at three of us, one of whom was myself. We were to follow him to his study at once. We knew what was in store, and my two fellow culprits began to cry in advance. I looked with indifference at their premature contrition, at their faces deformed by sudden weeping as if with the onset of tears the human mask had fallen off and disclosed a formless pulp of weeping flesh. I myself was calm: with the stoicism of fair and moral natures I submitted myself to the course of events, ready to face the consequences of my actions. That strength of character, which resembled obstinacy, did not please the headmaster, as we three culprits stood facing him in his study, the instructor standing by with a cane in his hand. I undid my belt with indifference, but the headmaster, looking at me, exclaimed:

"Shame on you! How is it possible, at your age?" and looked indignantly at the instructor.

"A strange freak of nature," he added with a look of disgust. Then, having sent the two small boys away, he made a long and earnest speech, full of regrets and disapproval. But I did not understand him. Biting my nails, I looked stupidly ahead of me and then said lisping:

"Please, Shir, it was Andy who shpat at the other Shir's roll."

I had become a complete child.

For gymnastics and art we went to another school building, which had a special room and equipment for these subjects. We marched in pairs, talking passionately, filling every street we passed with the sudden tumult of our mingled sopranos.

The other school was in a large wooden building, reconstructed from an old theater hall, and with many outhouses. The art class resembled an enormous bathhouse; the ceiling rested on wooden pillars, and there was a gallery all around the room, to which we climbed at once, storming the stairs, which resounded thunderously under our feet. The numerous smaller rooms and recesses were wonderfully well-suited to the game of hide-and-seek. The art master never appeared, so we could play to our heart's content. From time to time the headmaster of that other school rushed into the hall, put the noisiest boys into corners, and pulled the ears of the wildest. Hardly had his back been turned than the noise began anew.

We did not hear the bell announcing the end of the class. The afternoon came, short and colorful as usual in fall. Some boys were fetched by their mothers, who, scolding and smacking them, carried them off home. But for the others and those deprived of such solicitous care, the proper playtime only started at that moment. It was late evening before the old beadle who came to lock up the school finally chased us away.

At that time of the year, there was dense darkness in the mornings when we walked to school, and the city was still asleep. We moved blindly with outstretched hands, dragging our feet in the rustling leaves that lay thick on the pavements. We groped along the walls of houses so as not to lose our way. Unexpectedly in a window recess we would feel under our hands the face of one of our mates, coming from the opposite direction. How we laughed, guessing whom it might be, how many surprises we had! Some boys would carry lighted bits of tallow candle, and the city was punctuated with these wandering lights, advancing low above ground in a trembling zigzag, meeting, then stopping to shed light on a tree, a clump of earth, a pile of yellow leaves among which very small boys looked for horse chestnuts. In some houses the first lamps

168

were lighted, and the hazy glow from the upper floors, magnified by the squares of windows, fell in irregular patches on the pavements, on the town hall, on the blind facades of houses. And when somebody, lamp in hand, walked from one room to another, enormous rectangles of light outside would turn like the pages of a colossal book and the market square seemed to shift the houses and shadows and pick them up as if it were playing patience with an outsize pack of cards.

At last we reached school. The candles were extinguished, darkness surrounded us as we groped for our places. Then the instructor entered, put an end of a tallow candle into a bottle, and the boring questions about declension of the irregular verbs would begin. As there was not yet sufficient light, the lesson remained oral and had to be memorized. While one of us was reciting monotonously, we looked, blinking, at the golden arrows shooting up from the candle, at lines that cut across one another like blades of straw on our half-closed eyelashes. The instructor poured ink into inkwells, yawned, looked out through the low window into the blackness. Under the seats it was completely dark. We dived there, giggling, walked on all fours, smelling one another like animals, and performing blindly and in whispers the usual transactions. I shall never forget those blissful early morning hours at school while a slow dawn matured beyond the windowpanes.

At last came the season of autumnal winds. On its first day, early in the morning, the sky became yellow and modeled itself against that background in dirty gray lines of imaginary landscapes, of great misty wastes, receding in an eastward direction into a perspective of diminishing hills and folds, more numerous as they became smaller, until the sky tore itself off like the wavy edge of a rising curtain and disclosed a farther plan, a deeper sky, a gap of frightened whiteness, a pale and scared light of remote distance, discolored and watery, that like final amazement closed the horizon. As in Rembrandt's etchings one could see on such a day distant microscopic regions that, under the streak of brightness usually hard to locate, now rose from beyond the horizon under that clear crevice of sky.

In that miniature landscape, one could see with sharp precision a railway train usually not visible at that distance, moving on a wavy track and crowned with a plume of silvery white smoke, which in turn dissolved into bright nothingness.

And then, the wind rose. As if thrown from the clear gap in the sky, it circled and spread all over the city. It was woven of softness and gentleness, but it pretended to be brutal and fierce. It kneaded, turned over, and tortured the air until it felt like dying from bliss. Then it stiffened in space and reared, spread itself like canvas sails — enormous, taut, flapping like drying sheets — tangled itself in hard knots, trembling with tension, as if it wanted to move the whole atmosphere into a higher space; and then it pulled and untied the false knot and, a mile further away, threw again its hissing lasso, that lariat which could catch nothing.

And the dance the wind led the chimney smoke! The smoke did not know how to avoid its scolding, how to turn, whether left or right, how to escape its blows. Thus the wind lorded it over the city as if on that memorable day it had wanted to give a telling example of its infinite willfulness.

From early in the morning, I had a premonition of disaster. I made my way in the gale only with difficulty. On street corners, where the crosswinds met, my schoolmates held me by my coattails. So I sailed across the city and all was well. Later we went for gymnastics to the other school. On our way we bought some crescent rolls. Talking incessantly, our long crocodile wound through the gate and into the courtyard. One more minute and I should have been safe, in a secure spot, safe until the evening. If need be, I might have spent the night in the hall. My loyal friends would have stayed with me. But as fate had it, Vicky had that day been given a new top as a present, and he let it spin in front of the school. The top spun, a crowd formed at the entrance, I was pushed outside the gate and was immediately swept away.

"Boys, help, help!" I shouted, already suspended in the air. I could still see their outstretched arms and their shouting, open mouths, but the next moment, I turned a somersault and ascended in a magnificent parabola. I was flying high above the roofs. Breathless I saw in my mind's eye how my schoolmates raised their arms, and called out to the instructor: "Please, sir, please, Simon has been swept away!"

The instructor looked at them from under his spectacles. He went slowly over to the window and, screening his eyes with his hands,

scanned the horizon. But he could not see me. In the dull glare of the pale sky, his face had the color of parchment.

"We must cross his name off the register," he said with a bitter smile and returned to the rostrum. I was carried higher and higher into the unexplored yellow space.

LONELINESS

It is with great relief that I feel able to go out again. But for what a long time was I confined to my room! These have been bitter months and years.

I cannot explain why I have been living in my old nursery — the back room of the apartment, with access from the balcony — which was rarely used in the past, forgotten, as if it did not belong to us. I cannot remember how I got there. I believe it was during a bright watery-white moonless night. I could see every detail in the dim light. The bed was unmade, as if someone had just left it, and I listened in the stillness for the breathing of people asleep. But who was likely to be breathing here? Since then, this has been my home. I have been here for years and am rather bored. Why didn't I think in advance about stocking up! Ah, you who still can do it, who still are given the time, make provisions, save up grain — good, nourishing, sweet grain — for a great winter of lean and hungry years lies ahead, and the earth will not bear fruit in the land of Egypt. Alas, I was not provident, like a hamster. I have always been a light-hearted field mouse, I have lived from day to day without a care for the morrow, trusting in my starveling's talent. Like a mouse, I thought, What do I care about hunger? If worst comes to worst, I can gnaw wood or nibble paper. The poorest of animals, a gray church mouse, at the tail end of the Book of Creation, I can exist on nothing. And so I live in this dead room. Many flies died in it a long time ago. I put my ear against wood, to hear the sound of a woodworm. Deadly silence. Only I, the immortal mouse, lonely and posthumous, rustle in this room, running endlessly on the table, on the shelf, on the chairs. I run around, resembling Aunt Thecla in a long gray frock reaching to the ground — agile, quick, and small, pulling behind me a mobile tail. I am now sitting in bright daylight on the table, immobile, as if stuffed, my eyes like two protruding shiny beads. Only the end of my muzzle pulsates imperceptibly, by force of habit, in minute chewing movements.

This, of course, is to be understood as a metaphor. I am really an old-age pensioner, not a mouse. It is part of my existence to be the parasite of metaphors, so easily am I carried away by the first simile that comes along. Having been carried away, I have to find my difficult way back, and slowly return to my senses.

What do I look like? Sometimes I see myself in the mirror. A strange, ridiculous, and painful thing! I am ashamed to admit it: I never look at myself full face. Somewhat deeper, somewhat farther away I stand inside the mirror a little off center, slightly in profile, thoughtful and glancing sideways. Our looks have stopped meeting. When I move, my reflection moves too, but half-turned back, as if it did not know about me, as if it had got behind a number of mirrors and could not come back. My heart bleeds when I see it so distant and indifferent. It is you, I want to exclaim; you have always been my faithful reflection, you have accompanied me for so many years and now you don't recognize me! Oh, my God! Unfamiliar and looking to one side, my reflection stands there and seems to be listening for something, awaiting a word from the mirrored depths, obedient to someone else, waiting for orders from another place.

Mostly I sit at the table and turn the pages of my yellowed university notes — my only reading.

I look at the sun-bleached curtain, stiff with dust, waving slightly in the cold breeze from the window. I could do exercises on the curtain rod, an excellent bar. How lightly one could turn somersaults on it in the sterile, tired air. Almost casually one could make an elegant *salto mortale*, coolly, without too much involvement — a speculative exercise, as it were. When one stands on tiptoe, balancing oneself on the bar, with one's head touching the ceiling, one has the impression that it is slightly warmer higher up — the illusion of being in a warmer zone. Ever since my childhood, I have liked to have a bird's-eye view of my room.

So I sit and listen to the silence. The room is whitewashed. Sometimes on the white ceiling a wrinklelike crack appears, sometimes a flake of plaster breaks off with a click. Am I to reveal that the room is walled in? How can that be? Walled in? How could I leave it? That is just it: where there is a will, there is a way; a passionate determination can conquer all. I must only imagine a door, a good old door, like the one in the kitchen of my childhood, with an iron handle and a bolt. There is no walled-in room that could not be opened by such a trusted door, provided one were strong enough to suggest that such a door exists.

FATHER'S LAST ESCAPE

It happened in the late and forlorn period of complete disruption, at the time of the liquidation of our business. The signboard had been removed from over our shop, the shutters were halfway down, and inside the shop my mother was conducting an unauthorized trade in remnants. Adela had gone to America, and it was said that the boat on which she had sailed had sunk and that all the passengers had lost their lives. We were unable to verify this rumor, but all trace of the girl was lost and we never heard of her again.

A new age began — empty, sober, and joyless, like a sheet of white paper. A new servant girl, Genya, anemic, pale, and boneless, mooned about the rooms. When one patted her on the back, she wriggled, stretched like a snake, or purred like a cat. She had a dull white complexion, and even the insides of her eyelids were white. She was so absent-minded that she sometimes made a white sauce from old letters and invoices: it was sickly and inedible.

At that time, my father was definitely dead. He had been dying a number of times, always with some reservations that forced us to revise our attitude toward the fact of his death. This had its advantages. By dividing his death into installments, Father had familiarized us with his demise. We became gradually indifferent to his returns — each one shorter, each one more pitiful. His features were already dispersed throughout the room in which he had lived, and were sprouting in it, creating at some points strange knots of likeness that were most expressive. The wallpaper began in certain places to imitate his habitual nervous tic; the flower designs arranged themselves into the doleful elements of his smile, symmetrical as the fossilized imprint of a trilobite. For a time, we gave a wide berth to his fur coat lined with polecat skins. The fur coat breathed. The panic of small animals sewn together and biting into one another passed through it in helpless currents and lost itself in the folds of the fur. Putting one's ear against it, one could hear the melodious purring unison of the animals' sleep. In this well-tanned form, amid the faint smell of polecat, murder, and nighttime matings, my father might have lasted for many years. But he did not last.

One day, Mother returned home from town with a preoccupied face.

"Look, Joseph," she said, "what a lucky coincidence. I caught him on the stairs, jumping from step to step" — and she lifted a handkerchief that covered something on a plate. I recognized him at once. The resemblance was striking, although now he was a crab or a large scorpion. Mother and I exchanged looks: in spite of the metamorphosis, the resemblance was incredible.

"Is he alive?" I asked.

"Of course. I can hardly hold him," Mother said. "Shall I place him on the floor?"

She put the plate down, and leaning over him, we observed him closely. There was a hollow place between his numerous curved legs, which he was moving slightly. His uplifted pincers and feelers seemed to be listening. I tipped the plate, and Father moved cautiously and with a certain hesitation onto the floor. Upon touching the flat surface under him, he gave a sudden start with all of his legs, while his hard arthropod joints made a clacking sound. I barred his way. He hesitated, investigated the obstacle with his feelers, then lifted his pincers and turned aside. We let him run in his chosen direction, where there was no furniture to give him shelter. Running in wavy jerks on his many legs, he reached the wall and, before we could stop him, ran lightly up it, not pausing anywhere. I shuddered with instinctive revulsion as I watched his progress up the wallpaper. Meanwhile, Father reached a small built-in kitchen cupboard, hung for a moment on its edge, testing the terrain with his pincers, and then crawled into it.

He was discovering the apartment afresh from the new point of view of a crab; evidently, he perceived all objects by his sense of smell, for, in spite of careful checking, I could not find on him any organ of sight. He seemed to consider carefully the objects he encountered in his path, stopping and feeling them with his antennae, then embracing them with his pincers, as if to test them and make their acquaintance; after a time, he left them and continued on his run, pulling his abdomen behind him, lifted slightly from the floor. He acted the same way with the pieces of bread and meat that we threw on the floor for him, hoping he would eat them. He gave them a perfunctory examination and ran on, not recognizing that they were edible.

Watching these patient surveys of the room, one could assume that he was obstinately and indefatigably looking for something. From time to time, he ran to a corner of the kitchen, crept under a barrel of water that was leaking, and, upon reaching the puddle, seemed to drink.

Sometimes he disappeared for days on end. He seemed to manage perfectly well without food, but this did not seem to affect his vitality. With mixed feelings of shame and repugnance, we concealed by day our secret fear that he might visit us in bed during the night. But this never occurred, although in the daytime he would wander all over the furniture. He particularly liked to stay in the spaces between the wardrobes and the wall.

We could not discount certain manifestations of reason and even a sense of humor. For instance, Father never failed to appear in the dining room during mealtimes, although his participation in them was purely symbolic. If the dining-room door was by chance closed during dinner and he had been left in the next room, he scratched at the bottom of the door, running up and down along the crack, until we opened it for him. In time, he learned how to insert his pincers and legs under the door, and after some elaborate maneuvers he finally succeeded in insinuating his body through it sideways into the dining room. This seemed to give him pleasure. He would then stop under the table, lying quite still, his abdomen slightly pulsating. What the meaning of these rhythmic pulsations was, we could not imagine. They seemed obscene and malicious, but at the same time expressed a rather gross and lustful satisfaction. Our dog, Nimrod, would approach him slowly and, without conviction, sniff at him cautiously, sneeze, and turn away indifferently, not having reached any conclusions.

Meanwhile, the demoralization in our household was increasing. Genya slept all day long, her slim body bonelessly undulating with her deep breaths. We often found in the soup reels of cotton, which she had thrown in unthinkingly with the vegetables. Our shop was open nonstop, day and night. A continuous sale took place amid complicated bargainings and discussions. To crown it all, Uncle Charles came to stay.

He was strangely depressed and silent. He declared with a sigh that after his recent unfortunate experiences he had decided to change his way of life and devote himself to the study of languages. He never went out but remained locked in the most remote room — from which Genya had removed all the carpets and curtains, as she did not approve of our visitor. There he spent his time, reading old price lists. Several times he tried viciously to step on Father. Screaming with horror, we told him to stop it. Afterward he only smiled wryly to himself, while Father, not realizing the danger he had been in, hung around and studied some spots on the floor.

My father, quick and mobile as long as he was on his feet, shared with all crustaceans the characteristic that when turned on his back he became largely immobile. It was sad and pitiful to see him desperately moving all his limbs and rotating helplessly around his own axis. We could hardly force ourselves to look at the conspicuous, almost shameless mechanism of his anatomy, completely exposed under the bare articulated belly. At such moments, Uncle Charles could hardly restrain himself from stamping on Father. We ran to his rescue with some object at hand, which he caught tightly with his pincers, quickly regaining his normal position; then at once he started a lightning, zigzag run at double speed, as if wanting to obliterate the memory of his unsightly fall.

I must force myself to report truthfully the unbelievable deed, from which my memory recoils even now. To this day I cannot understand how we became the conscious perpetrators of it. A strange fatality must have been driving us to it; for fate does not evade consciousness or will but engulfs them in its mechanism, so that we are able to admit and accept, as in a hypnotic trance, things that under normal circumstances would fill us with horror.

Shaken badly, I asked my mother in despair, again and again, "How could you have done it? If it were Genya who had done it — but you yourself?" Mother cried, wrung her hands, and could find no answer. Had she thought that Father would be better off? Had she seen in that act the only solution to a hopeless situation, or did she do it out of inconceivable thoughtlessness and frivolity? Fate has a thousand wiles when it chooses to impose on us its incomprehensible whims. A temporary blackout, a moment of inattention or blindness, is enough to insinuate an act between the Scylla and Charybdis of decision. Afterward, with hindsight, we may endlessly ponder that act, explain our motives, try to discover our true intentions; but the act remains irrevocable.

When Father was brought in on a dish, we came to our senses and understood fully what had happened. He lay large and swollen from the boiling, pale gray and jellified. We sat in silence, dumbfounded. Only Uncle Charles lifted his fork toward the dish, but at once he put it down uncertainly, looking at us askance. Mother ordered it to be taken to the sitting room. It stood there afterward on a table covered with a velvet cloth, next to the album of family photographs and a musical cigarette box. Avoided by us all, it just stood there.

But my father's earthly wanderings were not yet at an end, and the next installment — the extension of the story beyond permissible limits — is the most painful of all. Why didn't he give up, why didn't he admit that he was beaten when there was every reason to do so and when even Fate could go no farther in utterly confounding him? After several weeks of immobility in the sitting room, he somehow rallied and seemed to be slowly recovering. One morning, we found the plate empty. One leg lay on the edge of the dish, in some congealed tomato sauce and aspic that bore the traces of his escape. Although boiled and shedding his legs on the way, with his remaining strength he had dragged himself somewhere to begin a homeless wandering, and we never saw him again.

A selection of books published by Penguin is listed on the following pages.

For a complete list of books available from Penguin in the United States, write to Dept. DG, Penguin Books, 299 Murray Hill Parkway, East Rutherford, New Jersey 07073.

For a complete list of books available from Penguin in Canada, write to Penguin Books Canada Limited, 2801 John Street, Markham, Ontario L3R 1B4.

WRITERS FROM THE OTHER EUROPE
General Editor: Philip Roth

A DREAMBOOK FOR OUR TIME

Tadeusz Konwicki
Introduction by Leszek Kołakowski

The world of dreams and the world of waking meet in this extraordinary book, called "one of the most terrifying novels in postwar Polish literature" and "a major literary sensation." The time is the early 1960s; the narrator, a young Pole, emerges from a coma after trying to poison himself. He is surrounded by provincial villagers, whose lives were forever shattered by the trauma of World War II. The incoherent mass of his own wartime memories arises—nightmarish images of guerrilla warfare, of blood, cruelty, betrayal, and guilt. As the past and the present succeed each other in his mind with frightening illogicality, he sees his choice to be between self-assertive survival and the peace of self-destruction. He chooses to live and is condemned to death-in-life. Tadeusz Konwicki's sensitivity to human anguish and despair makes this novel a passionate variation on the theme of *Heart of Darkness*: "We live, as we dream—alone."

WRITERS FROM THE OTHER EUROPE
General Editor: Philip Roth

THE STREET OF CROCODILES

Bruno Schulz
Introduction by Jerzy Ficowski

The Street of Crocodiles in the Polish city of Drogobych is a street of memories and dreams where recollections of Bruno Schulz's uncommon boyhood and the eerie side of his merchant family's life are evoked in a startling blend of the real and the fantastic. Most memorable—and most chilling—is the portrait of the author's father, a maddened shopkeeper who imports rare birds' eggs to hatch in his attic, who believes tailors' dummies should be treated like people, and whose obsessive fear of cockroaches causes him to resemble one. Bruno Schulz is considered by many to have been the leading Polish writer between the two world wars. As Isaac Bashevis Singer has written: "Schulz cannot be easily classified. He can be called a surrealist, a symbolist, an expressionist, a modernist. . . . He wrote sometimes like Kafka, sometimes like Proust, and at times succeeded in reaching depths that neither of them reached."

WRITERS FROM THE OTHER EUROPE
General Editor: Philip Roth

THE FAREWELL PARTY

Milan Kundera
Introduction by Elizabeth Pochoda

A telephone call announcing an unwanted pregnancy sends Klima, jazz trumpeter from Prague, back to the fertility spa where he had spent a night with a pretty nurse named Ruzena. As Klima tries to persuade Ruzena to have an abortion, as Ruzena wavers between compliance and refusal, others are drawn into the conflict: Klima's lovely wife, Ruzena's jealous boyfriend, a mysterious and saintly American millionaire, a persecuted political dissident, and the spa's Dr. Skreta, who gleefully injects his own sperm into patients, thereby advancing his dream of the brotherhood of man. All these people are sharply etched by Milan Kundera's pen in a novel that exposes the crumbling illusions to which we cling, the swirling ambiguities that surround us. "Kundera, himself an internal exile in post-Dubček Czechoslovakia . . . remains faithful to his subtle, wily, devious talent for a fiction of 'erotic possibilities.' . . . *The Farewell Party* is the kind of 'political novel' a cunning, resourceful, gifted writer writes when it is no longer possible to write political novels"—Saul Maloff, *The New York Times Book Review*.

WRITERS FROM THE OTHER EUROPE
General Editor: Philip Roth

LAUGHABLE LOVES

Milan Kundera
Introduction by Philip Roth

Here are seven dazzling stories of sexual comedy by Czechoslovakia's foremost contemporary writer. Praised by literary
figures as diverse as Jean-Paul Sartre, Louis Aragon, and
Philip Roth, Milan Kundera is master of graceful illusion and
illuminating surprise. In one of these tales a young man and
his girl friend pretend that she is a stranger he picked up on a
road . . . only to become strangers to each other in reality as
their game proceeds. In another, a teacher fakes piety in order to seduce a devout girl, then jilts her and yearns for God.
In yet another, girls wait in bars, on beaches, and on station
platforms for the same lover, a middle-aged Don Juan gone
home to his wife. Games, fantasies, and schemes abound in
all of the stories while different characters react in varying
ways to the sudden release of erotic impulses. As one critic
has noted, "Kundera's stories are dances . . . experienced by
Chekhov . . . X-rayed by Freud." "What is so often laughable, in the stories of Kundera's Czechoslovakia, is how
grimly serious just about everything turns out to be, jokes and
games and pleasure included; what's laughable is how terribly
little there is to laugh at with any joy"—From the Introduction by Philip Roth.

WRITERS FROM THE OTHER EUROPE
General Editor: Philip Roth

THIS WAY FOR THE GAS, LADIES AND GENTLEMEN

Tadeusz Borowski
Introduction by Jan Kott

Published in Poland after World War II, Tadeusz Borowski's concentration-camp stories show atrocious crimes becoming an unremarkable part of a daily routine. Prisoners eat, work, sleep, and fall in love a few yards from where other prisoners are systematically slaughtered. The will to survive overrides compassion, and the line between the normal and the abnormal wavers, then vanishes. At Auschwitz an athletic field and a brothel flank the crematoriums. Himself a concentration-camp victim, Borowski understood what human beings will do to endure the unendurable. As one critic observed: "Borowski looks at the concentration camp as if it were first of all a community of men and women, governed by unalterable instincts and formed by necessary habits. The constant need for human contact—in the persecutors as well as in the condemned—the clinging to ridiculous hopes and useless possessions; and at the same time the grotesque corruptions that become accepted as the consequence of the gift for survival. These terse descriptions, almost anecdotal in form, become an oblique commentary on the negotiations we conduct daily in our own, civilized ways."

Maxim Gorky

MY CHILDHOOD

My Childhood, which appeared in 1913, is the first part of
Maxim Gorky's autobiographical trilogy. The ordinary experiences of a Russian boy in the nineteenth century are recalled
by an altogether extraordinary man, whose gift of recapturing
the world of a child is uncanny. Across the vision of the boy
perched above the stove the Russian contrasts flicker—barbaric gaiety and deep gloom, satanic cruelty and saintly
forbearance, clownish knaves and holy fools.

MY APPRENTICESHIP

My Apprenticeship begins where *My Childhood* leaves off—
when the eleven-year-old Gorky is sent out into the world to
fend for himself. The world he encounters is one of almost
incredible squalor, misery, and barbaric violence, in the period of Russia's belated and ruthless Industrial Revolution.
Nevertheless, Gorky's resilience and strength of character,
his ultimate optimism, and the brilliant clarity with which he
recalls his experiences shine through the book.

MY UNIVERSITIES

First published in 1923, *My Universities* is the third (and Le-
nin's favorite) volume of Gorky's autobiography, recording
his life from 1884 to 1888, when he was twenty. Frustrated in
his desire to become a university student, Gorky seeks an
education in clandestine discussions with revolutionaries and
in arguments with religious fanatics and eccentric school-
teachers. Throughout this volume Gorky repeatedly stresses
his disenchantment with the workers and peasants—with
their apathy, drunkenness, and inertia. He submits himself to
a ruthless self-analysis and describes his attempted suicide.
My Universities offers incidents of enormous breadth and variety, and writing of rare power and conviction.

THE SHADOW OF THE WINTER PALACE
The Drift to Revolution 1825–1917

Edward Crankshaw

The panoramic survey of the reigns of the last four czars shows us the imperial origins of many aspects of the modern Soviet state. Dynastic, diplomatic, military, economic, and social history all enter the picture as Edward Crankshaw introduces Nicholas I, the archetypal autocrat; Alexander II, who liberated the serfs; Alexander III, who reacted by founding the first police state; and Nicholas II, upon whose head the whole system collapsed in ruins. Around these four central figures swirls a host of others—nobles, landowners, generals, bureaucrats, intellectuals, artists, revolutionaries—all forming a vast tapestry whose tangled paradoxes seem to be with us still. "The author's careful selection of detail . . . the quality of his prose . . . his beautiful combination of warm sympathy and civilized fastidiousness—these enable him to convey the style of a people. . . . To have many writers like Mr. Crankshaw in one field, we would have to be living in a golden age of literature"—Rebecca West.